Kat felt like she was flying.

Sebastian turned to look at her over his shoulder and grinned. "You like it?"

She smiled back, "I feel like I'm almost part of the horse, somehow, you know?"

He nodded. "That's exactly right. That's just how it should feel."

Kat felt the adrenaline surge through her as Sebastian gave the horse another little kick and the pony went even faster. Sebastian turned back to her again. He laughed when he saw her face. "You look drunk with pleasure," he said.

Kat grinned. "I kind of am!"

They slowed to a trot and then a walk. Sebastian pulled the horse to a stop, swung down, and then reached up to help Kat off.

Her feet hit the floor and her legs felt like jelly. She kept her hand in Sebastian's and leaned her cheek against the horse's neck. "That was amazing. Thank you," she breathed. She wasn't sure if she was talking to Sebastian, or the pony.

Sebastian took a step closer to her, "Katarina," he said. His voice caught in his throat. She turned away from the pony and looked into his eyes. They were dark with longing.

Nacho Figueras Presents:
Wild One

NACHO FIGUERAS
PRESENTS:

Wild
One

Jessica Whitman

Book Two in The Polo Season Series

FOREVER

New York Boston

Copyright © 2016 by Ignacio Figueras
Excerpt from *Ride Free* copyright © 2016 by Ignacio Figueras
Cover design by Elizabeth Turner
Cover illustration by Alan Ayers
Author photograph by Claudio Marinesco
Horse images © Steve Greer/GettyImages
Cover copyright © 2016 by Hachette Book Group, Inc.

Forever
Hachette Book Group
1290 Avenue of the Americas
New York, NY 10104
hachettebookgroup.com
twitter.com/foreverromance

Printed in the United States of America

OPM

First Edition: June 2016
10 9 8 7 6 5 4 3 2 1

Forever is an imprint of Grand Central Publishing.
The Forever name and logo are trademarks of Hachette Book Group, Inc.

The publisher is not responsible for websites (or their content) that are not owned by the publisher.

The Hachette Speakers Bureau provides a wide range of authors for speaking events. To find out more, go to www.hachettespeakersbureau.com or call (866) 376-6591.

ISBN 978-1-4555-6366-1 (trade paperback edition)
ISBN 978-1-4555-6368-5 (mass market edition edition)
ISBN 978-1-4555-6365-4 (ebook edition)

I want to dedicate the second book in this great series to my parents, Horacio and Mercedes, who gave me every opportunity in their power and more to enable me to learn the sport that I love. They were always so supportive and I would not be playing polo if it were not for them.

Thank you for being such great examples of what being a parent means—and to all parents out there who do everything and more for their children.

—Nacho Figueras

Dear Reader,

I first learned to ride a horse when I was four years old and started playing the sport of polo by the time I was nine. Tango was the horse on which I learned to play, and Tango was my first love. I fell in love with the beauty of horses and idolized the strength and bravery of the best players. In my native Argentina, everyone has a chance to go to polo matches and see how thrilling they are. It has been my dream to share the game that I love, the game that has given me so much—as a person and athlete—with the rest of the world.

I think polo is very appealing. After all, there's a reason Ralph Lauren chose it. There is something undeniably sexy about a man and a horse and the speed and the adrenaline.

It was at a polo match that I met my wife. I was in the stands and she was coming up the stairs, and I looked at her and she looked at me, and we looked at each other. I had to know more, so I asked her cousin Sofia to introduce us and she told me, "That's funny; she just asked me the same thing." So the cousin introduced us, and we talked for a little bit. It was the beginning of the summer, and we didn't see each other for two or three months. After the holiday, we started dating, and we have been together ever since...

I am very excited to present the Polo Season series, which blends my favorite sport with a little bit of romance. Whether you're already a polo fan or completely new to the game, I hope you will enjoy these characters and their stories.

Nacho Figueras Presents:
Wild One

Chapter One

Katherine Ann Parker looked in the bathroom mirror and carefully applied a layer of dark red lipstick.

And then, just as carefully, she wiped it back off.

Too much. The last thing she wanted was to look like she was desperate.

She dug some ChapStick out of her bag and slicked it on, trying to ignore the Silver Lake hipster breathing behind her, impatiently waiting to wash her hands.

Yes, that was better. And everything else seemed to be working—her black hair, pulled back into a sleek chignon; the crisp white fitted button-down showing just a hint of cleavage; the modest gold hoops in her ears; the dark wash jeans that were tailored just so, the six-inch-heeled ankle boots . . .

She frowned. She knew her manager, Honey Kimmelman, would nix the boots. As a general rule, the men in Hollywood were short and didn't like to be reminded of that fact. And Kat was already tall, even without the heels. The boots pushed her up over six feet.

"Well, too damned bad," she said out loud. "This is a job, not a date."

"Um, excuse me?" said the hipster.

Kat blinked, embarrassed. She had forgotten she was not alone. "Sorry. Personal pep talk," she mumbled, and she moved aside so the girl could use the sink.

The girl washed her hands and left, shooting one last quizzical look at Kat as the door swung shut behind her.

Kat lingered at the window, looking out over the panorama of West Hollywood. She sighed dreamily. Even the bathroom at Soho House had an amazing view.

She checked her watch—it was time. She smoothed her hair, almost went for the lipstick again, and then stilled her hand and forced a deep breath. It was just a meeting, she told herself. She'd been to a million meetings. She could do this.

* * *

As Kat eased her way to the back of the restaurant, she made a point of pretending not to notice the multitude of celebrities and A-listers scattered around the private club. Soho House was, above all, discreet. A place where even the biggest stars could have lunch, take meetings, gossip, and relax, and be sure to go unbothered. Kat had reluctantly let her membership lapse when she could no longer afford the annual fees, but she was always happy to come back as a guest.

The movie exec, Dee Yang, rose from her seat, smiling, as Kat approached the table. Dee was younger than Kat, dark haired and pretty, wearing a navy sheath that showed off her toned arms. Kat liked her at once, could see the intelligence written all over face, and recognized her warm smile as genuine.

"Kat, so great to finally meet you," said Dee as they shook hands. "I'm such a huge fan."

Kat waved the compliment off, smiling. "Thank you. It's so good to meet you, too."

"And this is Steve Meyers," said Dee as she and Kat sat down. "He's producing the project."

A fiftyish man with graying hair, in jeans and a baseball cap, nodded but did not look up from his phone. "Hang on. Just one second," he said, texting away.

Kat glanced at Dee, who raised her eyebrows apologetically and passed her a menu. "Have you had the burrata?" she said. "I can't resist it."

"And ooookay," said Steve, putting down his phone at last. "Sorry about that. Couldn't wait." He gave Kat an obvious head-to-toe once-over before he stuck out his hand. "Nice to meet you, Kay."

"Kat," Dee corrected.

"Right, sorry. Kat."

Kat's heart sank as she watched his eyes dart right back to his phone. It wasn't hard to read the room. He didn't want to be here. Dee had obviously talked him into this meeting. He probably already had someone else lined up for the job.

She forced herself to look at her menu, trying not to let the disappointment show on her face.

"So, Kat," said Dee, "I notice a little Southern accent. Where are you from?"

Kat smiled. "My folks are originally from Georgia, but I grew up in Wellington, Florida."

"Wellington?" Steve said, momentarily interested, "I think my first wife went down there once for some expensive thing she had to buy a crazy hat for. Tennis? Cricket?"

"Polo, probably," said Kat. "Or some other horse-related activity. It's pretty much all horses all the time in Wellington."

She could just imagine Steve's first wife, tan and toned, her face a mask of Botox, taking out her frustrations about her jerk of a husband as she violently stomped divots on the field in her Chanel suit and oversized hat.

"That's right," said Steve, "polo. You ride?"

Kat shook her head. "Nope. I am not what you would call a horsey person."

Steve nodded. His phone pinged. "Oh man, it's a text from Michael." His voice sank to a conspiratorial whisper. "You know, *Bay*. I have to answer this."

As he turned away from the table, Kat tried to push down a rising wave of annoyance.

"So anyway," said Dee hurriedly, "I absolutely love *Winter's Passing*. It's one of my all-time favorites. I cry every time I watch it. And you were practically still in school when you made it, right?"

"About a year out," said Kat.

"It was a crime that it lost the Oscar," said Dee.

Kat smiled ruefully. "Well, you know what they say, just an honor to be nominated."

Steve looked up from his phone again, smirking. "But then...*Red Hawk*."

Kat felt the smile freeze on her face. "Yes. *Red Hawk*."

Steve made a clucking sound with his tongue. "Man, how much money did that one lose? It was some kind of record, wasn't it?"

Kat met his beady eyes defiantly. "Came this close to making the Guinness book."

Dee laughed. Steve didn't even crack a smile.

"Hell of a thing to be remembered for," he said. "And didn't you have a fling with Jack Hayes while you were filming? He dumped you right after the box office numbers came in, right?"

Kat fought the urge to stab him with her fork. "Something like that."

"Well, they should have known better, really. Talk about ruining the source material. I mean, what little boy was going to want to see a girly version of *Red Hawk* comics?"

Kat stiffened. "And what Hollywood producer is so out of touch that he still thinks a bunch of little boys are driving the box office?"

Steve sniffed. "Yeah, because stunt-casting a female director obviously brought the audience out in droves."

Kat slowly counted to ten in her head before speaking again. "You know, I made a lot of mistakes on that film, but I'm pretty sure that being born female wasn't one of them."

He shook his head. "Shoulda stuck with what you know."

She cocked her head. "Oh? And what, exactly, do I know?"

"Rom-coms. Princess movies. Fifty Shades of Crap."

She stared at him. "You're kidding, right?"

He shrugged and looked back at his phone. "Your movie tanked. That says it all."

Kat felt her face flush, and some very choice words rose to her lips, but Dee hurriedly interrupted. "But that was all years ago," she said in a placating tone. "I'm sure you've done a ton since then, right?"

Kat took a deep breath and forced herself to turn away from Steve so she could give Dee her usual spiel about having some work in development, about how she was working on a new spec—but before she could even really start, Steve's phone pinged again.

"Oh, yep, gotta take this one, too," he interrupted.

That was it. She'd had enough.

She put her hand on his wrist and gave him her sweetest smile. "You know, Steve, I feel like we kind of got off on the wrong foot. Can we start over?"

He looked back at her, suspicious at first, but she just kept smiling until she saw the exact moment when he relaxed and a new kind of interest kindled in his eyes. His gaze slid down to her chest.

Bingo. She licked her lips in anticipation.

"It's cool," he finally said. "But I seriously gotta answer this text."

"Oh, is that Michael Bay again? Are you really friends with him?" Her Southern accent was suddenly thicker.

He smirked. "Played tennis with him just last week."

She looked up at him from under her lashes. "That is so amazing. I heard he only works with the best. You must be really good at what you do."

He straightened his shoulders. "I think it's fair to say that I know what I'm doing."

"I can see that." She smiled again, squeezing his arm. "I bet there's a lot you could teach me."

He raised his eyebrows. "I bet you're right."

She giggled. "Oh, hey, is that the latest iPhone? So neat. Do you mind if I take a look at it for just one little second?"

Steve chuckled. "Haven't seen it yet, eh? I had my assistant stand in line for twelve hours to get this thing." He passed it over.

Kat stood up, dropped the phone on the floor, and ground it under her heel.

"What the hell?" yelled Steve, his face going beet red.

Kat looked him in the face. "Oops. I'm so sorry," she said, deadpan. She stomped down again. "It must have slipped."

She smiled blissfully as she leaned even harder, enjoying the satisfying crunch of metal against metal.

Chapter Two

Sebastian," giggled the blonde, halfheartedly swatting away his hand, "stop it!"

Seb grinned and splashed her again. "Stop what, Lily?"

The blonde stopped giggling and pouted as she bobbed in the pool. "I'm Jilly, not Lily."

Sebastian turned to the redhead stretched out on a float next to him, "Then you must be Lily."

She huffed in protest, wrinkling her little nose. "I'm Amy!"

"Come into the water, Amy." Sebastian pulled her into the pool with a splash.

"Sebastian!" she cried, pushing her sopping wet hair out of her face, "you are the worst!"

Sebastian grinned. "Indeed I am. Now, should we have a bit more champagne?"

He was just reaching for the bottle sitting by the pool when a pair of boots stepped between him and the wine. The two women looked up and squealed, sinking under the water, trying to cover up their nakedness. Sebastian squinted up into the night.

Sebastian's older brother, Alejandro, loomed over him like a judgmental Greek statue.

"*Perdón*," he said, calmly, "but might I have a word with you in the pool house, Sebastian?"

"Of course," murmured Sebastian. "*Un momento, hermano.*"

Alejandro retreated into the pool house, shutting the door behind him.

"Oh my God," sputtered Jilly as she emerged from under the water, "was that Alejandro Del Campo? Holy shit, he's even better looking than his Instagram!"

Seb rolled his eyes. "Those are Photoshopped."

He climbed out of the water, not bothering to put on his clothes, and joined his brother in the pool house. Alejandro looked down at him, shaking his head.

"What can I do for you?" said Seb.

"Well, for one, you could put on some pants," said Alejandro.

Sebastian shrugged. "Why bother? Did you see those ladies? I'd just have to take them off again. So much work."

Alejandro's jaw tightened. "You know, my wife and eight-month-old son are sleeping in the house."

"Oh, please, they're all the way in the west wing. They can't hear a thing. They might as well be in Argentina."

"And our mother—"

Seb snorted. "She had three glasses of wine with dinner. You and I both know she is sleeping like the dead."

Alejandro looked upward in frustration and ran his hands through his hair. "And I suppose it's useless for me to remind you that we have a match tomorrow?"

Sebastian nodded. "We do. So you better get your rest, *Capitán*. Don't worry, I'll do my best to keep things quiet. Though I cannot promise much." Sebastian winked at his brother. "That Jilly is quite a lively girl."

Alejandro shook his head, a tired look on his face. "You

know, Sebastian," he said, "what was cute at twenty-two is no longer so charming at thirty-four."

"Thirty-three," said Sebastian automatically.

Alejandro shrugged. "I just hope you are fit to play tomorrow," he said as he turned away. "I would hate to have to pull you off the field."

Chapter Three

Well," said Honey, "the good news is that Steve Meyers said he wouldn't press charges if you replaced the phone and apologized."

Kat struggled with her house key as she balanced her own phone between her ear and shoulder. The lock had been sticking lately. She bumped the door with her hip a couple of times and finally felt it give. "And the bad news is that I didn't get the job," she said as she stumbled into the entryway and flipped on the light. "Right?"

"Um, duh, babe. But actually, Dee liked you. She told me that she definitely wants to work with you down the line."

Kat rolled her eyes as she bent to gather the mail on her floor. "Fat lot of good that does me now."

"Listen, you never know, okay? Maybe Steve will get caught screwing a studio head's wife and get thrown out of town. Or maybe Dee will get a promotion and end up running the whole place. The Industry works in mysterious ways."

Kat sighed in frustration as she sorted through the stack of envelopes and magazines. She needed a job now, not down the line. "What about the rewrite at Paramount? What happened with that?"

"One of the producers hired her boyfriend. Sorry."

"What about the open call at Fox?"

"Filled by some Diablo Cody wannabe."

"Well, what about—"

Honey cut her off. "Listen, Kat, what we need—aside from you learning to control your horrible, horrible temper—is a fresh writing sample. Something I can send out wide. A reason for everyone to remember just how good you really are. We gotta get that spec out. How's it coming? Are you close?"

Kat hesitated for a split second. "Yeah," she said. "Yeah, I mean, it's still in first-draft shape, but it's—you know, coming along. It shouldn't be too much longer."

"Great, great. I'm excited to read."

"But Honey, listen, if anything comes up—directing or writing—even like, you know, a commercial or maybe even a web series—"

"Just put your energy into finishing that script, girl. That's the key. And try not to break any more phones, okay?"

Kat sat down at her kitchen table and closed her eyes. "Okay. Got it. Will do. Thanks, Honey."

"Sure, babe. And no worries, okay?" Kat felt a pang of dread at the slight note of defeat in Honey's voice. "You know this business. Everyone has their ups and downs. I'm sure things will get better soon."

Kat put her phone down and tried not to cry. She hated lying to Honey, but she couldn't bear to tell her the truth either. She had abandoned her spec weeks ago. She'd read through the first act (which was as far as she'd written) and admitted to herself what she had known all along—that it was uninspired garbage. The same story she had already told and sold in a dozen different ways without ever getting another movie actually made.

No one wanted another plucky-small-town-girl-makes-good story anymore. And the fact was, Kat was sick of writing them. Especially since the days when she could identify with that kind of character were all but dead, burned, and buried.

She knew she had to start over, find something bigger, more personal, more essential, to write about. But for the first time in her life, she didn't know where to begin.

Kat hadn't had paid work for over a year. She had taken meeting after meeting, mining all her contacts, but nothing seemed to stick. She'd plowed through her savings, sure that the next job was just around the corner. Her agent, Jimmy, had stopped calling about three months ago, and now even Honey, who had always been as much a friend as a manager, was beginning to sound defeated. Kat was sure that, if she told her that she had writer's block, it would be the final straw.

She sighed and began pulling the pins out of her hair, releasing the wild black curls in a halo around her face. She stared at the stack of mail. Bills. Mortgage. Student loans. Overdue credit cards...

She stood up and made herself a pot of coffee. The kitchen was beautiful but depressing. She'd let her housekeeper go last month, and it showed. It smelled like last night's leftovers. There were two days' worth of dirty dishes stacked in the sink. Even the things that usually gave her pleasure—the way the golden California light slanted through the big Palladian window above her sink, the brightly colored Talavera tiles on her backsplash, the cheerful robin's egg blue of her La Cornue stove—couldn't cheer her up.

In fact, the whole house felt like a rebuke.

Buying a home was one of the first thing she did after

signing the contracts for *Red Hawk*. She'd been living like a college student in a tiny apartment in the valley with a revolving series of roommates, and she wanted to feel like a grown-up. She had a real career now, she reasoned, it was time to have a real home. And everyone assured her it was the thing to do, even at the height of the California real estate boom.

She'd tried to be sensible at first—looking at a sagging fixer upper in Huntington Park, a dark industrial loft in a marginal neighborhood downtown, a ranch house in Studio City that had once been owned by a somewhat famous B-list actor, but now smelled like cats and fifty years of cigarettes...But then, as if sensing her weakness, the Realtor had taken her to see this house, a 1920s three-bedroom Spanish-style cottage, tucked high up in the Hollywood Hills.

Kat had been filled with longing from the moment she walked in. The warm afternoon light poured in through every window and danced over the gleaming pine floors, the thick plaster walls, and the cheerful little beehive fireplace in the sunken living room. She got even more excited when she saw the snug, colorful kitchen with its intricately painted tiles and pretty blue stove. And when she discovered the copper slipper tub in the master bathroom, she almost made an offer on the spot. But it was when she'd walked out back and had been faced with the sparkling infinity pool overlooking the endless view of the city that she finally lost all reason. It was way out of her planned budget, but she had decided to bank on her future success and somehow make it work.

And it had worked for a little while. Jobs were offered, and checks kept coming in, and she'd started accumulating beautiful things to fill her beautiful house. She combed every flea market she stumbled across. Picking out mismatched china and silver flatware piece by intricate piece, never buying even a single fork unless she absolutely loved it, until she had a wild, colorful set big enough to feed twenty people if she wanted to. She sought out copper cookware in every size and shape, loving the substantial feeling of the heavy metal under her hands, the bright-penny look of them lined up on her stove. She drank her coffee from dusky green Wedgewood cups, the bone china so delicate and thin that she could see the shadow of her hand when she raised the cup to the light. She haunted the little boutiques on La Brea, looking for just the right mother-of-pearl inlaid side table, the softest hand-knotted wool rug, a beautifully tarnished silver platter big enough to serve an entire suckling pig if she ever had the need.

She unearthed a perfectly distressed harvest table in the back of a barn in Ojai, worn with the patina of a hundred years of farm wives shelling peas and hulling strawberries on its surface. She worked at an enormous Arts and Crafts desk in her office. It was bursting with pocket drawers, sliding doors, and secret compartments. She had a couch upholstered in yards and yards of the prettiest Liberty of London calico print, and so overstuffed with down that it felt like she had fallen into a cloud whenever she sat upon it. She found local artists she liked and splurged on their paintings and photographs for her walls. She filled her shelves with novels and cookbooks, art books, and biographies. She had a solid silver tea service and a queen-sized bed carved with such intricate designs of birds and roses that Frida Kahlo herself would have been thrilled to sleep on it. She slept under a crazy quilt so beautifully embroidered, it should have been in a museum instead of draped over her at night...

And she didn't stop with just household stuff. She had a closet stuffed with designer clothes tailored to fit her exactly right. There was a bureau bursting with silk and lace lingerie. She had expensive lotions, vials of perfume, and countless pots and tubes of high-end cosmetics. She never bathed in her slipper tub without dropping in some scented oil or a handful of dried herbs and petals that she had specially mixed for her at a little shop in Silver Lake. Afterward, she would dry herself off with huge, thirsty Egyptian cotton towels and then slip between her antique linen sheets.

These things used to make her feel safe. They made her feel surrounded by treasures so beautiful that they somehow lent their magic to her work and day-to-day life. But now they just made her panic because she had spent, she hadn't saved, and all she could see around her now were things to lose, things that were slipping from her hands.

Ten years in L.A. and what did she have left? A couple thousand dollars in the bank; this beautiful house full of beautiful things that she could no longer afford; a string of broken relationships; one small, good movie—*Winter's Passing*—and one huge, horrendous bomb—*Red Hawk*.

Red Hawk was the film that was supposed to propel her firmly onto the A-list, to smash the tinsel ceiling for women writer-directors once and for all. A film that, instead, had broken her heart and pretty much ruined her career.

She had been so young. And everyone had made such a big deal about what a pioneering moment it would be—a woman director taking on a major comic book franchise. It was a huge opportunity. The money was great. She loved the source material. The project already had an enormous, built-in fan base. She knew that there were hundreds of directors who would've happily crawled over broken glass and her own dead body to get the kind of break she was being offered. It seemed like a home run.

So she signed on. Even though the script they gave her had already gone through half a dozen writers and still needed serious work. Even though the producers managed to say at least one incredibly offensive and/or sexist thing to her in almost every conversation she had with them. Even though her only real experience had been with a low-budget indie. Even though she hadn't been given the cast she wanted. Even though she was refused final cut.

It had been a disaster from day one. There were swarms of producers and studio execs on set. There was a huge cast, many of whom were A-list stars. There were agents and managers, all watching from the sides. Everyone had an opinion. Everyone had an agenda. Everyone felt she needed to be micromanaged. And no one thought twice about foisting their point of view onto Kat.

She tried to make everyone happy, and that was terrible. And then she tried to just make herself happy, and that was even worse. She lost her temper on an almost daily basis. She nearly cried in front of the entire cast and crew twice. And then, one day, while she was hiding in a supply closet, trying to will herself to take on the next scene, Jack Hayes stumbled in, looking for a hidden place to smoke a cigarette. It was his first big movie, he had a sizable part, and he was cocky and gorgeous—everyone could already see what a huge star he was going to become—and he offered to share his forbidden cigarette with Kat, and then suddenly, before she knew it, Kat was sleeping with one of her actors.

It went downhill from there. The film ran way over budget. The execs second-guessed every creative decision she made. The lead actress quit to go to rehab halfway through. The release date was pushed twice. And then the studio commandeered the final cut and butchered her vision of the story. Kat actually did cry when she saw the version they released. It was terrible, nothing like what she had imagined—she wished she could take her name off the whole thing. And the critics had agreed with her; the reviews were merciless. The box office had been painfully small. On lots all over town, people had clucked their tongues and made jokes about sending in a girl to do a man's job.

Plus, she came home one night to find Jack in bed with her Pilates instructor.

Overnight, Kat went from being a wunderkind to the purest type of poison. People literally turned their eyes away from her when she entered a room. She became invisible in an industry that was all about being seen.

She'd survived on dribs and drabs of work after that, waiting to break in again, but nothing ever stuck, and now it seemed that even the regular trickle of rewrites and punch-ups she'd been able to count on had dried up at last.

Kat sighed and sipped her coffee. She knew that Honey was right, there was only one way back in. As much as everyone enjoyed gloating over an epic failure, they loved a comeback even more, and industry memories could be conveniently short when it suited them. Kat knew that people would, at least, still read what she wrote. And if she wrote something great, all would be forgiven.

Kat looked at the dirty dishes in the sink, the kitchen full of high-end appliances, the view out the window of her glimmering pool, the house full of her intricate, lovely things that she had thoughtlessly spent her money on, always expecting more cash to come. None of this was inspiring greatness.

Her phone rang and a capital *M* appeared on the screen.

"Hi, Mama."

"Katy Ann?" Her mother's voice sounded far away and worried. "It's about your daddy..."

Chapter Four

"Her husband is in the hospital, *pobrecita*," said Sebastian's mother, Pilar, as she poured him a cup of morning coffee. "A stroke apparently."

Sebastian accepted the cup gratefully, rubbing his temple. The bright morning light pouring in through the kitchen windows made him wince. The girls had finally left just before dawn. "I'm sorry," he said, "but which maid? Surely not the blond one—I didn't even know she was married."

Alejandro snorted as he leaned over to his baby son and spooned some cereal into his mouth. "Not that it would make any difference to you if she was."

Pilar *tsk*'d, distracted. "*Ay*, don't say such things, Jandro. Your brother would never be involved with a married *doña*."

Alejandro shrugged. "One would hope."

"Well, I suppose it depends on just how big her husband might be," Seb joked.

Pilar gave him a little punch in the arm. "*Basta ya, hijo.* Anyway, I am not talking about a maid. I'm talking about Corinne. The housekeeper. Really, Sebastian, she's worked for us for years."

"Oh, poor Corinne! When did this happen?" asked Alejandro's wife, Georgia.

Unlike her husband and mother-in-law, who were both immaculately dressed and groomed, Georgia was still in her pajamas, her caramel-colored hair in casual disarray. Sebastian glanced at her and smiled, glad to have a *compañera* in his dislike for early mornings.

Pilar spooned some sugar into her tea. "Two days ago. It was a small stroke, but still, he will need time and rehabilitation. I only just found out now. Corinne called to let me know she wouldn't be in this week. I told her not to worry—*por supuesto*, we would be fine—but she's insisting that she'll bring in some help. She has a daughter who used to work for her apparently."

Georgia put down her fork. "Well, I'm going to call and see if there's anything we can do. Surely a meal or two at least?"

Alejandro smiled at his wife and reached out to touch her arm. "That is very sweet of you, *querida*."

They gazed at each other for a moment, exchanging a glance so private and charged that it made Sebastian look away, embarrassed.

He smiled ruefully. If he didn't see proof of it on a daily basis, he never would have believed that his brother could fall so hard and so deep for a woman.

Having grown up under the shadow of a father who regularly and openly strayed from their mother, the two brothers had each struggled to find their own ways of coping with their paternal legacy.

But as much as he admired his brother's marriage, Sebastian couldn't see himself taking the same path. He'd figured out quite young that no one could get hurt the way his mother had been if no one ever got attached. So he flitted from one woman to the next, having his fun along the way, and being certain that he never paused long enough to form any real connection.

Pilar cleared her throat, and Alejandro and Georgia jumped, suddenly seeming to remember that they were not actually alone. "Yes, well," said Pilar, "let me know what Corinne says. And I'll order flowers. But I'll need one of you to deliver them to her house. You know *el hospital* cannot be trusted."

Sebastian snorted. Ever since his mother had once sent flowers to an ailing friend that had been misdirected to the maternity ward, she refused to believe that anything would be delivered properly. "Send Jandro, *Mamá.* Old ladies like him better than me."

Georgia giggled and then quickly covered up with a cough when her husband shot her a look.

Pilar frowned at Sebastian. "Between the match and the award he is getting tonight for mentoring those *barrio* children, your brother has enough to do." She smiled at her elder son and patted him on the arm.

Alejandro smirked at Seb like he was nine years old again and had just been given the last piece of cake.

Sebastian rolled his eyes. "Fine, then, wouldn't want to interrupt Saint Alejandro's quest for a Nobel Prize." He turned to his brother. "Pity I won't make it to the barn this morning, though, but obviously, this is much more important."

Pilar shook her head. "No, no, the flowers won't be delivered until later today. You can do both, *no problema.*"

Alejandro smiled smugly at Seb. "*Sí, hermano,* you can do both, *no problema.*"

* * *

Sebastian headed for the barn, annoyed. He was hungover and exhausted, and the last thing he wanted to do was ride, but he had skipped practice twice already this week, and he knew he should get some warm-up time on the pitch before the game. Plus, it wasn't worth seeing the pissed-off look on his brother's face if he insisted on taking the morning off.

He sighed as he brushed out his pony. When did things get so bad between him and Jandro? Of course, Alejandro had always been more responsible, more conservative. He'd had to be. He was the older brother, the head of the family since their father had died. But Sebastian's lifestyle—his drinking, his partying, the women—had never seemed to bother his brother before. In fact, Jandro had always seemed amused by it all, if anything, enjoying his younger brother's sense of humor and lust for life.

The pony snorted her protest at Seb's heavy hand with the curry comb. Seb instinctively lightened his touch.

He knew that Alejandro had gone through a lot. His brother had been unhappily married, and then widowed, very young. For years he'd raised his daughter, Valentina, on his own while he also led the polo team and managed the family dynasty. He'd definitely carried the weight of the world on his shoulders.

But things were different now. Georgia was more than his match in every way. Valentina was safely off to college in New York City. They had little Tomás, who was a bright and easy baby. The team was winning again. The Del Campos were respected and admired just as much, if not more, as they had been when their father was still alive.

Really, in most ways, Alejandro was happier than Seb had ever seen him.

And yet his relationship with Sebastian was worse than it had ever been. Whenever Jandro turned to his little brother, it seemed that the happiness simply slid off his face. He was brusque, sharp, and disappointed. It was almost as if, once Alejandro had managed to get his own affairs in order, his focus had simply shifted onto Sebastian's life. And, thought Sebastian ruefully, his brother had obviously found it to be greatly wanting.

Seb put down the curry comb, annoyed. Why should he try to please Alejandro when his brother treated him with so little respect? Why should he practice when he was exhausted? If he was going to play at all decently this afternoon, what he really needed was a nap.

He patted his pony as he led her back into her stall. "Sorry, *chiquita*. I'll make it up to you later."

He passed his mother behind the wheel of her Mercedes as he made his way back to the *hacienda*. She stopped her car and rolled down her window. "*Bueno*, Sebastian. I'm glad you're back. The flowers should be delivered within the hour. I left Corinne's address on the kitchen table. Run them over with our regards as soon as they arrive, okay?"

Seb reluctantly nodded. So much for his nap.

Instead of going back to bed, he made his way down to the home theater in the basement, yawning as he sank into the butter-soft leather sofa. He started to scroll through the menu of movies on the flat screen, but nothing looked appealing. Maybe just a quick little rest, he thought as his eyes slowly closed.

Chapter Five

It never failed to amaze Kat how her parents managed to keep every last detail of their home exactly as it had always been. It was as if the cottage were encased in amber. The worn, indescribably comfortable red sofa in the living room, the cheerful grass green tile on the kitchen floor, the round pine table in the dining room with the cut-glass cruets of olive oil and balsamic vinegar—subtle evidence of her mother's Italian-American heritage. Even the succession of identical, slightly mangy black cats who all seemed to enjoy the same sunny spot in the living room window. Kat's father was an animal lover, and he always said that no one ever wanted black cats, so he made it a special point to give them a home.

She had not seen her father yet. Her mother had picked her up from the airport, and they had gone straight to the hospital, but her father had just been whisked away for tests, the doctors said it might be a few hours before he could receive visitors. Her mother had insisted that Kat go home so she had could unpack and rest a little before coming back to the hospital. She assured Kat that her father was not bad at all. "Just a little stroke," she'd said. "A teeny tiny one. He'll be absolutely fine." And Kat desperately wanted to believe her.

Kat drifted into her old bedroom, which was also untouched but strikingly different from the rest of the cottage. Instead of perfect cleanliness and order, here were messy clues to her past and a chaotic map of her future. The walls were papered with movie posters and pictures torn from magazines: Susan Sarandon and Geena Davis grinning out from *Thelma and Louise*; Holly Hunter from Jane Campion's *The Piano*; stills from *Clueless*, *9 to 5*, *Bull Durham*, *Breakfast Club*, *She's Gotta Have It*...a whole collection of Katharine Hepburn, Bette Davis, and Marlene Dietrich. On one wall, she had pinned up her tickets from every movie she had seen from the time she was ten years old.

She smiled as she touched the overlapping collage of film stubs and memories—she had seen some great films, but a lot of terrible ones as well. She hadn't known how to differentiate yet. All she knew was that there was no place she was happier than the air-conditioned multiplex on a Sunday afternoon.

On another wall were pictures of her favorite film couples—Bogie and Bacall, Liz and Dick, Maria and Tony, Edward and Vivian, Rose and Jack, Harry and Sally, Satine and Christian, Buttercup and Westley...These made her feel wistful, remembering the girl she had been—endlessly lying in bed, staring up at these images of true love, feverishly spinning her own romantic future...God, that's probably why she'd never found the right guy. All these expectations. There was no way real-life romance could hold a candle to the glories of the silver screen.

She sighed and sank down onto her narrow bed. Her body fit into the mattress as if she were sixteen all over again. She turned her head on the pillow and took a deep breath. She could almost smell the Anaïs Anaïs perfume, Noxzema face wash, and Mane 'n Tail shampoo.

Oh, if she could only go back to that girl and give her some advice—let her know that the braces would come off, her skin would clear up, that being tall and smart were not such bad things after all. She would tell her what mistakes to avoid, what men to stay away from, not to spend so much time worrying that she'd be stuck in Wellington forever.

Except, of course, here she was, home again.

She tried to tell herself she'd come home for her parents' sake, but deep down she couldn't ignore the niggling suspicion that she would have ended up back here anyway. There had simply been nowhere else to go. And prospects seemed dim that she'd make it back out this time. Unless she could finally find the way back to her work.

The buzz of the doorbell startled her. She groaned and buried her head in her pillow. Her first instinct was to ignore it—hoping that whoever it was would go away—but then, she reprimanded herself, she had come here to help, not hide in her room like a recalcitrant teen.

* * *

Sebastian felt foolish. A gigantic bouquet of purple, hot pink, and orange blooms—wisteria, peonies, and birds of paradise—blocked his view. The florist must have made a mistake. There was no way his mother would have ordered something so ostentatious. But he'd overslept and the flowers had been delivered before he had woken from his nap. He knew that if he bothered to take the time to return them and negotiate the exchange, he'd never get them dropped off and still make it to the club for the opening chukka.

The door swung open, and instead of the motherly-looking maid he was expecting, a tall woman with golden skin, high cheekbones, riotous black curls, and cool gray eyes looked back at him.

"Uh," he said, "Mrs. Parker?"

The woman shook her head. "She's out. Can I help you?" Her voice was low and husky.

He blinked, momentarily forgetting why he was even there. There was something about her steady gaze that unnerved him. That, and the little beauty mark just above her upper lip. It looked like a tiny smudge of chocolate. "I—uh—Mrs. Parker—"

"My mother," she prompted.

He nodded. Right. He'd forgotten that her daughter was in town. He looked at the flowers in his hands. "Ah, oh yes, these are for your *papá*. Your father." He thrust the enormous bouquet into her arms. "Courtesy of the Del Campo family."

The woman raised her brows, looking amused. "Wow. Well, I'm pretty sure this is the biggest bouquet my daddy's ever received." She ducked her head and smelled a peony, looking up at him through the fringe of her long, dark lashes. "Actually they're probably the only flowers he's ever received," she added, and smiled.

Sebastian's heart constricted. Her smile was slow and sweet and absolutely dazzling. He felt breathless.

She looked at him expectantly for a moment longer, and then said, "Oh! Sorry! Wait. Hang on," and left him standing in the doorway.

He blinked, confused, and then she was back with her purse in her hand. She dug out a five-dollar bill and tried to hand it to him.

He stared at her bewildered.

She wrinkled her nose. "Is it—is it not enough?"

"What?"

"The tip?"

He almost laughed. She thought he was the delivery boy. She waited earnestly for his answer.

He smiled, mischievous. "Oh, well, normally it would be fine, but you know, for around here..." He shrugged.

She flushed and added a ten-dollar bill to the five and offered it to him. He grinned and took the money from her.

A tingling bolt of electricity passed through his body as his fingers brushed hers.

Her eyes widened. She obviously felt it, too. He gazed at her for a moment—noticing the tight curves of her body beneath the simple jeans and tank top she was wearing, her shapely legs that seemed to go on forever. Suddenly, he felt a little less playful.

"I'm sorry," he said, "I didn't catch your name."

She frowned. "I didn't give it."

He took a step toward her. She didn't move. He smelled something sweet and dark, like caramel. He wondered if it was her or the flowers. "Maybe you should," he said.

She looked at him, her cheeks flushing an even deeper pink. "I—I don't think so."

She took a step back.

"Wait—" he said.

But she had already shut the door in his face.

Chapter Six

O*h my God*, thought Kat as she dropped the flowers on the table and leaned back against the wall, feeling her heart beat a tattoo against her chest. What the hell was *that*?

She shook her head, trying to get ahold of herself. She had been in Hollywood for ten years. She'd met George Clooney, Denzel Washington, Brad Pitt, Ryan frigging Gosling, and yet she would swear on the family Bible that she had never seen a more attractive man than the one who had just been standing there on her front porch, holding a monster bouquet of flowers and looking for all the world like he wanted to eat her alive.

"And I'm pretty sure I'd enjoy every single minute of it," she muttered to herself.

The thick, wavy hair, the pale green eyes, the lightning flash of a smile, the broad shoulders, and the luscious golden skin with just enough of a five o'clock shadow to make her wonder what he'd been doing last night that left him with so little time to shave this morning...It was as if all her daydreaming about impossible teen love and romance had conjured up this vision and handed it over—along with the slightest tantalizing hint of a mysterious accent—lock, stock, and barrel, right to her front door.

And a delivery guy, no less, she thought. Slap a mustache on the man and it was like a bad porn film.

God, she had totally lost her cool. Why hadn't she told him her name? Why had she slammed the door in his face? It was like she was a gawky teen all over again, giggling and blushing every time a boy even looked her way.

She looked at the flowers on the table. Of course. That was it. A second impression. She would find an excuse to go to the florist where he worked, just casually bump into him as she perused the roses and daisies...

She imagined the surprised look on his face when he saw her, the knowing way he would smile at her. Maybe she'd dress up just the tiniest bit—a little skirt with a tee. That black Chanel skirt that showed off her legs so well, and that perfect, soft faded green tee she'd found in the boutique on Melrose, the one that fit her just so and made her eyes look more blue than gray...

She put the flowers back down. "No. No. No. No. Just stop," she said aloud. Jesus. This was ridiculous. What was she thinking? She was going to date a delivery guy? She was a grown woman plotting like a girl desperate for a date to the prom. She'd seen this guy once. One time. She knew nothing about him except that he delivered flowers for a living and he was scorchingly hot. She was here to help her parents. To clear her head. To get back to her work. The very last thing she needed was some out-of-control crush—or worse yet, another inappropriate romance—to distract her from her tasks.

She unceremoniously dumped the flowers into a pink plastic pitcher that usually held Kool-Aid and plunked it next to the roses on the table. Her plate was more than full. And she was definitely not looking for love.

Chapter Seven

Sebastian dismounted from his horse and threw down his mallet in disgust. All around him his teammates and their well-wishers celebrated and congratulated one another, but he could not wait to get off the field. He'd been an embarrassment. The team had won, but he had played terribly.

He tossed the reins of his pony over to the nearest groom and shouldered his way through the crowd. He caught a glimpse of his brother's smiling face as Alejandro leaned down and kissed his beaming wife. Alejandro looked up for a second and locked eyes with Sebastian. His ecstatic smile quickly darkened, and he opened his mouth to speak, but Sebastian just kept walking. The last thing he needed right now was the inevitable dressing down and I-told-you-so he knew he had coming.

He stalked through the parking lot and threw himself into his dark green Porsche Spyder, slamming the door behind him. He sat for a moment in sullen silence before smashing his hands against the steering wheel in frustration, and then starting up the car with a roar and peeling out of the lot.

As he drove, he replayed all the mistakes he'd made on the

field that afternoon. He'd been slow and inattentive. He'd let his pony get bumped off the line of the ball. He'd been hooked three times by an absolute *choto*, and then missed his penalty shots. In fact, he'd missed nearly all of his shots. It was a miracle, really, that the team had won.

It was a new and uncomfortable feeling for Sebastian— this awareness that he'd been subpar on the pitch. Even if he avoided practice, even if he played hungover more often than not, his natural talent and athleticism had always carried him along. His father used to rail at him, telling him that he had more inborn ability in his little finger than the rest of the team put together, and if he would just apply himself, show a little self-discipline, practice and train like the rest of the team did, he could have a 10-goal handicap. He could be among the very best. But Sebastian had never wanted to be the best. He'd just wanted to have his fun, be good enough, and let Jandro have the glory.

But today he had not been good enough. Not even close. And this had just been the worst in a steady series of lackluster games for him lately. He hated to admit it, but Alejandro was right. He needed to buckle down, pull his weight, pay attention. No more drinking, no more late nights, no more missed practices. He would turn over a new leaf.

Starting tomorrow.

He made a brutal left-hand turn into the parking lot of a run-down bar outside of town and skidded the car to a halt. He reached into his kit bag in the backseat and pulled out a clean T-shirt and tennis shoes, stripping off his telltale La Victoria jersey and riding boots. He didn't want to see anyone he knew, and he did not want to be recognized either. What he wanted was a stiff drink or two, and to find a woman he could lose himself in for the night and then never have to see again after the morning.

One more time to get it all out of his system, he promised himself as he pushed through the bar door.

After that, he'd be a changed man.

Chapter Eight

The hospital room was dim and quiet. The only noises were the occasional beep of the heart monitor and the sound of her father softly breathing in and out. Kat sat by his bed and watched him as he slept.

She rubbed her eyes, trying to hold back the tears. Even ill, Joe Parker's face was so handsome, with his firm jaw, strong cheekbones, and jaunty mustache. At seventy, his hair was more pepper than salt and still thick and wavy.

The doctor had told her that he'd been lucky. Though the right side of his body had been severely weakened, there didn't seem to be any cognitive damage. They said that he'd need a month or so in a rehabilitation clinic to get enough of his strength back so that he could walk again, but they thought none of the damage would be permanent.

Her father had always been a big, strong man. A man who could fix or build anything, a man who could easily carry her on his shoulders even when she'd been the tallest kid in the fourth grade. But now she had to admit, as she bent over his bed, he looked smaller somehow, shrunken, a little bit diminished, and definitely older than the last time she'd seen him.

God, how long had it been? Three years since her folks had come to see her in L.A.? Yes, because she'd still been working then, though on nothing much more than a script that had eventually been rewritten by another screenwriter and then left to languish on the studio shelf, never to be made. But at the time, it had seemed of immeasurable importance, and she'd resented every moment her parents had taken her away from it.

She'd been terrible when they were there, she thought with a wince. She had promised to take them to see all the sights—Grauman's Chinese Theatre and the La Brea Tar Pits, the Hollywood Bowl, and a tour of the studios. Her mom had even shyly mentioned that they wouldn't mind spending a day at Disneyland. And instead of showing them around, Kat had blown them off, made excuses, and pawned them off on her assistant while she was holed up in her office with her laptop, desperate to make her deadline for a producer who had already lost interest in the project.

And to make it worse, they had been ridiculously understanding about the whole thing, insisting that, of course Kat's work should come first, that they didn't need her assistant's help, that they would find their own way around the city if they wanted to see anything, that it was just nice to spend whatever time with their daughter that she could give them. Her mother had cooked dinner for her practically every night, for Pete's sake, and her father had spent the week fixing whatever he could find wrong in her house. They'd hardly seen more than a five-block radius of her place the entire time they were there.

And now, seeing her dad like this...She shook her head at her own selfishness. How could she have wasted time with them? How could she just blithely assumed there would always be another visit? Another chance to make up for her negligence?

Her father stirred and opened his eyes. For a moment, he looked panicked and confused, and Kat's heart clenched as she reached for his hand. "Daddy, I'm here. It's me, Kat."

Her dad turned toward her voice and, blinking, slowly focused on her face. Relief flooded through her as she felt him relax and a look of recognition sprang into his eyes.

"Katy, honey?" he said. His voice was raspy but sounded stronger than she'd expected. "What in the ever-lovin' hell are you doing here?"

She smiled, happy to hear him sound mostly like himself, happy to see the bright blue of his eyes, filled with the same kindness and laughter as always. "I've come to see you, Daddy."

He nodded, understanding, and his voice dropped to a whisper. "Let me tell you something important, Katy Kat."

She leaned forward to hear him.

"Getting old is for the goddamned birds."

She laughed. "Better than the alternative, though, right?"

He smiled ruefully. "I suppose."

She felt tears sting her eyes. "I'm so glad to see you, Daddy."

He shook his head. "Now, Katy, I hope you didn't stop work just to come out here. I know this might look a little bad, but really, I'll be fine."

She looked away for a moment, trying to gain some control. "Of course you will, Daddy. Actually, I'm taking a little break from Hollywood. Or rather"—she smiled ruefully—"maybe Hollywood's taking a little break from me."

"What about your house?"

"I rented it to a friend. I can write from here. I just

thought it was time to come home for a while. I've missed you guys."

He squeezed her hand. "Well, then, I'm happy you're here, baby." His smile suddenly faded, and he struggled to sit up. "How are you and Mama getting by with one car? Because you know my truck isn't safe for either of you to drive, but I can call up Jimmy and ask him for—"

She gently held his shoulders, trying to guide him back down. "No, no, don't worry, Daddy. Please, lie back down. We're fine with one. I don't have anywhere much I need to go, and we know better than to drive your old beater. That truck doesn't start for anyone but you."

He slumped back into the bed and gave her a weak smile. "Well, maybe that's because you call her an old beater."

She smiled back, worried about how tired he suddenly looked. "Maybe so. But you don't need to concern yourself with that. I'll take care of Mama. You just concentrate on getting better."

He nodded and closed his eyes, patting her hand. "Thank you, honey. You're a good girl, Katy Ann."

After he drifted back to sleep, when she knew for certain that he was absolutely out, Kat turned her face away and finally let the tears fall.

Chapter Nine

Sebastian slammed back his shot of tequila and then ordered another as he scanned the room. The bar was exactly what he had hoped for—sawdust and peanut shells on the floor, throbbing 1970s Southern rock on the jukebox, and a delightful array of available women. He had chosen a seat at the very back of the room to make sure he had a full view of his options. There were, he thought, several girls here tonight who would do nicely. The little blonde in the cowboy boots and cut-off shorts sitting at the bar and giving him the eye, a cocoa-skinned girl with long braids who had smiled at him as he walked past her, and a shapely red-head who actually seemed to be here on a date, but looked so bored that Seb was sure it wouldn't take much to lure her away.

Suddenly the image of a pair of eyes so gray that they were almost silver, a lush pair of soft, pink lips accented by a little chocolate freckle, and a head full of tumultuous black curls flashed into his mind. Now, if *she* were here, he would have no problem forgetting the game. In fact, if she were here, he was pretty sure all his troubles would be solved. At least temporarily.

Sebastian belted his second shot and the cheap liquor burned his throat as it slid down. For a moment, his body tightened, thinking of the high color that had bloomed in her cheeks when they had brushed hands, the golden slope of her bare shoulders, the way she had looked at him, her eyes sparking, just before she slammed the door in his face...God, what a woman. He must have thought of her a dozen times since meeting her that morning.

The redhead's date got up and headed toward the restrooms, leaving her alone.

It was now or never.

Shaking off the images of the gray-eyed girl, Seb stood up and casually strolled over to the redhead's table.

"Good evening," he said as he took her date's seat. "I couldn't help but notice that you look bored out of your mind with your gentleman friend. Are you, perhaps, open to other options?"

The redhead bit her lip and looked at him appraisingly. "What'd you have in mind?"

Sebastian grinned. He found—nine times out of ten—that a simple smile and then being brutally direct usually got him exactly what he wanted. "Well, a drink to start, then a drive, and then maybe—"

Suddenly, his entire body was jerked backward and out of his chair. He wrenched away and whirled to face the absentee date, and behind him, two more of his hulking, glowering friends. Each one was bigger than the next, and all looked as if they'd like nothing better than to teach Sebastian yet another lesson in humility.

Chapter Ten

Are you sure you don't want more, hon?" asked Kat's mother as she bustled around the immaculate kitchen. "Everything is still nice and hot."

Kat used her biscuit to mop up the last of the gravy on her pink Fiestaware plate and popped it into her mouth. She washed the bite down with a sip of sweet, creamy coffee and sighed contentedly. "No, thank you, Mama. It was so good, truly, but I couldn't eat another bite."

Corinne shook her head of neatly tended iron gray curls. "I wish you'd eat more, baby. You're nothing but skin and bones."

Kat laughed. "Mama, I'm already at least three sizes bigger than any woman is supposed to be in Hollywood, and if I keep eating your biscuits and gravy, they're never going to let me back over the border."

"Oh, *pish*," said Corinne, "that is nonsense. And even if it was true, you're behind the camera, not in front of it. No one cares about your dress size."

Kat brought her dishes to the sink and began to wash up. "You'd think that would be so, wouldn't you?"

Her mother joined her at the sink, drying the dishes as Kat cleaned them. "Isn't it?"

Kat snorted. "Heaven forbid any woman in Hollywood should forget that they are, first and foremost, eye candy."

Corinne's brow wrinkled. "Well, that must be an awful hard place," she said, "if someone as beautiful as you is convinced that they aren't good enough."

Kat smiled. "It's not so bad, Mama. I'm just telling you about the worst parts, is all. There's a lot of good stuff, too."

"Like what?"

"Oh, lots of things. There's the weather, for one."

Her mother rolled her eyes. "We have perfectly good weather here."

"You have humidity so thick you can practically eat it with a spoon. The weather in L.A. is always warm and dry, but not too hot, and the sky is always a perfect blue."

"Well, the sky is blue here, too."

Kat laughed. "And everyone thinks that Hollywood is full of mean, selfish people just looking to make a buck, but actually, if you think about it, it's full of artists. Deep down, almost everyone in Hollywood is a dreamer. Even the people making the worst movies and the crappiest TV shows started out planning to make something great."

Corinne frowned. "Katy Ann, are you sure you're going to be okay cleaning for me today? I just haven't had a chance to replace the maid that quit last week, and I need someone I can trust to fill in. But it seems like an awful lot to ask of you."

"Oh, Mama, I did it with you all through high school. I guess I'm not too proud to pick up a broom."

"How about scrub a toilet?"

"I don't suppose I've forgotten how to do that either."

"I could always go to work—and you could go to the hospital."

"I was with Daddy for hours last night. He needs you. He's trying too hard to be strong for me. He needs someone he can lean on."

Corinne nodded. "True enough." She sighed. "You know I hate to even ask, Katy Ann."

"I know, Mama."

"But with the hospital bills and your daddy missing work for a while..."

Kat looked at her mother. "Mama, I'm going to help you however I can. I just wish I could do more."

"You're doing plenty."

Kat put her arm around her mother's shoulder and squeezed. "You go on. I got this. I'll take care of those Del Campos, no problem. I'll do such a good job, they won't even miss you."

Corinne looked at her daughter, deadpan, "Well, maybe don't do *that* good a job, hon."

* * *

Sebastian lay on his back, squinting at his brother through his one good eye, his broken wrist propped up on the back of the couch. "I told you," he said. "This is not my fault."

The muscles in Alejandro's jaw twitched. "Then just whose fault is it, Sebastian? Because I do not see anyone else to blame at the moment."

Sebastian struggled to sit up, ignoring the pain in his sore ribs. "I could have just as easily broken my wrist on the field, Jandro. It's not as if we don't get injuries all the time."

"But you didn't hurt yourself on the field. You broke it in a bar fight."

"It wasn't even a fight. It was a more like *una masacre*. There were three of them. And they were huge—gigantic."

"And please tell me again, why did they attack you?"

"Because a girl one of them was with—okay, she turned out to be his wife, but I didn't know that part—gave me a little attention. As I said, not my fault."

Alejandro groaned in frustration. "We have another two months of games, Sebastian."

Sebastian held up the cast on his wrist. "I know. And I'm truly sorry. But obviously you're going to have to find someone else. Unless you'd like me to play *zurdo*—left handed."

For a moment, Alejandro looked like he was going to explode, then he shut his eyes, took a long, deep breath, and let it out again. "Maybe this is for the best anyway."

Sebastian looked at him. "What is that supposed to mean?"

His brother ran his hands through his hair. "I think you taking a break from the game isn't the worst idea. Your heart hasn't been in it lately. Perhaps some time off will help."

Sebastian felt stung by the truth of what Alejandro was saying, but forced himself to smile, determined not to show his feelings. "Maybe so. Who will you get to replace me?"

"I'm sure Hendy knows someone. Or perhaps Enzo can take it on."

"Great idea," said Sebastian casually. "Give the *piloto* some time on the field. I'm sure he'll be thrilled. Now"—he used his one good hand to fluff his pillow before he lay back down on the couch and grabbed the remote control—"I'm going to drown my disappointment in a bottle of tequila and a marathon of terrible movies."

Alejandro sighed as he left the room. "But of course you are, *hermano*. I expected no less of you."

Chapter Eleven

The house was enormous. Beautiful, but enormous. Filled with high coved ceilings and sweeping arches, Aubusson carpets and silk window dressings, dark wood floors and jewel-colored velvet upholstery. The whole place was lush and luxurious and brimming with art and books and glorious natural light from the countless floor-to-ceiling leaded glass windows. Kat now understood how it kept her mother busy full time, even with the small army of regular staff helping her.

Before Kat left for college, Corinne had worked for a dozen different clients around Wellington, cleaning houses from top to bottom all on her own. But this job for the Del Campos was different, Kat realized. Her mother had kept telling her that she was a housekeeper now, not just a maid. But it was only seeing the scope of Corinne's duties in person that made Kat finally understand. This was not just a cleaning job—this was a production. One that was, in some ways, every bit as complicated as any movie set Kat had ever been on.

Her mother supervised the other workers in the house, making sure every corner of the home was immaculate. She worked with the head gardener to keep the grounds up to par. She kept shopping lists, and hired and fired staff when needed. She made sure that there was nothing left unnoticed, no task left undone, and judging from the list of tasks Corinne had written out for Kat, she wasn't afraid of rolling up her sleeves and doing some of the dirty work herself when it was needed.

Kat had started cleaning early that morning in the enormous kitchen, taking note of the twelve-burner Wolf range, the huge glass-fronted refrigerator, and the way every bit of food inside it was arranged like a still life.

After living in Hollywood for so long, Kat was used to a certain level of luxury. Wealth no longer intimidated or impressed her in the same way it had when she was a girl. But this home was truly unlike any place she'd ever seen.

There was something old world about it. It was an estate—not just a house—but despite its size, it felt lived in and welcoming. As she wandered through the house, taking note of what needed to be done, and contemplating its most intimate spaces, Kat sensed a kindred soul in whoever had carefully curated the pieces in this home.

The bedrooms were restful and luxurious, painted in the kind of soft, glowing colors that would change with the light throughout the day and fade into a tranquil whisper at night. The shining dark wood floors were softened with subtly patterned silk carpets that tempted Kat to slide off her shoes and sink into them with her bare feet. The huge windows were tempered with linen drapes just the right thickness to change the light to a flattering twilight glow when they were pulled. The beds were covered in generously fluffy down comforters, with enough pillows to make them feel lush, but not smothered. In a few of the rooms, there were fireplaces abutted by big, comfortable chairs that Kat imagined would be perfect to curl up in and spend the day reading.

The en suite bathrooms were equally luxurious, with deep soaking tubs and glassed-in showers. In one bathroom, Kat admired what she imagined must be Pilar Del Campo's Art Deco dressing table. It was made of rosewood and topped with an elegant triple-folding mirror framed in light green Murano glass.

Kat decided to start her cleaning right then and there. She wanted an excuse to handle every little thing on that table. As she dusted and polished, she gripped the heavy silver and horn comb in her hand, enjoying its substantial weight; brought the cut glass bottle of Joy perfume to her nose for a delighted sniff; ran the tips of her fingers over the beautiful sable and tortoiseshell makeup brushes; and opened a heavily carved teak box to find a pirate's chest of gleaming, multicolored jewels.

Expensive jewelry had been the one thing that Kat had never really indulged in, reasoning that it was too easily lost or damaged, but these sparkling pieces made her gasp—they were so alluring—and she couldn't help reaching to touch them, softly running her finger over the glowing stones before she carefully shut the box and left the room.

Kat had been in houses this big before, but never one that also managed the trick of feeling like a real home. This place was full of pretty patinas and soft surfaces, sun-lit corners to curl up in, gorgeous art to get lost in, a snug little library brimming with books. Kat smiled when she found the playroom. It was filled with cushy, child-sized furniture, an antique rocking horse with a real saddle, and in the corner there was a large birdcage, where several canaries cheerfully hopped about and sang. One wall was painted with an enormous mural of life-sized horses and foals. She sighed, looking over the carefully arranged toys, games, and books. It almost made her ache to imagine the kind of magical childhood the Del Campo children must be experiencing.

She got to work, and by late afternoon, Kat had lost count of the number of bedrooms and bathrooms she'd been through. So many beds to make, so many floors to mop.

She supposed she should have felt miserable, going from meetings at Soho House to changing some stranger's Frette sheets, but there was something oddly soothing about the work. She'd helped her mother on and off in high school, earning pocket money by pitching in on weekends. Kat knew precisely the most efficient way to whirl through a room, knew how to reach the places that most people didn't ever think of cleaning. And though it had been years since she'd last done this kind of work, she fell back into her old rhythms in no time at all.

She didn't have to think. She didn't have to worry about meeting deadlines or propping up egos. Nobody cared what she was wearing or who she knew . . . It was just hospital corners and dusting, tidying up and running the vacuum. Every room started out beautiful, but looked even better after she left it, and that felt good. More tangible, at least, than staring at a blinking cursor on her laptop, wondering whether she'd ever write anything decent again.

She was dragging the Dyson down the stairs to the bottom floor when she heard it—music so familiar that, in a split second, she felt she was back in sound mixing, arguing with the producers about which version of the song they would use to score the credits.

It was, unmistakably, the bombastic closing number they'd used for *Red Hawk*.

She dropped the vacuum and followed the song into a room at the end of the hallway, where she saw, projected on a screen almost as big as the wall, the scrolling names of her entire cast and crew, intercut with what the execs had deemed to be "hilarious" outtakes and bloopers from the film. Kat scowled. She hated the credits. She'd fought and lost her battle over them just as she'd lost control of every other part of the movie.

For a moment, she froze, thinking that this had to be an elaborate joke someone was playing on her. What were the chances, after all, of this particular film being mysteriously played just at the moment she had walked down the stairs?

But then someone laughed. A low, rich chuckle over one of the more obvious pratfalls in the outtakes. Kat craned her neck to see who was lying on the enormous tufted leather couch in front of her and gasped when she spied the bruised and battered version of the man who had delivered her father's flowers just a day ago.

"What are you doing here?" she blurted out.

The man's face popped up from behind the couch and blinked in surprise. "Me?" he said incredulously. "I live here. What are *you* doing here?"

Kat's mind whirred. Oh, for Pete's sake, so he wasn't a delivery guy, he was a Del Campo brother. She should have known. Her mother had been talking about these guys for years...

"Okay. I'm guessing you're Sebastian, not Alejandro."

A smile played around his mouth. "What makes you so sure?"

"From what my mother has said, Alejandro would never pretend to be a delivery guy."

"And Sebastian would?"

"Definitely."

"Well, I didn't actually pretend. You assumed."

"You didn't exactly correct me."

"I didn't have a chance. You slammed the door in my face."

Kat looked away, embarrassed. "You gave me the flowers," she pointed out. "What else was supposed to happen?"

He raised an eyebrow. "I guess we'll never know."

Kat felt herself flush.

"But I find myself at a disadvantage. You have now gathered that I am neither a delivery boy nor Alejandro, but I still don't know what your name is or why, exactly, you are in my house."

"I'm Kat," she said. "And I'm temporarily working here. To help my mother."

The music changed on the screen, and she couldn't help looking up at it.

"A terrible movie," Sebastian said. "I mean, I'd heard it was bad, but it actually exceeded my expectations of just how horrible it could be."

She fought to keep her face neutral. "Oh?"

"Yes, it's all over the place. One minute a comedy, the next a dark drama. It made no sense."

Kat jutted her chin out defensively. "Well, there were a lot of people involved in the production."

"I mean, there were all these scenes where it would get interesting, and start to really pull you in, and then suddenly something ridiculous would happen. Like the female lead— why was she wearing a bikini while being chased through Detroit?"

Kat sighed in frustration. "She was wearing a bikini because she was sunbathing in the park when the Silver Shadow found her. But originally she was supposed to be wearing running gear because she was training for a marathon."

He looked at her. "What? I don't remember a marathon."

"No, the marathon's not in the movie. It was in the original version, but after the actress playing that part quit, they had to recast and the new actress didn't have as much clout, and so, when the producers suggested a bikini instead of running shorts and a tank top, she had to agree."

He stared at her. "How do you know that?"

She shrugged and looked away from him. "I think I saw a documentary."

"There's a documentary about this movie?"

"Or maybe it was in a magazine or something. I don't know." She looked back at him, determined to change the subject. "What happened to your face anyway? You look like you got hit by a truck."

He smiled ruefully. "Three trucks, as a matter of fact."

She locked eyes with him for a second and felt her heart speed up. Even with the bruises and scrapes and his eye half swollen shut, he was still ridiculously good looking.

He reached for the half-empty bottle of tequila sitting in front of him. "Would you like a drink?"

She laughed, almost tempted to take him up on it. "I need to finish cleaning your house."

"How much do you have left?"

"Just this room."

He leaned forward and straightened some magazines on the coffee table. "There. It's clean. Now would you like a drink?"

She couldn't help laughing again. "No."

"How about dinner?"

"Hey, wait a moment," she said, suddenly remembering something. "You took my tip! You owe me fifteen dollars!"

Sebastian's face split into a grin. "Well then, it's settled. I shall return your tip, and *you* can buy *me* a drink."

She was about to say no again, but then he reached out and lightly touched her hand with his, and it was as if the small throb of heat from his fingers entered her bloodstream and entwined itself throughout her body. She was flushed with a tingling warmth.

She stared at him as the mischievous smile faded from his face and something much more serious shone through his sea green eyes.

"Truly," he said softly, "it would be my pleasure."

He skimmed his hand over the back of hers and wrapped his fingers around her wrist, searching out her pulse with his thumb. She realized he could feel how fast her heart was beating and pulled her hand away, embarrassed.

His eyes met hers. "What have you got to lose, *linda*?"

She almost laughed. *Not much, that's for sure.*

"Fine," she said. "Why not?"

He looked at her for another moment and then his charming, self-assured smile locked back into place. "Excellent," he said, struggling to his feet. "Well, if we are to go out in public, I think it would be a good idea if I put on a nicer shirt to distract from my mangled face. And although you look perfectly charming in your apron and rubber gloves, I assume you would like to change as well. So I shall pick you up in an hour or so?"

She nodded, a little flustered, as behind her, the roll of credits finally came to an end.

Chapter Twelve

Kat ran her fingers through her curls, slid a pair of large silver hoops into her ears, and then stood back and surveyed her outfit in the mirror. She was thankful that the friend who had rented her house in L.A. had needed closet space so that Kat had been forced to bring most of her clothes with her. She knew that Wellington nightlife was somewhat formal—there were places that wouldn't let her through the door in her usual L.A. uniform of jeans, flip-flops, and a well-fitted tee, so she had chosen a short, silvery gray tank dress with a plunging back. She looked into her closet for a moment, hesitating between a pair of flat beaded sandals and a pair of red Jimmy Choo cage heels. Happily thinking of the way she'd had to tilt her head up to look into Sebastian's face when he delivered the flowers, she went for the heels. Then a little eyeliner, some mascara, and a slash of red lipstick to match the shoes.

She turned around to check her rear view, liking the way the dress dipped into a dramatic vee down her back, but frowning at the noticeable panty line. She quickly slid her underwear off and fished out a black lace thong from her dresser. She tugged it on, smiling wickedly to herself as she imagined Sebastian pulling up her dress and seeing the low-backed corset she was wearing, the lacy underwear, the look of desire flashing in his moss green eyes as he softly skimmed her body with his hands...

What was she doing? She squeezed her eyes shut for a moment and then threw herself down onto her bed, staring at a poster on the ceiling emblazoned with Bette Davis's shrewd little face. Bette would never be so dumb, she thought. Bette would have seen right through this guy.

Kat knew a million men like Sebastian. She'd dated dozens of them over the years. Okay, maybe not quite as good looking, but basically the same. Hollywood was filled with his type—cocky, sexy, rich, and completely unreliable. A one-way ticket to heartbreak. Kat knew better. She had stopped dating altogether in the last year because she had been burned so many times. And yet here she was, back home with her mother and sick father, and the first thing she managed to do was get picked up by the kind of playboy she had learned to avoid at all costs in L.A.

This was ridiculous. He was going to be here any moment. She should just call him and cancel.

Except, of course, she never got his number.

Her mother would have the Del Campo house number, of course. But her mother was at the hospital for the night, and Kat really, really did not want to call her father's sick room and have to explain to her mom why she needed to talk to Sebastian Del Campo.

The doorbell rang and Kat shot up. She hurriedly gave herself one last glance in the mirror and then strode through the house to the front door. She would just tell him in person. Say she wasn't feeling well. Or why not be blunt and simply admit that she had changed her mind? After all, she didn't owe this guy anything. She had just met him.

She threw open the door and was met with an enormous bouquet of flowers—peonies, roses, lilies, and lilacs—even bigger than the one he had brought for her father.

Sebastian peeked over the top. "Delivery for *Señorita* Parker," he said with a grin.

Oh for God's sake, he was even slicker than she'd imagined.

Her eyes slid over him, taking in his glossy dark hair, the crisp cotton shirt that matched his sea green eyes, the way his perfectly tailored pants were just the right kind of tight. He was also, she thought hopelessly, even better looking than she remembered.

Damn it.

She sighed, and smiled, and took the flowers.

Chapter Thirteen

Can you actually drive with that thing?" asked Kat, eyeing the cast on Sebastian's wrist.

Sebastian winked at her as he put the car in reverse, using just the tips of his fingers on the gearshift. "You'd be surprised at what I can do with only one hand, *linda.*"

As they drove, Sebastian told Kat that they had to make one quick stop at the barn before they went on to dinner. "I just realized that I left my phone there," he said sheepishly. "I haven't been able to find it since my last match."

As they pulled up to barn, Kat turned to him with her eyebrows raised. "That's a barn?" she said.

Sebastian shrugged. He knew the barn, with its pillars and enormous windows, was more impressive than most Beverly Hills mansions, but the ponies were everything to the Del Campo family. It only made sense to give them the very best.

It was the end of the day, and the grooms and students were shutting down for the night, throwing in flakes of hay, securing doors, and making sure all the ponies were bedded down safe and sound.

Sebastian dug through the office desk, searching for his phone, while Kat trailed down the hallway, seemingly more interested in the framed pictures of Del Campo family polo players and their ponies than the actual, live horses in the barn. Sebastian watched her, enjoying the contrast of her strappy red stilettos against the barn floor littered with the straw and dust of a working day.

She stopped in front of a black-and-white photo of a young woman with dark eyes, wearing jodhpurs and a polo shirt, and holding a black pony on a lead. "Who's this?" she called back to him.

"*Mi abuela*," said Sebastian as he triumphantly unearthed his phone from the desk and walked over to join her. "My father's mother. She was very scandalous. Beautiful and hard-headed."

"Did she play polo?"

"*Sí.* She was quite good."

"I didn't know women could play."

"Well, back then they really didn't. She was the exception. But more and more play now."

Kat nodded, peering closer at the picture.

Suddenly a voice echoed down the hall. "Katy? Katy Ann?"

Kat turned, and her face split into a grin. "Oh my God, Camelia Montalvo!"

One of the grooms, a curvy and muscular woman in a red shirt and jeans, threw her shovel aside and ran over to hug Kat, her long, dark brown braid flying behind her.

"Katy Ann, holy shit! What in the world are you doing here?"

"Camelia, I can't believe it!"

Sebastian looked at them jumping up and down in each other's arms. "I take it that introductions are unnecessary, then?"

Kat turned to him. "Camelia and I went to high school together."

"And middle school! And grade school!" interjected Camelia. "That was before Katy ran off to be a hot-shot Hollywood director, though."

Sebastian turned his head toward Kat, surprised. "Wait, you're a director?"

"Are you kidding, Seb?" said Camelia. "Katy is probably more famous than you are."

Kat shook her head. "Definitely not."

"Oh, come on," said Camelia. "She was only nominated for an Oscar for the first film she ever made."

Seb blinked. "What was the film?"

"It was called *Winter's Passing*," muttered Kat. "I'm sure you've never seen it."

Sebastian laughed. "I certainly have. Twice. And I cried like a little girl both times."

Kat blushed and looked pleased.

"And then she made that big comic book movie," said Camelia. "You know the one—with the girl in the bikini—what was it called? *Black Hawk*?"

Sebastian choked. "*Red Hawk*?"

"Yeah, that's right," enthused Camelia. "Big film!"

Kat raised her eyebrows at Sebastian. "Amazing coincidence, eh?"

Sebastian didn't know whether to laugh or apologize. "But I thought you cleaned houses," he finally said.

"And I thought you delivered flowers."

He laughed. "I did say that there were parts I liked, didn't I?"

"Oh no, hey, listen. You were right. It's a terrible movie."

"It is not!" said Camelia indignantly. "It was a great film. Super good."

Kat shook her head and put her arm back around Camelia.

"And what about you? Last time we talked, you were heading to the Olympic trials."

The smile on Camelia's face dimmed. "Oh well, that didn't exactly work out. Finances fell through."

"What happened?" said Kat.

She shrugged. "It's not even worth telling. How long are you in town? Can we have a lunch date?"

Sebastian rubbed the nose of the nearest pony and watched the women make plans. The horse nuzzled his neck as he checked the time.

"I'm sorry to break up such a lovely reunion, but if we are to make our reservation, we should probably go."

Camelia looked at them, her eyes wide. "Wait, you guys are together?"

"Just dinner," said Kat hurriedly.

"A first date," said Sebastian. "But who knows where that will lead?"

Kat rolled her eyes. "Dessert, if I'm lucky."

* * *

As they walked out of the barn, Sebastian looked over at Kat and noted the way her dress dipped in the back and exposed a swath of her smooth, bronzed skin. For a moment, he vividly imagined reaching out to run his fingers over that flesh and then dipping even farther down, beneath the fabric, to cup the curve of her shapely bottom. He felt himself quicken at the thought of what she would feel like under his hands.

She stumbled in her heels, and he took the excuse to reach over and place his hand on her arm. His breath caught in his throat as he felt her tense under his fingers, but she did not move away. He kept his hand in place, just barely touching her, until they reached the car. When he finally removed his hand so he could open the door for her, he was surprised to feel a sharp pang of deprivation, as if he'd lost something he did not want to be without.

He shut the door behind her and then stood for a moment, feeling slightly shaken. There was something about this woman, he thought, something *different*. And he was not sure he entirely understood or liked what that meant.

Chapter Fourteen

Kat knew that offering Sebastian a bite of her pie was the right thing to do, but she really didn't want to do it.

She had watched, amazed, as he plowed through his dessert—a piece of molten chocolate cake almost as big as his plate—in no time at all, and then let his gaze rest hungrily upon her key lime pie. She felt, based upon the way he had devoured his own dessert, that if she offered him a bite, he might simply eat the whole thing, and frankly, she very much liked pie and didn't particularly want to give it up.

Still, she supposed she should show some measure of generosity. After all, he had taken her to this beautiful restaurant, right on the beach, and ordered a ridiculously nice bottle of wine and a delicious dinner of paella and lobster, and then proceeded to charm the pants off her (not literally, at least not yet) with funny and thrilling stories about polo, and Argentina, and his family. And not only that, he had been careful to ask her questions about her own life as well, her work and her family, and really did seem interested in her answers. Plus, he kept smiling at her, and every time he smiled at her, she felt herself get just a little more hot and bothered, as if he was incrementally turning up the temperature underneath her seat bit by excruciating bit.

Considering all this, she sighed in defeat and pushed her pie over to him. "Would you like a bite?"

His eyes lit up, and he dug in with his fork and broke off a large piece.

She snatched her plate back before he could go in for a second time. "Good lord, I said a bite," she laughed, "not the whole thing."

He innocently held up his broken wrist. "I can't help it. I am eating left handed. I cannot control the fork. Plus," he added, and grinned slyly, "I have a most terrible sweet tooth."

Kat felt her temperature rise again. He had a tiny smudge of cream on his mouth, and it was all she could do not to lean over the table and kiss it off right then and there. But then he licked his lip and the cream disappeared, and Kat sighed again, ruing the lost opportunity.

He looked at her questioningly.

She quickly brought up a new topic. "Tell me more about your grandmother," she said. "The one in the picture."

"Ah," he said. "What do you want to know?"

"Well, what was her name, to start with?"

"Victoria Del Campo. But we just called her *Abuelita*."

"That's beautiful."

"My father named the Del Campo team after her. La Victoria. *Abuelita* was *una viuda*—a widow, like *mi mamá*—but her husband died very young and left her with my father to raise."

"That must have been hard. Did she ever marry again?'

"No, no. Not that she didn't have many opportunities. She was rich, and charming, and a great beauty. My half sister, Antonia, looks very much like her actually. But she never fell out of love with my grandfather. Certainly, *Abuelita* was never without male attention, and I think she had many affairs after he died. But nothing serious. She always said that it was not her destiny to marry again, that one great love was enough for anyone."

Kat smiled. "Do you think that's true?"

Sebastian met her gaze. "I think that what they had was real, but rare," he said softly.

Kat lowered her eyes, suddenly self-conscious. "And she played polo. You said she was good?"

"Well, yes. She was on a team—all men except for her, of course. And she was position number three—which is like *el capitán*. Even now, not many women play that position. And you know, she taught my father to play, and my father, well, he taught Alejandro and me."

"And you two are decent, I guess?"

Sebastian laughed. "You really don't know much about polo, do you?"

Kat shook her head. "Not a thing. You said your grandmother was scandalous, though. Why—because she played?"

"*Sí.* She played, of course, which was quite shocking for a woman of her time, but she was also a bit of a libertine, you know? A free thinker."

Kat smiled. "Sounds like someone I know."

Sebastian laughed. "No, no, she was far more wild than I could ever hope to be. There is one story that I love about how she had a dinner at her country estate in England with her team and King George, and she showed up to the table wearing nothing but her jodhpurs, diamonds, riding boots, and a smile."

Kat felt her eyes widen. "Topless with royalty? Oh my God, that's fantastic! But why?"

"She liked to shock, you know? And she said that she had to put up with these men doubting her abilities on the field, she had to put up with everyone trying to tell her how to live her life, how to raise her son. And she wanted to show them that no one told her what to do. That she was her own woman. And of course, she was very proud of her rather magnificent breasts apparently. She said that old George had a very hard time looking her in the eyes while trying to make polite conversation."

Kat laughed. She could just picture the scene. An elegant manor house. A formal dining room, lit with candles and perfectly set. The men would all be sexy and dashing and wearing evening clothes. The liveried servants would come and go, bringing course after extravagant course. Everyone would drink champagne, and Victoria would stride in and take her place at the table, straight backed and beautiful, looking like a queen and daring anyone to say anything...

Suddenly Kat's heart beat a little faster. "Sebastian," she said urgently, "do you know any other stories about your grandmother?"

Sebastian cocked his head, "Oh, *sí*. Hundreds of them. And actually, I think *Mamá* has all her journals somewhere. *Abuelita* kept a diary for most of her life."

Kat's felt a thrill of excitement. "Do you think your mother would let me see them?"

"But why?" He laughed. "Are you going to make a movie about my grandmother?"

Kat looked at him for a moment. "Maybe. If your family is willing."

He blinked. "Seriously?"

"I mean, I don't know. Let's not jump the gun. It's just that sometimes"—she ran her finger along the edge of her plate, a little embarrassed—"sometimes I read about something, or hear a story, and I get this feeling—something inside of me just kind of blooms, if that makes sense? Like, I can just *see* the story, you know? Hear the voices..." She shook her head. "Sometimes it's nothing. In fact, most of the time it's usually nothing. But I would love to hear more about Victoria if you're willing."

She felt a little shiver of pleasure as Sebastian reached across the table and took her hand. "I would be more than happy to tell you every story I know, *linda*," he said softly. "Let's take a walk."

Chapter Fifteen

Kat and Sebastian took off their shoes and walked along the edge of the sea. The sand was wet and warm, and the water hissed in and out over their bare feet as the tide came in. The beach was empty, and the moon was bright, and when she looked at him, her gray eyes gleamed silver in the pale light.

She was, thought Sebastian, even *more* than he had imagined she would be. She was beautiful, of course, but in an effortless way. Seb had grown so used to the "stick chicks" that flocked around the games and clubhouse, with all their glossy, hypergroomed surfaces and surgically enhanced lips and tits proudly on display, that he found himself oddly mesmerized by Kat's imperfections and flaws. The beauty mark above her lip, the two-inch scar on the inside of her elbow that shone silvery white against her smooth tan skin (a childhood accident, she told him, trailing her finger over it self-consciously), the way that her glossy black curls sprang out around her head like an unruly corona in the Florida humidity, the faint laugh lines that appeared around her pretty eyes every time she smiled...

And she was smart, and funny, and she told him scandalous, gossipy, hilarious stories about Hollywood, and made him laugh so hard his belly ached. And when he flattered or flirted, her cheeks would flush pink and her eyes sparkled, but at the same time, if he went over the top, he knew that she did not buy his bullshit. Not even one little bit. Because nothing got past this woman. *Nada.*

She had argued with him playfully when the check arrived, demanding that he return her fifteen dollars so she could pay at least some of her share. He had grinned and handed the waiter his credit card, and told her that she was never getting that money back, he had earned it fair and square.

And now she walked alongside him, laughing and chattering about this and that in her husky, honey-sweet voice. Her legs were long enough that he barely had to adjust his stride, and her swinging hand kept grazing his arm and sending little shocks of pleasure through his body. All he could think about was the fact that he wanted to grab hold of her shoulders, lay her down in the sand, and kiss her until they both lost their breath.

"Wait," he said, suddenly catching the last bit of her sentence, "did you just say that you've never ridden a horse?"

She bent to examine something shiny on the ground, poking at it with her toe, her long, black curls swinging perilously close to the wet sand. "Nope. Never have."

"But you grew up in Wellington. How is that possible?"

She shot him a look over her shoulder. "We're not all in the horsey set around here, Sebastian. There are other parts of Wellington, you know."

He frowned. "Well, of course, but—"

"I asked my parents for lessons once, when I was eight," she said.

"And?"

"And they told me that they could afford to buy me one lesson, if that's what I really wanted, but that it would just be that one time and then not again."

"So why didn't you do it?"

She straightened up. "I was afraid I'd like it too much," she said lightly. "I thought it would better not to have tried it at all than to try it and miss it after."

"Ah, is that why you were looking at the pictures in the barn instead of the ponies?"

She wrinkled her nose, surprised. "What do you mean? I looked at the ponies."

"No, you passed right by them. You went straight for the photographs. I've never seen anyone do that. It's very hard not to look at those ponies."

She shrugged. "Well, I'm a director. I'm visual. I like photographs."

"I think you were still afraid you would like the ponies too much. Still holding back."

She laughed. "Maybe so. Though I always thought the ability to hold back was the sign of high intelligence in a child."

"Well, that reflects rather poorly on me, then, because I was the opposite as a boy. No impulse control whatsoever. I wanted what I wanted, and I did not like to wait."

She raised an eyebrow. "Why do I have a feeling that you never quite grew out of that?"

He put his hand on his heart. "You wound me, *linda*."

She laughed. "I'm fairly certain you'll recover."

Her laughter, the way she teased him, it just made him want her even more. He caught her hand and pulled her toward him. "*Besame*," he said softly.

She blinked. "Forgive my rusty Spanish, but doesn't that mean—"

He cut her off by gently placing his mouth upon hers.

Her lips were soft and warm, and he searched them slowly, first with his own lips and then with his tongue, just barely touching the outline of her mouth until she exhaled and stepped closer to him.

She settled her body against his and twined her hands into his hair, and he could feel her lush curves melting against him, her soft breasts pushing up against his chest, the way her hips cradled his groin, making him pulse with desire.

He loved kissing a woman this tall. He didn't have to bend to her mouth at all, and it was so easy to pull her even closer and go deep. She tasted amazing, like sweet lime and champagne and a trace of salt, and she smelled of that same intriguing bittersweet caramel fragrance he had noticed the first day they met. He went deeper still, and she pushed up against him and made a soft, warm sound in the back of her throat, and suddenly he was flooded with an electric hunger so sharp that he felt that he might lose control.

And so he did what he had been fantasizing about doing all night. He led her away from the water and laid her down upon the warm sand and covered her body with his own.

He held himself just barely above her with his one good arm as he reached down and crushed his mouth to hers, trying desperately to fill all the space between them.

She responded avidly, moaning and twisting under him, and he pulled back for a second to search her face.

"Please," she said, and that was all the encouragement he needed, dipping his mouth to her throat and tasting her skin, trailing his way down to her collarbone, dragging his tongue across her salty-sweet flesh.

She closed her eyes and arched up toward him, and he throbbed against her in response and wanted to rip her clothes from her body, but then growled in frustration since his one good hand was being used to hold himself up.

She opened her eyes, and her gaze flicked to the cast on his wrist. "Switch with me," she whispered.

He rolled over onto his back, and she followed, straddling him in the sand and leaning down to kiss him, her tongue exploring his mouth as he caressed her long, graceful neck and then finally reached the sweet, bare skin on her back, now gritty with sand, that had been haunting him all evening. He trailed his hand down farther and found her almost naked bottom, and it was as exquisite as he had known it would be, firm and round and warm, and he groaned happily as he fit his palm against her, wishing he had two good hands so he could feel all of her at once.

She broke off kissing him. "Do you think," she said hoarsely, "that we should find someplace more private?"

He pushed himself up and looked around. The beach was deserted. The only light from the restaurant was far behind. "I think we're alone," he said.

She responded by reaching down and unbuttoning his shirt, kissing her way down his chest with every button she opened.

He inhaled sharply. Each touch of her mouth was like a lit match against his skin. He could feel her all through his body, and he was so hard that he thought he might explode like a schoolboy if he let her go any longer.

He brought his mouth to her soft, full breast, feeling the rough pattern of lace under the cotton of her dress and then the bud of her nipple. He cupped her with his hand and sucked through the cloth until she gasped and bucked her hips, and he felt the nub rise and harden under the wet fabric.

"Sebastian," she moaned. "Oh God, that feels so good."

She reached down and unzipped his pants, pulling down his boxer briefs so that he sprang free, hard as a rock and aching under her hand. She rubbed herself against him, sliding up and down, pleasuring herself. She was so hot and soft and wet, and the friction of her G-string against his sensitive skin nearly drove him mad with desire.

"*Linda*," he panted, "I don't have a—"

She hushed him with a kiss and reached for the purse that she had discarded in the sand next to them, pulling out a foil chain of condoms.

He grinned at her appreciatively, and she shrugged, looking the tiniest bit embarrassed.

"I like a girl who comes prepared," he murmured.

She ripped open a packet with her teeth and, looking at the cast on his wrist, said, "Let me help you," as she rolled it down over his throbbing cock and then straddled him again, and slowly, ever so slowly, slid herself down onto him. He watched her face as he filled her, as she arched her head back, and her cheeks flushed, and her eyes closed in pleasure. He thought that he had never seen a woman so breathtaking, so uninhibitedly beautiful. She seemed to be holding nothing back, taking everything she wanted as she slowly stroked up and then down again.

He let her take the lead until he could stand it no longer, and then he thrust himself up into her, making her shudder and cry out. He reached underneath her dress and touched the warm, wet center of her, slowly circling with his thumb as he rocked his hips and moved within her. She bent her face to his, gasping against his cheek, and her hair fell around his neck like heavy, warm silk. Her breasts flattened against his chest, and he could feel her tighten and start to clench and shake, and suddenly her hips were jerking against his. She cried out his name, and he felt her muscles contract over and over again. She threw her head back, met his gaze, and in that excruciatingly powerful moment, he found his release.

And it was like nothing, *nothing*, he had ever felt before.

He felt shattered, enraptured, pierced through with the beauty of the moment—as if there was nothing in his entire world but her glimmering gray eyes, the sound of her voice calling out his name, and the glorious feeling of his body dissolving into hers.

He thrust into her one final time, and then she collapsed on top of him, laying her body over his as their breathing finally slowed. They listened to the hiss of the sea and rested in the soft, warm sand.

He gently kissed her face, and thought to himself that she felt so good, so *right*, and that he never wanted to be anywhere else. That he would stay here forever if she let him...

And then he laughed softly, because he really had never felt these things before. And honestly?

It kind of scared the living hell out of him.

Chapter Sixteen

The next day, Kat opened her door and found Sebastian standing on her front porch, holding a stack of compact leather-bound journals. They smelled faintly floral. "They're *en español*," he said. "You will need me to translate. It might take days, but I am willing to make the sacrifice."

Kat smiled at his boldness, but inwardly she squirmed. She had awoken that morning with a groan of remorse. She never slept with a man on the first date (or at least, not since college) and yet not only had she had sex with Sebastian—she'd had sex with him *in public*. They had been out there for anyone to see. They could have been arrested, for God's sake. She cringed, imagining calling her mother at the hospital.

"Oh hi, Mama. I know you're at Daddy's sick bed, but do you mind mortgaging the cottage and coming down to jail to bail me out for public indecency and exhibitionism?"

And she couldn't even blame it on the wine. She'd had a few glasses, but she'd been perfectly clearheaded by the time things had really started up with Sebastian. No, it hadn't been the wine at all—it had been *him*. He had made her drunk with his intoxicating mix of sweetness, and wicked humor, and wit, and his outrageous, absurd, ridiculous amount of sex appeal.

The man was just hot. When he'd kissed her, that was the end and the beginning and everything in between. No one had ever made her feel the things he had just by simply placing his mouth over hers. She had been helpless to deny his need.

No, she corrected herself, the truth was, she'd been helpless to deny her *own* need.

And afterward, when they had been shamelessly lying there on the sand, in full view of God and whoever might stroll by, she had thought, *a busload of nuns could pull up and see us in this moment, and I wouldn't even bother to raise my head from his shoulder. I would just wave and smile and let them all judge. I don't care. It was worth it.*

But now here she was, face to face with him again, and she could hardly look him in the eye. Though she had to admit to herself that she wasn't sure if her inability to look at him grew out of regret or because she knew that, when she finally met his gaze, things would simply start up all over again.

Her mother had gone to work for the day, and her father had been moved to the rehabilitation center and had made it very clear he did not want Kat there looking over his shoulder while he learned to walk again. So she had her days free. They would be alone in the house for hours.

This was not a good idea.

But still, he had brought the journals. And he was willing to translate, which was incredibly thoughtful, and—she finally allowed herself to really look at him—oh no, he looked *so good*.

He was wearing jeans and a thin white shirt with the sleeves rolled up to accommodate the cast on one side and his muscular brown forearm on the other. The shirt looked soft and perfectly worn, and was exquisitely tailored to fit his broad shoulders and chest, tapering down to his narrow waist. His jet-black hair was just long enough to curl under his ears and past his open collar. His eye was still bruised, but no longer swollen.

She could smell him. A heady, clean mix of salt and musk, with just a hint of something sweet and citrusy. She glanced into his bright green eyes and she suddenly had a flash of him under her, filling her, the sharp thrust of him that had sent convulsive shivers through her body, that made her skin burn and the breath leave her lungs. The way his eyes had seared into hers in that final moment of release...

She briefly squeezed her eyes shut and then opened them again. "Come in," she said, trying to sound as casual as possible. "I'll make you some lunch in trade for your translation services."

He smiled slyly. "I am willing to start with lunch, Katarina, but translating *español* can be very taxing work, you know. There might have to be better incentives."

Kat swallowed and tried to sound brisk. "Well then, maybe I can make dessert as well."

And then, before he could answer, she whirled around and headed toward the kitchen. "I have some amazing tomatoes from my mama's garden," she called out to him. *Damn.* Her voice had the slightest tremor; she was sure he would notice. "I'll make a Caprese salad, does that sound good?"

"*Sí*, delicious." He sounded amused. He definitely knew that she was holding herself back.

She studiously avoided looking his way as she busied herself in the kitchen, slicing cheese and tomatoes and warming a loaf of bread.

"What can I do to help?" he asked.

"Oh, actually, you can go out back to the garden and pick some basil. You know what that looks like, right?"

He shot her an insolent look. "Yes, I know what basil looks like."

He went outside, and she continued to prepare the salad. After the cheese and tomatoes were arranged in perfect scalloped slices on a big green platter, she opened the back door and walked barefoot out into the yard to find him.

From the backyard, Kat could hear, but not see, the ocean. Her parents never had the kind of money that would allow for a view, but if Kat followed a crooked little path that skirted the house across the way, she could be on a small, pebbly beach within five minutes.

The garden was small but absolutely packed with vegetation. Her mother had an extremely green thumb and had turned their quarter-acre lot into a carefully cultivated jungle of greenery.

There was a white picket fence around the edges of the yard, draped in pink rambling roses and twining vines of fragrant yellow honeysuckle. There was a cluster of citrus trees—lime and lemon and orange—which smelled heavenly no matter what the season and provided leafy green privacy from the neighbors. There was a small reflecting pool, choked with flowering water lilies, where the occasional wavering flash of an overgrown goldfish came into view amid the dark leaves and waxy white petals.

The kitchen garden was the crown jewel, though, surrounded by neatly trimmed hedges of rosemary and partially shaded by an arbor covered in grapevines. It was packed with an astounding amount of fruit, vegetables, and flowers for cutting. Her mother hadn't let a single inch of space go unused.

Kat laughed when she found Sebastian standing amid the herbs, looking lost, while staring at a particularly brilliant patch of jade green plants.

The exact color of his eyes, she thought to herself, and smiled.

"I thought you said you knew what basil looked like," she teased him.

He looked up. "I do. This is basil, I'm sure of it. But"—he swept his arm toward another cluster of darker green—"I am fairly certain that this is as well. And that, too," he said as he pointed to the other end of the garden. "I did not want to bring you the wrong kind."

Kat squinted and looked. He was right. "Oh. Maybe there's more than one kind."

He raised his eyebrow. "Something you failed to mention."

She moved into the garden, feeling the round, warm pea gravel crunch underneath her feet. She bent and picked a large leaf of the herb and inhaled the spicy-sweet scent. "This kind will do."

"All this"—he waved his arms around as if to take it all in—"it's like the Garden of Eden. So much...what's the word? *Abundancia.*"

She smiled as she picked the basil. "My mother's motto has always been 'Why not more?'"

He laughed and stepped toward her, wrapping his arm around her waist. "I like your mother," he said. "We have a similar outlook on life."

Kat knew she should move away, but instead, she turned toward him, resting her hands full of basil around his neck and nestling her hips up against his.

"Ah, *linda,*" he murmured, smiling down at her and

stroking her hair, "you look so pretty in this garden. Like a barefoot *gitana*—a gypsy queen."

Kat shook her head at his over-the-top poetics, but felt her cheeks warm, secretly pleased.

He smiled at her some more, and she couldn't help herself. "*Besame*," she whispered.

He laughed. A deep, seductive chuckle. "*Ay, mandona*—bossy girl—using my own words against me. Are you always this demanding?"

He leaned forward and placed his mouth close to hers. She could feel his breath tremble against her lips.

"Of course I am," she sighed. "I'm a director, after all."

He laughed again and closed the distance between them, kissing her tenderly—searching and slow—but she didn't have patience for that. She didn't need warming up. She wanted the deep, urgent kisses he had given her the night before. She wanted to be kissed so hard that it would leave her lips bruised and swollen. She felt flushed with need, as if she could throw herself into his arms and wrap herself around him, meld her body to his, and still not get close enough.

He seemed to sense her craving because he suddenly pulled her toward him with a deep, masculine sound, and gave her exactly the kind of kiss she had been yearning for. He kissed her with such furious desire that she could practically taste blood in her mouth, and when she ground her hips against him and felt him throb in response, her entire body seemed to go up in flames.

He broke the kiss and looked at her. "Katarina," he panted raggedly, "you don't know what you do to me."

But she did know. She knew exactly what she did to him. Because he did it to *her*.

She wanted him. She wanted him right where they were

standing, in her mother's garden. She ached for this man in a way that felt almost dangerous. But she peeled herself away and forced herself to gather up the basil she had dropped and tried to calm her breathing. "Let's eat lunch," she said. "And maybe have a glass of wine. And while we eat, you can read me a little from Victoria's journals."

"And after lunch?" he said. His voice was tight with desire.

She met his eyes, and the pupils were so dark and dilated that his gaze had practically gone black.

Her mouth had gone dry. It was hard to swallow. "Like I said earlier," she said. "Dessert."

He looked at her for another moment, his face naked with longing, and then he sighed and said, "You know, I understand that you mean something else when you say 'dessert' and please know that I absolutely want what you are hinting at, and all that it implies, but"—a smile tugged at the corners of his mouth—"I really must know. Will there be actual dessert?"

She snorted, the tension broken. "Did I not just tell you about my mother? That kitchen is full of sweets."

"*Sí, sí.* 'Why not more?'" he quoted happily. "Okay, good. Because," he said slyly, "there is absolutely no reason why we can't have *both* kinds of dessert."

She let out a groan and turned back toward the cottage.

"In fact," he said, hurrying after her, "I bet we can think of some very clever ways to combine the two..."

Chapter Seventeen

Is there another piece?" Sebastian asked hopefully.

"You've had four!"

"And you've had three, *linda*."

"I've had two and a half!" Kat shook her spoon at him.
"And it is not polite to count."

He moaned as he ate the last bite in his bowl. "It's just so
good. If I had known that your mother could cook like this,
I would have fired her as our housekeeper and settled her in
la cocina ages ago."

"Can't your mother cook?"

"*Sí.* She is a magnificent cook. But she doesn't make this
peach—what did you call it again?"

"Cobbler."

"Yes." He sucked his spoon. "Cobbler."

She sighed and sat back in her chair. "I did miss my
mother's cooking. Not that there isn't great food in L.A.
but—"

"No cobbler."

She laughed and then looked at him. "So why do you still
live with your mother?"

"Why do you?"

"Touché." She clinked her spoon against his as if they were wielding tiny swords.

He pushed his bowl away. "I live with *mi mamá* because that's what is expected, *sabes?* I'm unmarried. She's a widow. And there is plenty of room, of course. Even Alejandro and his wife and children still live in the *hacienda* when we're in Wellington. They have their own places in Argentina and New York, though."

She raised her eyebrows. "Three houses?"

He shrugged. "The family travels a great deal. That's what we do. Follow the stick and ball. It's easier if we don't have to rent every time we move."

"But you could move out if you wanted to? Have your own place?"

He nodded. "I suppose. But why would I?"

She stood up and cleared their dishes off the table into the sink. "It's just very different than how most people do things here. As soon as I hit eighteen, I was out the door. I couldn't wait to leave."

He looked around the snug little cottage. It seemed cheerful and warm in the early afternoon light. "Was it so very bad here?"

She shook her head. "No, not at all. I love my parents. They're great. But you know, big dreams and all that. Couldn't make movies in Wellington."

He nodded. "I suppose it's different when you always know you're going to join the family business."

"You always knew it would be polo?"

He smiled. "They put me on a horse before I could walk."

"I'd like to see you ride."

He laughed. "You're one of the few people I know who hasn't. It's rather a refreshing change actually."

She sat back down at the table. "Why? Don't you like polo?"

He considered this. "Like it? Sure. Of course. I just sometimes wonder what it would be like to do something else."

"Like what?"

He shrugged. "I was born a Del Campo. I'm not sure what else I'd be good at, honestly. But I wasn't ever given much of a chance to find out."

"The way you talked about it last night, I thought it was your passion."

He thought for a moment. "I love the ponies, of course...but passion? Like putting my whole heart into it? I honestly don't know." He felt surprised by this realization. "It's Alejandro's passion. That is certain. Which is funny because I'm actually—" He stopped himself.

"You're actually what?"

He laughed ruefully. "I was going to say that I'm actually the better player. But that's not really true. I have...more natural talent, I guess you could say. Polo has always come very easily to me. But Jandro works harder and cares more. So he's better when it counts, *sabes?*"

He shrugged and pulled the pile of journals over. "Anyway, shall I read you some?"

She nodded.

He opened the top book on the stack and gazed down at the first page. He smiled as he recognized his grandmother's distinctive slanted script. He remembered countless birthday cards and notes she had sent him over the years. He had been a terrible grandson who rarely, if ever, wrote back, but she never seemed to hold it against him.

He squinted for a moment, translating in his head.

"Ah, this is very early. When she was sixteen. She is

writing about selling flowers in the marketplace in Argentina. I should explain to you that my grandmother and grandfather came from very different backgrounds. *Abuelita* was a *campesina*, you know, a country girl. Very poor. And *mi abuelo*—my grandfather—was *un ladino*. His family was mainly European and came from great wealth. And according to the family story, they met at the market."

He scanned the page. "Yes, here it is. She is saying that a handsome older boy came to the market and bought out all her roses and then gave them back to her as a gift. But she says she had to give away all the flowers but one before she went home that night because her parents would wonder why she'd sold so few...Ah, and look! *La rosa!*"

He showed Kat a brown, crumbling flower pressed between the pages.

Kat gasped and reached out to touch it. "That's amazing."

"*Sí.*" He bent his head to the pages again. "She says that she hopes he will come back to the market tomorrow..." He turned the page, and yet another dried rose fell out. He chuckled. "Which, apparently, he did."

Kat took the journal from him and carefully flipped through the pages, counting under her breath. "Twenty-five roses. Oh my gosh, Sebastian," she said. She looked up at him, a dawning look of wonder on her face. "I think we just found the title of the movie."

Chapter Eighteen

Kat went to her room for paper and a pen to take notes, and Sebastian followed her. She riffled through her desk as he threw himself upon her bed and lay, sprawled out, curiously looking around the room.

She couldn't help feeling a little thrill, seeing him on her bed.

"So this is the make-out den where you brought all your high school *novios*, eh?" he said, raising a brow.

She laughed. "Sure. If by 'all,' you mean none."

"Your parents were strict?"

"Um, no. I mean I had no high school boyfriends."

Sebastian made a face. "That's ridiculous. Of course you had boyfriends. Look at you."

She smiled and shook her head, picking up a framed photo off her desk and showing him. "Yes, look at me."

Seb took the photo. It was a picture of her and Camelia—arms around each other. Camelia looked almost exactly the same—wide, dark eyes and a mischievous smile. But Kat had braces and a regrettable hairstyle. Above her smile, her eyes looked distant.

"Hot, eh?" said Kat.

Seb cocked his head. "You look sweet and innocent and like you're just counting the hours until you can get out of town."

She nodded. "You got it."

"And I'm sorry, but you were a knockout even then."

Kat snatched the photo back. "Don't be ridiculous."

Seb laughed and leaned back on the bed. "There's nothing like a beautiful woman who doesn't have a clue how gorgeous she really is."

"Oh, for Pete's sake," said Kat. "Really? Do you honestly think there is a woman on earth who isn't excruciatingly aware of just how attractive or unattractive society deems her to be?"

He blinked. "But you just said—"

"I'm not an idiot, Sebastian. I know that I no longer look like"—she shoved her finger at the photo—"that. I'm fully aware of the fact that I'm not a total troll anymore."

"You never looked like a troll."

She shook her head. "You didn't know me then."

He sighed. "Fine. What I meant to say is that there is nothing like a woman who is fully aware of the incredible power she wields over nearly every man in the room."

"You're the only man in the room."

"I rest my case."

She snorted and went back to looking for a pen.

He smiled and looked around some more. "So it's always been movies, eh?" he said, taking note of her wall of tickets. "Just like for me, it's always been polo."

"Well, except no one expected me to make movies. I wasn't raised and groomed for Hollywood. I just really liked film."

"I like it, too," he said. "Jandro complains that I spend more time watching movies than I do on horseback."

"What's your favorite?" she said.

He wrinkled his nose, thinking. "I like big, epic films. *Lawrence of Arabia. Doctor Zhivago.*"

"So you're a romantic."

"No. No. I'm a realist. But I like to escape."

She smiled dubiously.

"Come on," he said. "What's your favorite then?"

"I have too many to choose."

"That's not fair. You made me pick."

"Yes, but you don't make movies for a living."

He sat up in her bed. "But I practically do. Remember what Alejandro said."

She laughed. "Do you want to watch a movie right now? I have kind of an amazing collection." She walked to the closet and pushed open the accordion door. Instead of clothes, there was a wall of VHS tapes, all arranged in alphabetical order.

Sebastian whistled and came over to look closer. "Wow. Who has tapes anymore?"

"I couldn't throw them away. This was my film school before I went to film school."

He looked closer and wrinkled his nose. "I think you have every single John Hughes film ever made."

She laughed. "Oh, I know I do. Want to watch *Pretty in Pink*?"

He glanced back at her. "No. I definitely do not."

She bent over, squinting at the titles. "Well then, do you want to watch—"

"*Linda*," he said, cutting her off. His voice sounded dangerous. "For how long will we be alone in this house?"

She looked at him. "Why?"

He returned her gaze. "Because I want to know if I have enough time to properly make love to you."

"Oh," she said softly.

"So how much time do we have? An hour? Two?"

"Um..." Her eyes darted to the clock radio by her bed. "Um, more like four or five."

He smiled. A slow, satisfied, devastating smile. "Take off your clothes," he said.

She swallowed. "All of them?"

"*Si, toda.*"

She felt a rush of heat that started at her cheeks and flooded to her toes. "Is there any particular order you'd like me to go about this?"

He bit his lip. "I'll let you choose."

She took a deep breath and reached for her shirt, unbuttoning the top button. "Like this?"

His eyes went dark, and his nostrils slightly flared. He nodded slowly. "Yes. Like that. Now do the next one."

She undid the next one, and then another, relieved that she was wearing a pretty bra underneath. "How's that?" she asked. Her voice was trembling.

"Take off the shirt."

She slowly slipped the shirt off, then met his eyes again.

"Now the bra."

She unhooked her bra and dropped it to the floor.

He stared at her. "Katarina," he said hoarsely, "you are so beautiful."

She could barely breathe. "Sebastian, I don't want to—I need you to..."

He moved across the room toward her with what felt like lightning speed. He crushed her into his arms and then he was kissing her—deeply, passionately, as if he couldn't get enough. He ran his hand through her hair, over her cheek, down her neck, and then cupped her breast, stroking her nipple with his thumb.

She gasped and felt him smile against her mouth.

He continued to tease her—splaying his hand over her breast, catching her nipple between his fingers, sending thrills throughout her body as he tantalized her with his expert touch. She arched against him, wanting more, and he broke the kiss with a moan and lowered his mouth to her breasts, ravenously licking and kissing until she couldn't stand it anymore.

"Please, Sebastian," she groaned, and then he took her nipple into his mouth and softly sucked, using his tongue to torment her until she cried out with desire and thrust herself at him.

He lifted his head. "It kills me," he said in a hiss, "not to have both my hands. All I want to do is touch you everywhere, to run my fingers through your hair, down your body, to put my fingers inside you where I know you are so soft and wet—"

"If this is what you can do to me with just one hand," she said breathlessly, "I'm not sure I could survive two."

He grinned and returned his attention to her breasts. She sighed and then pushed him away so she could unbutton his shirt, baring his glorious chest. His skin was golden and smooth. His muscles were so hard and defined that she actually stopped for a moment and laughed at his perfection. He was so beautiful. *Who actually looks like this in real life?*

She thought of the actors on the movie sets she'd seen getting airbrushed and made up, the lighting, the wardrobe, the digital enhancement...Sebastian looked better, standing here, half naked in her childhood bedroom, than any movie star she'd ever seen, on or off the screen.

His beauty made her greedy. She fumbled at his jeans, popping open the button at his waistline, yanking off his pants, and then taking a step back—holding him at arm's length—wanting to see him in all his masculine glory. He stared back at her, his eyes burning as she found herself actually walking a slow circle around him, absorbing the width of his shoulders, the ropes of muscles on his back, the sharp, strong curve of his behind, his powerful thighs and calves.

She took a deep breath as she slowly reached out and touched the hardness of his pecs, felt the bud of his dark brown nipple rise to her touch, traced the striated lines of abdominal muscle that stretched, quivering, across his stomach, the dark, rough path of hair that led southward. And then she took his cock into her hand, feeling the pulse of velvet over steel, listening to his breath hiss out, watching his eyes clench shut.

"Katarina," he whispered hoarsely.

She sank to her knees, placed her hands on the hard contours of his behind, pulling him toward her, as she took him as far into her mouth as she could, her tongue tasting the salt and copper tang of him, her body clenching with pleasure as she heard him moan, and his hips rocked, slowly pushing himself in and out of her mouth.

Then he froze, and his hand clenched into her hair. "*No más*," he said. "It feels too good." He pulled her up, roughly stripping off the rest of her clothes in what felt like seconds, and then, oh mercy, he swept her up with just one arm, and carried her to her bed, spreading her thighs and kissing the very core of her.

She groaned, and the groan almost twisted into a scream as white-hot flashes of pleasure rocketed through her with every flick of his tongue, every slow, swirling lick, every deep kiss, every pulsating sensation.

He paused and looked up at her, his green eyes shining.

"You taste so sweet, *linda*," he said wonderingly. "I've never tasted a woman as sweet as you."

He buried his face back into her and then reached up to hold her breast, softly pinching her nipple between his thumb and finger while his tongue continued to swirl round and round, and suddenly she was tumbling over the edge, a hot, dark, brutal feeling pulsing through her, stars exploding behind her eyes, the sweet agony rolling through her with the unstoppable force of thunder, her whole body melting into liquid. And she lost her breath and she lost her sense of where she was or who she was and all she could think of was *him*. Sebastian. The man who was making her feel things she had never felt before.

She shuddered with loss as his mouth left her. She heard the sound of a condom wrapper being ripped open. Then his lips were on hers, hot and strong, and his tongue pushed into her mouth as he settled himself between her thighs and slowly thrust up into her. And she was peaking all over again as his body pressed against hers. He filled her and teased her and thrust back into her, over and over again as she was driven to greater and greater heights. Until she felt that she might not ever regain her breath, it was all so much.

And finally, she felt him shake and buck and call her name and say things in Spanish that she understood without translation, and she was filled with one last burst of pure, aching sweetness—a feeling so strong that she felt lifted out of her own body, couldn't find where she ended and he began. Then, with a deep moan, he fell against her, deliciously crushing her under him, as she lay there in his arms, trembling and breathless and in awe of the searing power of what had just passed between them.

Chapter Nineteen

The next two weeks passed in an idyll. Kat slept late every morning, rising after her mother left for work, and by noon the doorbell would ring. Sebastian would be on her doorstep, always with some small gift in his hand. A cup of iced coffee with cream, a paperback book he thought she'd like, a silver-plated pen, a bright red silk scarf because, he told her, he wanted to see it against her wild black curls.

They would eat, often picking their lunch straight from the garden. They would talk, making each other laugh. Sometimes they would take the hidden path down to the beach and walk along the edge of the sea together. When they returned home, Sebastian would translate and read Victoria's journals to Kat while she took notes—amazed at just how deep, sweet, and daring this woman's life had been—and then they would make love.

They were both insatiable. They spent hours poring over each other's bodies, licking and kissing and biting and losing themselves in each other, working themselves into a sweat-slicked haze of passion and pleasure. Kat had never felt so immersed, so splayed open, so greedy. There was so much heat between them. The smallest thing could set her off. The slightest brush of his hand, a quick glance across the table, the way the muscles in his wrist flexed as he handed her the salt, the sound of his laugh...

Afterward, spent and exhausted, Sebastian would doze on her bed while she worked at her desk, incorporating the day's notes into the ever-progressing story she was building. She liked the sound of his deep, even breathing filling the room, liked being able to turn in her chair and see him there, naked and sprawled, the late afternoon sun slanting over his bare chest and face, his dark hair glimmering in the light, his long, black lashes in repose against his high cheekbones, his full lips just slightly parted. She actually ached when she looked at him, he was that beautiful.

She often wondered what her teen self would have thought—seeing a man this mesmeric, this gorgeous, this masculine, in her own bed. Teenage Kat had always gone for the geeks and nerds. The shy boys who couldn't yet meet her eyes, the ones who aroused absolutely no real sexual interest or posed no threat whatsoever. It was so beyond her early imagination that someone this physically perfect could ever want her. Sebastian was like a mirage in her bed, a fever dream of physical perfection. Kat suddenly understood what it was to have a muse.

When it got late enough, Sebastian would rise from the bed, kiss her one last time, and exit before her mother got home. By unspoken agreement, they kept what was happening between themselves, a secret that only made their time together that much more intense, a flame they wanted to shield, not expose. They never talked about it, but there was never any question of Sebastian staying later, or any hint about leaving the bubble of their little world and going back out into the public eye.

After her mother arrived home, Kat would help her make dinner, and they would take it over to the rehab clinic to share with Kat's father. The three of them would eat, surrounded by people in various states of sickness and healing, content to be together as a family again. Her father made progress every day, and it seemed he would be released soon.

Kat and her mother would go home after, and sit in the kitchen with a cup of tea, chatting a little before Corinne went to bed. Kat had told her mother that she was working on a script about Victoria Del Campo, and that Sebastian was helping her translate the journals, but nothing more than that. Sometimes Kat, catching a glimpse of the rosy, satisfied glow of her own face in the mirror, couldn't quite believe that her mother hadn't put two and two together yet. But Corinne, distracted by the demands of her job and the ache of having her husband out of their home, never seemed to suspect anything.

After her mother went to bed, Kat would make herself a pot of coffee, turn on the little lamp on her desk, and write feverishly through the night. She sat in her small pool of buttery light until the gold and pink rays of dawn would creep through the windows, and the birds started to sing, and her back ached, and her eyes started to see double, and she had run out of words. Then she would crawl into her soft, warm bed, still redolent with the sea and musk scent of Sebastian's body, and sleep like the contented dead until she woke up in the early afternoon, and started her day all over again.

Victoria had taken hold of her, and the story of Sebastian's *abuelita*—her life and love—came pouring out onto the page in a torrent. Hearing Sebastian read Victoria's translated words every day left Kat feeling that she *knew* her somehow. That she had a direct line to Victoria's wants and fears, that she understood each loss, each love, her obsessions and passions. Victoria had loved her husband body, heart, and soul, and before he died, her life had been incredibly happy—filled with romance and riches. She had lived a beautiful, easy life with a man who had adored her.

But it was after he died, thrown from a horse that she had warned him he'd never break, that her truest self seemed to emerge. It was as if she had been tempered by the fire of her tragedy. She was left with her two-year-old son, a pack of in-laws who'd never wanted her in the family to begin with, and no idea what was next. But she believed in destiny. And she felt strongly that her destiny did not include spending the rest of her life as the obedient, widowed daughter-in-law to a bunch of people who had only barely tolerated her while her husband was still alive.

After her husband died, Victoria's in-laws made it very clear that they saw her and her child as nothing more than mistakes her late husband had made. So she took the money she had inherited from him—thank God he had left her more than well provided for—and left town. Only bothering to return when it was time for her son to claim the estate as the sole heir after her disagreeable in-laws had passed on.

Kat only wished that she'd had the chance to meet her—to actually know a woman as brave, smart, and fierce as this woman had been—but she was comforted by the fact that she saw her coming back to life on the page, that she could already envision the magnificent movie that was going to arise from a couple dozen pressed roses and the pages of some dusty diaries.

Still, there was only so much that Kat could gather from Victoria's words and Sebastian's stories, and so one day, as she lay naked and entwined with Sebastian on her small bed, feeling the breeze cool the heat of their skin, listening to the sound of his heart beat in his chest, watching the dappled sunlight dance across her bedroom wall, she looked up at him and sighed.

"It's time for me to actually see it," she said. "I need you to take me to a game."

Chapter Twenty

The day of the match, Sebastian sat on the terrace of the *hacienda* with his mother, having cocktails and discussing La Victoria's chances against the other team. It was an exhibition game and charity dinner, played to raise money for Alejandro's foundation for inner-city youth.

Pilar was already dressed for the event in a long, acid green tunic and jeweled sandals. Alejandro and Georgia had gone ahead to prepare the ponies.

"*Ay*," said Pilar, squinting at some dark clouds rolling in over the horizon, "do you think it might storm?"

Sebastian took a sip of his martini. "I have found that one of the benefits of this"—he held up his cast—"is that I do not have to follow the weather report any longer."

"It's still your team, *pibe*. Even if you're not playing."

He shrugged. "They seem to be doing just fine without me."

His mother lifted an eyebrow. "*¿Celoso?*"

He snorted. "No, I'm not jealous. I'm rather enjoying the break, actually."

She turned her sharp green eyes upon him. "La Victoria suffers when you're not on the pitch, *hijo*."

He shrugged. "I'm sure they don't even know I'm gone."

"You're the best player they have, Sebastian, whether you want to admit it or not."

He looked away, not comfortable with the line of conversation. "Now you sound like *Papá*. Besides, I've been keeping myself busy with other projects."

"*Sí*," she said meaningfully. "I've scarcely seen you these past few weeks."

He smiled and took another drink. "Apparently there is a whole world out there that is not polo, *Mamá*."

She pursed her lips. "So which car should we take to the match, *hijo*? Mine or yours or should we call the driver?"

His heart beat a bit faster. He was surprised by the sudden urge to tell her, to come clean, to share how he was feeling. He wanted his mother to know about Kat. "*Lo siento, Mamá.* I'm afraid we'll have to go separately. I must pick up a friend."

She arched an eyebrow. "A friend?"

"The filmmaker I told you about. Corinne's daughter."

She grimaced. "Corinne's daughter? Oh no, Sebastian. What are you thinking?"

"What do you mean?"

"I absolutely forbid you to date that girl. It's out of the question."

He felt himself go cold and still. "I am a grown man, *Mamá*. I hardly think you can tell me who I can or cannot date."

She shook her head. "Sebastian, Corinne has worked for us for almost five years now. I would not like to lose her."

"What are you talking about?"

"I am saying I do not want our housekeeper to quit because my son has toyed with her daughter's heart."

"And who says that I'm doing that?"

She lifted an eyebrow at him. "When have you not done that?"

He shook his head. "It's not that way, *Mamá*."

"Oh? What way is it then?"

He felt himself flush. Leave it to his mother to make him feel ten years old all over again. "It's...different," he said.

"You like her." It was not a question.

"*Sí.* She's smart. And funny."

His mother's eyes slightly widened. "I do not think I have ever heard you describe a woman in quite that way before."

He buried his face into his martini glass. "I think you'll like her, too."

Pilar slowly nodded, and then took sip of her gin and tonic. "Well, we will see. But if I lose my housekeeper, it will be you who will be making the beds, *hijo*."

Chapter Twenty-one

Kat had been to a lot of Hollywood events—parties, dinners, award shows, fund-raisers—and thought that she had pretty much seen the apex of glam and luxury. She was used to gift bags and haute couture, she'd seen life-sized polar bears carved out of ice (Endangered Wildlife Fund) and A-list movie stars arguing over who would take home the floral centerpieces at the end of the night (apparently, Julia and Reese both really liked orchids), but this, she thought, as she and Sebastian zoomed up the long, sun-dappled roadway towards the polo match, might just eclipse them all.

"This is a private estate?" she said as a perfectly manicured polo field and the huge white tent abutting it loomed into view. "These people actually have their own playing field?"

Sebastian shrugged. "A polo field is just ten acres. They have plenty of room."

"*Just* ten acres?" spluttered Kat. "Do they even play?"

"The husband is an enthusiast."

"So buy a commemorative T-shirt, then. Who needs an entire polo field?"

Sebastian smiled at her. "Everyone is allowed their hobbies, Katarina."

"Some hobby," muttered Kat as Sebastian pulled up onto the circular driveway and tossed the keys to the valet who magically appeared at his car door.

Kat smoothed her dress as she and Sebastian walked toward a line of model-handsome men, all clad in the same uniform of head-to-toe white. They stood at attention, bearing silver trays with flutes of pink champagne. Seb expertly scooped up two glasses and handed one to Kat without breaking stride.

Kat had agonized a bit over what to wear, but finally decided on an ankle-length white cotton sundress and flat sandals. Sebastian had warned her that it would be a rookie mistake to wear a fancy hat—that was horse racing, not polo—and so she just piled up her curls on top of her head and slipped on an enormous pair of Jackie O sunglasses. Looking around at what the rest of the women were wearing, she felt like she'd made a fairly solid choice. All the women drifted around in a sea of pale, billowing, expertly draped fabric, their long, blown-out hair streaming behind them. The younger girls were mainly in short, loose tunics and wedge heels, showing off their tanned and toned legs. And the more mature women tended toward pastel kaftans and floor-length, shoulder-baring sundresses. They all looked cool and casual and nonchalant, even as they were surrounded by the most unimaginable luxury.

Kat glanced over at Sebastian and felt a little thrill of appreciation. The men in attendance looked sharp in their brightly colored pants, striped button-down shirts, and white belts and shoes. But Sebastian was wearing a simple, untucked pale blue linen shirt—open just deeply enough to see a fair-sized triangle of his muscular golden chest—and loose white jeans with light brown loafers. He looked as if he had just wandered off the beach, stumbled upon the party, and decided to stay on a casual whim.

He looked better than any man there, Kat thought, feeling her cheeks flush.

Sebastian took her by the hand and led her into the tent. They weaved through dozens of round white-linen–draped tables set with gleaming china, crystal, and flatware. In the center of every table were silver vases overflowing with soft pink roses and peonies. Glittering chandeliers hung from the roof of the tent, and at the front, in a place of honor, was a life-sized statue of a horse made entirely out of red roses.

There were signs of the various sponsors of the event—the Veuve Clicquot was flowing, a black Bugatti Veyron was parked on the grass in front of the bar (Sebastian whistled when he saw it. "Fastest car in the world," he said, trailing his finger admiringly over the hood), a display of museum-quality Piaget jewelry was arranged on pedestals up front, as young models—tall, thin, beautiful waifs all wearing white goddess gowns—drifted among the guests, sporting some of the more intricate and costly pieces around their long necks and seemingly only allowed to say, "Price upon request," in answer to any questions.

Kat goggled at the casual opulence as Sebastian led her through the tent. Heading for the field, they passed a clutch of children, giggling and wielding miniature wooden polo mallets. They were wearing shrunken versions of their parents' outfits—tiny seersucker blazers and flowy sundresses—and they made a beeline for the kids' tent, where there were pony rides, a magician, and multiple crafts set up to entertain them.

A bevy of waiters and cooks darted around, offering canapés and expertly preparing a traditional Argentine barbecue for the post-match dinner. In the corner, a sculpted young blonde with a mohawk spun records at her DJ station.

"So this is for your brother's charity? How much do tickets cost anyway?"

Sebastian whistled for a moment, acting as if he was not going to answer.

"Sebastian?" pressed Kat.

"Ten thousand dollars," Sebastian said quickly. "*Mira*, isn't that Donna Karan?"

"Ten thousand dollars?" yelped Kat. "Did you actually pay that?"

"It's for charity," said Sebastian. "And anyway, you said you needed to see a game."

Kat shook her head. "You could have just taken me to a practice."

Sebastian tugged at his ear for a moment.

He's nervous, Kat realized.

"I want you to meet my mother," he said.

Kat stopped and dropped her hand out of his. "Your mother is here?" she gasped.

"Well, of course," said Sebastian. "She comes to every game."

"Sebastian—"

"Don't worry," said Sebastian, cutting her off. "She only knows that we're working on the script together, that we're friends, but nothing more. It won't be a big deal at all. And just think, you can ask her questions about Victoria. They were very close."

Kat frowned. "I don't know..."

Sebastian took her hand again and raised it to his mouth. One quick, warm kiss pressed upon her skin, and Kat suddenly felt giddy.

"Don't worry, *linda*," he said. "She'll love you."

Together they looked for the reserved seats marked "Del Campo" alongside the field. Pushing through the crowd, Kat couldn't help noticing the way that almost every woman's eyes widened and then intently tracked Sebastian as they passed. As one tanned and toned socialite after another shot him hungry looks, Kat moved just a bit closer, taking his arm.

"Ah, *Mamá*. Good," said Sebastian as they reached front row center, just a few yards behind the blue sideboards lining the field. Kat quickly dropped her hand away from Sebastian's arm.

An elegant older woman with eyes the same color as Sebastian's, wearing a long green kaftan and a rope of sparkling dark blue sapphires, stood up to greet them.

Kat smiled and felt vaguely discombobulated because she recognized the necklace as being a piece she had touched while cleaning.

"Hello, *hijo*," Pilar said as she kissed Sebastian.

The woman swept Kat with a curious, but not exactly unfriendly, look. Kat felt a little shock of worry. Even if Sebastian's mother didn't *know* there was something going on between Kat and her son, she obviously suspected it.

"This is Katarina Parker, *Mamá*," he said. "Katarina, this is *mi mamá*. Pilar Del Campo."

"Please, just call me Kat, Mrs. Del Campo. So nice to meet you."

Sebastian's mother took Kat's hand between her own and smiled. "And you must call me Pilar. Your mother has helped us out for many years now. She is very proud of you. Tell me," she said, patting Kat's hand before releasing it, "will your father be home soon?"

"Yes, he's doing much better. It should any time now."

"Shall we sit?" said Sebastian. "I believe the match is about to start."

As they settled into their seats, a short, pretty, sandy-haired woman wearing medical scrubs and carrying a fat little baby wearing a tiny polo jersey hurried over and flopped down next to Pilar.

"Ugh," she groaned, "the nanny got a migraine right after we got here. I've been trying to check horses and keep Tomás busy at the same time. I finally had to give up and let the other vet take over."

"This is my sister-in-law, Georgia," said Sebastian. "Georgia, this is my friend Katarina."

"Nice to meet you," said Kat.

Georgia looked a little surprised, but smiled warmly. She and the baby had the same wide hazel eyes and sprinkle of freckles across their noses. "Nice to meet you, too," she said.

Kat couldn't help noticing the quick questioning look Georgia shot at Pilar, who answered with a slight shrug.

"*Dame el bebé*," said Pilar as she pulled her curly-haired grandson into her lap. He immediately grabbed her sapphires and began to happily suck on the rope of jewels.

"I didn't have time to change," said Georgia, attempting to smooth down her hair. "I'm going to have to wear the scrubs for the whole game."

Pilar patted her daughter-in-law's hand. "You're working, *niña*. You're just as you should be."

As the announcer began calling the crowd to their seats, Kat looked over at the next row and then did a double take when she saw a shockingly familiar woman wearing a lilac-colored dress. "Whoa. Is that Liberty Smith?" she asked Sebastian.

Sebastian craned his neck to see. "Ah, *sí*, look at that. What do you know? I guess America's Sweetheart is a polo fan."

"*Que linda*," murmured Pilar.

"Oh," said Georgia, "I loved her in that movie where she met that man on the train, and then chased him through Tiffany's."

"Do you know her?" Sebastian asked Kat.

She shook her head. "No. I mean, I've been to a few events where she showed up, but I've never talked to her or anything. She's always got a bodyguard the size of a Buick keeping the little people away."

Sebastian laughed. "I don't know what's all that special about her. You're much more beautiful, *Katarina*."

Kat rolled her eyes. "She's one of the biggest stars in the world. Get her attached to a project, and no problem getting it made."

"*Sí*," interjected Pilar, "that's because her husband over there is worth thirty-eight billion dollars. He finances anything she wants to do."

Georgia turned to her mother-in-law, looking shocked. "Pilar, how in the world do you know that?"

Pilar shrugged. "My dentist has magazines."

They gave their attention to the field and stood up for the National Anthem. After the last note sounded, the players burst onto the field, entering on their ponies as the announcer introduced them by name.

Sebastian's brother certainly was handsome, thought Kat, as she watched Alejandro gallop by, the shoes on his white pony sparking silver in the Florida sun. But he looked rather stern and humorless, she mused. From what she could see, his face lacked Sebastian's merry sweetness and mischief.

Two of the other teammates on La Victoria were almost equally impressive on their horses as Alejandro—a dapper older man with a mustache, who was introduced as Lord Henderson, and a younger man, broad-shouldered and auburn-haired, with a wide and easy grin, named Rory Weymouth. The fourth man, though—Mark Stone—seemed unsure of himself on his shining black pony. He was young, and awkwardly handsome, and obviously just happy to be on the field, but always a bit behind his teammates and tugging at his reins as if he couldn't quite make the horse do what he wanted.

* * *

"Oh, come on," muttered Sebastian, watching Stone lurch around the field, "Stone is my replacement? What does he know about ponies? He's a computer nerd."

"*Shhh*," hissed Pilar. "He is the CEO of a multibillion-dollar company, and this is just an exhibition game."

"He gave a very generous donation to the foundation," whispered Georgia.

Sebastian snorted. "So he bought his way onto the field."

Pilar rolled her eyes. "At least he has two working arms."

"And he's going to use both of them to screw this up."

Kat looked at him. She seemed amused. "You can't stand it, can you?"

He shook his head. "I am merely worried for the sake of the team," he said primly.

She laughed. "Why, Sebastian Del Campo, I do believe you're jealous."

He frowned. "You are the second person to accuse me of that today, Katarina."

"I was the first," murmured Pilar, not taking her eyes off the field.

Kat laughed again.

Seb waved his hand in the air, frustrated. "That *choto* is riding my favorite pony!"

* * *

Kat had been around polo all her life, in the sense that it was not to be escaped in Wellington. There were always ads and billboards announcing the next match, idle chatter about it in every line in every store, the kids of grooms and estate workers discussing it with awe and appreciation at school. She knew the basics of the game through sheer osmosis— in her mind, it was pretty much soccer on horseback with a smaller ball and no goalie.

But even though she had been surrounded by it, she had never felt part of it. Her mother had not been working for the Del Campos when she was growing up. The children of the families who came to play for the season didn't attend her public school. And if Kat thought about polo at all, it was only, quite literally, in passing. A trip to the mall, when she would walk by a group of Argentine girls her own age, as glossy and well groomed as the ponies they rode, or once or twice, a party with Camelia, who had an after-school job at a barn, and would occasionally get invited to some of the lower-key events. Kat trailed along to a couple of horsey parties and stood on the edge of the room, feeling underdressed and ignored. It was Us versus Them, Rich versus Poor, Townies versus Tourists.

There was a coin toss, and the teams were off. Alejandro caught the ball and sent it hurling down the field with a mighty stroke of his arm and all the players followed it at breakneck speed.

The game was not what Kat had expected. She had imagined something more genteel. But seeing it live like this—taking it out of the imagined realm of British princes and ladies in white gloves—thrilled her. This was brutal, and fast and dangerous. There was incredible strength in these players and ponies. Sometimes the ball would get hit so hard, and go so fast, that Kat couldn't even track it. It would hurl up into the bright blue sky, and she would squint to see where it went, and she might as well have been looking for the stars at noonday—it would just be gone—and then, all of the sudden, it would come rushing back down and hit the ground, and the players and their ponies would foam around it in a wave of horseflesh, fighting it out, until it was caught up again.

The ponies thundered past them, mere inches from the sideboards, and Kat could hear the sounds of their hooves hitting the ground and the heavy, ragged snorts of the horses. She felt the strength and speed of the animals in her very bones and wondered how it would feel to be a player in this game, to be clinging to a flying beast as it forced its way through the other ponies, how anyone ever got up enough nerve to lean down and try to hit that tiny white ball while moving at an unbelievably rapid velocity.

Alejandro hit the ball to Rory, who knocked it back through the goal. The announcer yelled the score and Rory's name, and the crowd cheered wildly. The ball was thrown back in, and the players set off full-tilt back down the pitch.

Kat thought of Victoria—all those years before—insisting that she be allowed her place on the field. She watched the players rush by and could imagine the Del Campo matriarch among them—braver and better than them all—muscling her way through the other players, leaning dangerously to hit the ball right under her pony's neck, laughing as she scored, cantering her pony off the field when the horn blew and it was time for fresh horses.

It was all magnificently, beautifully, frighteningly fun and dangerous, and she suddenly understood its siren's call.

Kat turned to Sebastian, and she could see her own excitement reflected in his eyes. She grabbed his hand and squeezed. "Will you take me riding after this?" she whispered to him. "I want to feel it for myself."

Chapter Twenty-two

The Del Campo family team won, of course. Sebastian had never doubted that they would take the win, even with that joke of a player, Stone, in his place. Exhibition game or not, La Victoria had played with their usual passion and brio and had pretty much wiped the field.

As the team lined up at the presentation stand to receive their silver award plates, Sebastian couldn't help smiling as Alejandro's bay stallion, Temper, was led out and given the Best Playing Pony blanket. But the glow of warmth he felt for the headstrong little horse was erased as soon as they announced Mark Stone as MVP.

Alejandro took the mic, explaining to the crowd that, in polo, MVP wasn't always about who scored the most points, but rather, who showed the most heart, and since this had been Stone's first pro game ever, the team had decided that he had more than deserved the honor.

"How much more do you think he paid for that?" snorted Sebastian to his mother.

Pilar just shot him a sidelong look of warning in response and kept up her enthusiastic applause.

"Now, I hope you will all join us under the tent for a

wonderful dinner—traditional Argentine barbecue—and the chance for us to pick your pockets for even more donations for our foundation," said Alejandro, and the crowd laughed good-naturedly.

As he watched the spectators swarm around the players, shaking hands and taking pictures, Sebastian knew he was being an ass for feeling anything less than happy that his brother's foundation had just raised well over a million dollars for a bunch of kids who really needed it. He'd worked with some of these teens himself—teaching them to groom and ride, giving them an escape from the crushing poverty of the inner city—and he knew what a life-changing experience it could be for them. But he was surprised to find that he could not seem to get rid of the bitter taste in his mouth, watching the game from the outside.

He looked over at Kat, who was standing apart from the crowd, jotting down something in her notebook. She'd had exactly the reaction he had hoped—she had fallen for the game right before his eyes. She'd seen the power and beauty and the danger on the field, and it had obviously excited and inspired her. So why didn't he feel better about it?

He supposed that maybe she and his mother had been right—he *was* jealous, but not in the way they assumed. He was jealous because he had only been a spectator to Kat's feelings, not the direct cause. He wasn't really sure what version of himself she knew if she didn't know the man who rode and played.

He watched Kat write. A curl from her pinned-up hair had fallen, and it clung to her long, graceful neck. She looked up for a moment and caught him staring at her, and she threw him a slow and dazzling smile from behind her ridiculously oversized sunglasses before she bent her dark head back down to her work.

He felt a twist in his gut. She was so beautiful. She made him want things he had never known he could want before now. He felt a brand-new world open up when he looked at her.

Chapter Twenty-three

Kat spotted Camelia near the ponies and stopped writing to head over to her. As she crossed the pitch, she realized that Camelia was her one true connection to the horse world. From the time they were girls, Camelia had been horse crazy. And not just horse crazy in the way that most little girls were temporarily horse crazy—but truly in deep. She started trading farm work for lessons by the time she was twelve, doing grunt work at whatever barn was willing to hire her, learning how to groom, and finally finding a more permanent position at fourteen with a wealthy older couple who lived and breathed dressage.

Camelia fell in love with her horse, Skye, a high-stepping chestnut Oldenburg stallion, while he was being boarded at the barn where she worked. The owner, a wealthy horse world dilettante named Kurt Junkins, showed up only once every couple of months or so and was always frustrated by his inability to make the sensitive horse obey. But Camelia exercised the horse every day and built a bond with him that far surpassed anything the animal felt for his absentee owner.

One day, Camelia came up from the riding ring to see Junkins atop Skye, driving him with a whip and galloping down the gravel driveway. The high-strung horse was rolling his eyes and resisting, and, Camelia later told Kat, she knew what was going to happen seconds before it actually did. The horse slipped on the gravel, going to its knees, and the owner was catapulted off and fell heavily onto the driveway.

Camelia sprinted right past the man to the horse, running her hands down its legs, desperate to make sure the animal was okay.

Junkins got up eventually—he'd merely knocked the wind out of himself—and came at the horse with his whip.

Camelia threw herself between them before she could even think.

Kat liked to think of her fierce little friend, protectively backed up against the great big hulk of a horse, boldly facing down the enraged owner.

In the end, without any idea how she was going to do it, Camelia had desperately offered to buy the horse for even more than it was worth, and Junkins had spat on the ground and said he'd be better off without the dumb animal anyway.

Camelia worked off that debt, plus the cost of boarding Skye, for five more years at that farm, and she'd never complained.

Sometimes Camelia would try to get Kat to come with her to the farm, but Kat always had an excuse not to go, having convinced herself that she simply wasn't interested in horses. But deep down, Kat had nursed a sliver of jealousy, seeing her friend so deeply enmeshed in a world that she could only view from the outside.

It was, thought Kat, very strange to suddenly be so firmly on the inside of that world now.

"Hey," said Kat, giving Camelia a friendly little shove on the shoulder. "Fancy meeting you here."

Camelia looked up from the pile of halters she was sorting and grinned. "Holy shit, girl! Look at you! What are you doing here all dolled up like one of the beautiful people?"

Kat smiled ruefully. "I'm here with Sebastian."

Camelia's eyebrows flew up. "You guys are still together? But it's been, like, a month."

"So? A month isn't that long."

"Trust me, it is for Seb. So that's why you couldn't hang out with me—you've been boning my boss."

Kat rolled her eyes. "Still the same old Cam."

Camelia laughed. "Hey, I'd be boning him, too, if I ever got the chance." She looked over toward the tent. "Oh my God, is the *señora* here, too? You're hanging with the whole family?"

Kat shook her head. "I was ambushed. Sebastian says they don't know anything's going on, but I get the sense that he's being purposefully obtuse."

"Well, why should it matter? What do they care if you guys are seeing each other?"

Kat shrugged, a little embarrassed. "I don't know. From the looks Georgia and Pilar are giving each other behind my back, I get the feeling I'm not necessarily welcome."

"What? No way. Dr. Georgia isn't like that at all, she's no snob. And actually, I've never known the *señora* to be either. I mean, at least not about that sort of thing. If they're giving each other looks, I bet they're just in shock that Sebastian brought someone to meet them who wasn't pumped full of silicone."

Kat laughed. "Maybe. But it still feels a little weird. It's one thing when it's just me and Sebastian having a little fun, but my mom works for his mom, you know? I mean, I've actually cleaned the toilets in their mansion."

Camelia made a face. "I suppose that could be awkward."

Kat shook her head. "Anyway, I should go face down dinner. I just wanted to say hi real quick. I'll call you later, I swear."

"Okay, but hey, Kat, remember, you might have scrubbed their toilets, but none of them have been nominated for an Oscar, right?"

Kat smiled at her friend. "Not as far as I know anyway."

* * *

Sebastian had been cornered by Liberty Smith's billionaire husband, David Ansley. He was a short man with visible hair plugs, a barrel chest, and a deep, dark tan. He seemed to know absolutely nothing about polo, and didn't care to learn much more.

"Far as I can see, it's basically just croquet on horseback, eh?" he said to Seb with a shrug. "I'm only here because Liberty dragged me by the balls. She's got a thing for horses."

Sebastian looked over at the movie star, who was taking pictures with fans on the field. A group of admirers hovered around her, waiting their turns. "I see," he said politely.

"And I figured going to this thing was easier than buying her another horse."

"Oh, does she keep horses?"

"She's got, like, twenty, but she's so busy, she doesn't get a chance to ride very often. Which never stops her from buying another one, of course."

Sebastian nodded, looking around for an excuse to escape. "Of course."

"Yeah, well, I hear you're a pretty good rider, right? You need some work? Maybe you can give her lessons sometime or something."

Sebastian smiled, amused. "I do not generally teach. I'm really just a player. And right now"—he held up the cast on his arm—"I'm not even playing."

Ansley shrugged. "Everyone's got a price."

Sebastian saw Kat walking back toward him, her white dress molding to her curvy shape as she strode across the field. He took a deep breath. "If you'll excuse me," he said to Ansley without taking his eyes off her.

He met her halfway across the field, wishing he could steal a kiss but knowing they were on display. She smiled up at him.

"So just how good is this Argentine barbecue they keep talking about, huh?" she said.

He smiled. "The best," he said and couldn't resist taking her hand.

They found their seats at the Del Campo family table. Sebastian's mother and sister-in-law were already there. Pilar was still holding baby Tomás and nodding and smiling at a small crowd of well-wishers.

Georgia smiled at them as they sat down. "Did you enjoy the game, Kat?"

Kat smiled broadly in return. "It was amazing. I can't wait to write about it."

"Yes," said Pilar, turning away from her admirers, "Sebastian told us about your plan for Victoria's diaries. How exciting. My mother-in-law lived quite an interesting life, no?"

Alejandro and Mark Stone, both still wearing their game jerseys, joined them at the table.

"Who is living an interesting life?" said Alejandro, smiling at his mother and wife and taking his son onto his lap.

Pilar leaned over and kissed her son. "¡Ay, hijo! You were

increíble." She patted his cheek. She turned to Mark Stone. "You, too, *Señor* Stone. Excellent first game."

Sebastian snorted, and Georgia kicked him under the table.

"I'm Kat Parker," said Kat when Alejandro turned to her. "That was an amazing game."

Mark Stone looked at Kat like an adoring puppy. The obvious glow of admiration in his eyes did nothing to make Sebastian like him any better. "It was completely awesome," gushed Stone. "I can't believe I got anywhere near that field."

"Me neither," muttered Sebastian.

Alejandro shot him a warning look. "Ah, *Señora* Parker's daughter. *Sí*," he said, "I should thank you for keeping my brother busy with your project. Otherwise I'm afraid he'd be in a bar figuring out how to break his other arm."

Sebastian felt a flash of annoyance, but took a large drink of his wine and then turned to Stone, trying to keep his temper in check. "Good game," he said begrudgingly. "Did you enjoy riding Stella?"

Stone smiled and blinked foolishly. "Now, let's see, which one was Stella?"

Sebastian choked on his wine. Georgia looked worried, and his mother quickly shook her head at him. He ignored them and glared at Stone. "The first pony you rode. *My* pony. I trained her myself."

Stone didn't seem to notice Sebastian's displeasure. "Oh yes, the first one. She was the gray? No, wait—she was a roan, right? She was great. Well, they were all great, really. I mean, the whole thing was just a total blast."

Sebastian gritted his teeth. "Yes, well, they say that the pony makes the rider."

Stone nodded in agreement. "Totally. It's kind of like playing video games, you know? Like the horse is the joystick and you're just shooting all over the pitch."

Sebastian felt his mouth drop open.

"Anyway," Stone said, and stood up, "would anyone like a drink? I think I'm going to have something a little more celebratory than wine."

They all declined, and he wandered off toward the bar. Sebastian turned to Alejandro. "Nice choice," he said. "Seems that he really respects the ponies."

Alejandro held up his hand. "*Basta ya, Sebastian,*" he said quietly. "Not now."

"I notice that *choto* wasn't riding any of your favorites, though, eh?" he said to his brother.

"Well, it's not as if anyone is riding your ponies at the moment. And maybe he was not experienced, but he was playing with heart and joy, which is more than I can say for your time on the field lately."

Sebastian threw down his napkin and stood up, but Pilar put a restraining hand on his arm. "*Hijos,*" she murmured, looking at both of her boys, "not now. Not here."

Sebastian took a deep breath. He could see that people around them were starting to stare. He looked down at Kat, who gazed back at him with concern.

"*Lo siento,* Katarina, but I am afraid I have lost my appetite. Would you mind terribly if we left a bit early?"

Chapter Twenty-four

So," said Kat as she watched Sebastian furiously shift his way through the gears in his car, "your brother seems cool."

Sebastian whipped around to glare at her with a look of fury in his eyes.

"I'm kidding! I'm kidding!" she said. "Jeez, don't run us off the road."

He turned back to the wheel, a muscle jumping in his clenched jaw. God, she thought, even anger looked good on him.

She touched her hand to his shoulder. "You want to talk about it?"

He shrugged her off. "Nothing to talk about. He's an ass-hole and a bully. Just like my father was."

"Your father?"

"Never mind." He was quiet for a moment and then bit out, "He thinks I am lazy, but maybe I am just bored."

"Who?"

"Alejandro. He claims I don't work hard enough. Don't practice. I'm not committed to the team. He says I'm too old to be behaving this way. But he doesn't understand."

Kat raised her eyebrows.

"I think I liked him better when his own life was a mess because then, at least, he didn't feel any need to try fix mine."

"And is he right? Does your life need fixing?"

He flung his hand up. "My life is fine. My life is great."

"So what's the problem?"

"He thinks I drink too much, party too much, too many one-night—" He paused for a moment. "Never mind. But he thinks I should get serious. Do more."

"More?"

"He says I'm not living up to my potential."

"And what do you think?"

"I think he would actually hate it if I ever played at my full potential."

"What do you mean?"

He shook his head. "Forget it. It is not important."

She sat back in her seat. "Do you want to know what I think?"

"I doubt I have a choice in the matter."

She shot him a look, but went on. "I think maybe he's right."

"Oh, excellent. Thank you. That makes me feel so much better."

"But maybe polo isn't the place where you need to prove that."

He rolled his eyes.

"And you know what else I think?" she went on.

"Please do tell."

"I think that it's probably good you broke your wrist."

He groaned. "Believe it or not, I have heard this before."

"I mean, you've never not been a polo player. Maybe this is a chance for you to try something else."

"Just like you are trying something else at the moment?"

"I didn't start making movies when I was two years old. I wasn't born into Hollywood."

"But it's your passion."

"And is polo yours?"

Chapter Twenty-five

Fueled by the game, Kat wrote for almost forty-eight hours straight. Only taking an occasional break to sleep a few hours before she found herself wide awake again and compelled to return to her laptop. Seeing the polo game had unlocked something in her, given her an understanding of Victoria that she hadn't had before. It brought her story to life.

She turned Sebastian away that first day. He showed up at his usual time, a cup of chai for her in hand, and a sheepish look of apology on his face.

"I was an ass, Katarina," he said humbly, and though she did appreciate the sentiment, she was in the kind of creative flow that she hadn't felt in years and had no intention of letting anything get in its way.

She took the tea. "Come back tomorrow," she said, and gave him a quick kiss on the cheek before shutting the door in his face.

She turned him away on the second day. This time he showed up with yellow roses and a box of chocolates, those sovereign symbols of apology, but she was now running on three hours of sleep, bleary and overcaffeinated, unshowered, and still not finished with the script.

She took the chocolates. She smelled the roses. She didn't kiss him this time because she hadn't brushed her teeth yet. "Tomorrow," she said, and shut the door again.

On the third day he came, but this time it was she who handed over the gift. A printout of the finished screenplay for *Twenty-five Roses*. "Go," she said breathlessly. "Go, read it."

He smiled at her. A huge grin. "Really?" he said. "It's done?"

She nodded and smiled back, but resisted the urge to celebrate just yet. She honestly didn't know if it was any good. She was so tired. Much too exhausted to be able to judge all that had poured out over the past few weeks.

She swayed on her feet, barely able to keep her eyes open. "Call me as soon as you finish," she said giddily.

Then she staggered off to her bed and fell asleep before her head hit the pillow.

* * *

She awoke with a start a few hours later. Her mother was sitting on the bed next to her, smoothing her hair back from her brow.

"Mama?"

"Hey, kitty kat, sorry to wake you. I'm going to see Daddy. I didn't know whether you wanted to come or not."

Kat struggled up and blinked blearily. "I'll come with you. What time is it?"

"It's about six."

"Oh, okay, just let me get dressed, and I'll be right down."

Her mother stood up, and then hesitated for a moment. "Baby, I need to talk to you about something first, though."

Kat felt a little jolt of panic. "What's wrong? Is it Daddy?"

Corinne shook her head. "No, no. He's fine. I just—I heard something at work today, is all."

"At work?"

Her mother looked away and took a deep breath, and then looked back at Kat again and said, "Katy Ann, are you seeing Sebastian Del Campo?"

Kat blinked rapidly. "Who told you—"

"It doesn't matter. I run that house. I was going to hear eventually."

Kat looked down, nervously pleating the sheets between her fingers. "It's nothing, Mama. I mean, yes, we've been sort of...seeing each other, but it's not serious."

Corinne sighed. "Well, now, see, that is not what I wanted to hear."

Kat looked back up. "What did you want to hear?"

She laughed softly. "Well, I was really hoping to hear you weren't seeing him, but if you were, I guess I was thinking that maybe you two were madly in love. That you were you going to run off together and make me some green-eyed grandbabies."

Kat shook her head. "No, nothing like that."

Corinne nodded and sat back down on the bed. "You know, Katy Ann, Sebastian is a lovely boy, but sometimes...When you grow up with so much, you don't ever truly learn to value anything, you know? He means well, but I've never known him to be serious about any one thing—or person, for that matter—in all the time I've worked for his family. Do you understand me?"

Kat put her hand on her mother's arm. "Mama, it's okay. I know. I've got his number."

"I just don't want you to get hurt."

"I can handle him, Mama."

Corinne chewed her lip. "That's fine, but if this isn't serious, I'm just worried that after it's all over... Well, I do work for them, you know, baby."

Kat suddenly felt sick. "You're worried about your job."

"It's just with your daddy in the hospital, everything feels a little... precarious."

"Mama, I'm sure Seb would never—"

Corinne nodded, "Of course he wouldn't. I'm just being silly. And the Del Campos are fine people. But I'm sure they're not our kind of people, you know what I mean? I worry about you getting in too deep."

Kat put her arm around Corinne's shoulders. "I'm not, Mama, I swear. We're just having a little fun. It's all under control."

"Well, if you're sure..."

"I am," she said firmly. "Now, why don't you go pack up dinner for Daddy while I get dressed, okay?"

Her mother gave her one last searching look and left the room. Kat sat on the bed for a moment, thinking.

A series of images from the last month unspooled in her head. Sebastian laughing across the table from her at the restaurant, his hands flying as he told her a story about riding. Sebastian kissing her on the beach, the feel of the warm sand on her back as he lowered her to the ground. She and Sebastian standing in her mother's garden together, the basil dropping from her hands as he kissed her. Sebastian stealing a bite of her dessert from her plate. Sebastian hovering over her, licking his way down her naked body. The gentle way he took her hand on the pitch at the polo match. Sebastian reclining on her bed, occasionally glancing up at her through his long lashes as he read his grandmother's words to her in his deep, mischievous voice. Sebastian, his face flushed, his green eyes locked on hers, thrusting himself into her, sending her spiraling over the edge as she lost herself in the deep, pure pleasure of his beautiful body touching hers...

She shook her head.

They were just having fun.

Right?

Chapter Twenty-six

Sebastian stood outside Kat's bedroom window, a handful of gravel in one hand and a bottle of champagne in the other. He sent a rock pinging against the glass and then waited.

Nothing.

He tossed another stone. It was long past midnight on a moonless night, and he didn't want to wake Kat's mother, but Kat hadn't answered any of his calls or texts, and he simply couldn't wait any longer.

No answer.

The script was magnificent. Full of heart and fire and tension. Love infused every part of it—love between the main characters, yes, but also love for the game, for polo. He had been amazed that Kat had understood this part of his *abuela* so clearly.

Reading it had almost made him jealous. Kat's overwhelming talent and passion were apparent in every word. What would it feel like, he wondered, to truly be able to immerse yourself in the thing you were so clearly put on this earth to do?

He threw another stone, a little harder this time.

Ping.

"Come on, *linda*," he muttered as he lost patience and threw several rocks at once, harder than he had intended. They clattered against her window and the side of her house.

Her window flew open. Her face gleamed pale in the night, the inky shadows of her hair spilling down over her shoulders as she leaned out and peered into the darkness.

"Camelia," she hissed, "if that's you, I want you to remember that we are no longer sixteen years old and I have exactly zero interest in hearing about how you just went to third base with Joey Butkiewicz—"

"*Shh*, Katarina, it's me."

She squinted. "Sebastian? What in the hell? It's one in the morning."

"I finished the script."

Her face lit up. "Ah! Hang on! Don't move!" And she slammed the window shut behind her.

She was beside him in a moment, wearing a torn T-shirt and sweatpants that were several inches too short at the ankles, her hair a wild cloud around her face.

"This is what you wear to bed? *Que* sexy."

"Shut up. I need to do laundry. Now—tell me what you thought. Do not hold back. Do not worry about my feelings. I need to hear your honest opinion."

She gazed up at him with a burning light in her eyes. He smiled and gathered her into his arms.

"It was fantastic, *mi corazón*," he whispered. "I loved every page of it. *Mi abuelita* would have loved it, too."

Her face broke into a dazzling grin. "Really? You're not being easy on me, are you? Because I can take criticism."

He shrugged helplessly and pushed a lock of her hair off her face. "I wouldn't change a word."

She smiled even wider. "Seriously?"

"Well, except for some bad Spanish. Who taught you your Spanish?"

"*Señora* Paviola, ninth grade. But it wasn't her fault. I had a crush on the guy who sat in front of me and spent all my time doodling pictures of the back of his head in my notebook instead of conjugating verbs. But never mind that—you really liked it?"

He stepped back and presented her with the bottle of champagne. "I loved it. Let's celebrate."

* * *

Kat ducked back into the cottage to change out of her pajamas and gather up some wineglasses and a blanket. They took the little path down to the beach and spread the blanket upon the sand. Sebastian sent the champagne cork flying into the starry night sky, then he poured the wine and toasted her.

"To Katarina. I knew you were beautiful, intelligent, witty, and sexy as all hell, but I had no idea that your talent ran so deep. Here's to the amazing words you have put on the page, and to seeing those words come to life on the screen. *¡Salud!*"

Kat felt that she might burst from happiness as he leaned over and kissed her, his lips still damp from the champagne. "I couldn't have done it without you," she whispered to him, and he kissed her again, deeper this time, and then they settled back on the blanket.

"So," he said, "now that the script is done, what next?"

She laughed. "Now comes the hard part. Getting it made. Believe it or not, a period love story about the history of polo isn't going to be the easiest sell."

"Don't be silly," he said. "I'm sure that once they read it, the studios will be lining up."

She lifted an eyebrow. "Well, I'll send it to my manager first, and she'll probably have notes."

"Notes on what? It's perfect as is."

Kat smiled. "I'm glad you think so, but there are always notes. And then my manager will probably slip it to a few people—let them see it before it goes wide, you know? If we can get a big-name actress attached up front, or a really powerful producer, that will help. And as much as it pains me to say this, even if we can sell the script, I don't know if I can get a guarantee that I'll be the one to direct—"

Sebastian sat back up. "Wait, what? This is your project. Of course you'll direct."

She shook her head. "My name has been a liability ever since *Red Hawk*. If we really want to see this movie made, we should be open to all sorts of avenues. You have to be willing to compromise."

He stared at her. "How can you talk like that? You sound like a businessman, not an artist."

She felt a little pang of exasperation. "Hollywood is a business, Sebastian, and you have to approach it that way if you want to get anything done."

"But the business side is for the agents and managers and executives to figure out. That's their job. You are the artist. You should be protected from all that."

She laughed. "That sounds great, but that's not how it works."

He looked at her. "Well, then, we will make it work that way. I will be the producer."

She laughed. "What?"

He shrugged. "How hard can it be? I know movies. I have

money. I have contacts. I will put together the business end of things so that you can be the artist."

She blinked in astonishment. "That's—that's like me saying I've ridden a horse on a merry-go-round so now I should be a professional polo player."

He grabbed her hand, excited. "No, don't you see? This is perfect! We'll go to L.A., and we can stay at your place while we film. Then we'll probably have to go to Argentina at some point, but there's plenty of room at *el campo*—"

She shook her head. "Wait, slow down—"

"You will need horses, of course. And people who know polo. I can supply both."

"This is crazy. You can't just—"

"I have all this time on my hands, and you're the one who told me I should try something else, Katarina. You said I should stop being a polo player for a while. So why not a producer?"

She pulled her hand away from him, angry. "Sebastian, I don't think you understand just how important this movie is to me. I can't just let you pretend to be a producer because you're bored. This is my last chance. If this movie doesn't get made and made right, I won't work in Hollywood again."

He looked at her, a stubborn set to his jaw. "And that is precisely what I will do—make sure this movie is made right."

"You don't know anything about the industry."

"I can learn."

"You think this is a game, Sebastian? I have no money, no future, no other skills. I'll be cleaning houses for good if I can't make this film work out."

He put his hands on her shoulders. "Listen, *mi corazón*, I understand—"

131

She shrugged him off and stood up. "You cannot possibly understand. You've had everything just handed to you on a silver platter from the day you were born. Maybe you can do things on a whim because you have the means to simply start all over again if something goes wrong, but I don't have that luxury. I have to be careful. And thoughtful. And not take risks. This film is everything to me, Sebastian, everything!"

He stared at her. "Is that really what you think my life is like? So easy?"

"I don't think it, I know it."

"And you really think that I would ever do anything to harm you?"

She paused for a moment. Her mother's words about him echoed in her head. "Not on purpose, no. But I think—I think you would be careless." She met his eyes. "I think you would start the work and then get bored. I think I would be left to pick up the pieces."

He nodded slowly, not breaking the gaze between them. "So that's how you see me. As some child who simply pushes aside his toys when he tires of them."

She looked away. "I'm sorry. I just can't risk it."

He stood up. "Perhaps you're right then," he said quietly. "Perhaps working together would be a mistake. In fact, perhaps this whole thing was a mistake from the beginning."

She turned to him. "That's not what I meant."

He held up a hand. "I know what you meant, Katarina. You were very clear."

They walked back to the house in silence.

Chapter Twenty-seven

Sebastian led his little piebald mare, Elizabét, from the barn out toward the practice field. He'd had to ask one of the grooms to help him tack up since he still had only one working arm, but riding one-handed was not going to be a problem.

He swung up into the saddle and rode out onto the field. It was still early in the morning. The sun was just slanting over the horizon, and the air had a kiss of nighttime coolness.

He had briefly gone home after leaving Kat at her house, but found that sleep was elusive.

Lying there in his room, staring up at the ceiling, he'd felt hollow inside, gut-punched. He could still hear the way she had talked to him—like he was some stupid, reckless child.

He urged the mare into a trot as he remembered the first time he had met her—the look in Kat's eyes just before she'd slammed the door in his face. How had he not seen it? She'd been a mistake from the very beginning. What had possessed him to think of her any differently than the multitude of other women he'd been with? Why had he let his guard down?

He pushed the mare harder, urging her into a full-blown

gallop. He'd been a fool. Hanging around her like a lovesick puppy, bringing her gifts, introducing her to his family. He glowered at the thought.

He had actually imagined it was different with her. That she was different. That *he* was different with her. He'd let himself go soft, to fantasize about the kind of future he'd never allowed himself to imagine before. Talking about staying at her house in L.A., going home to Argentina together, assuming that this movie was their project to complete together...

He let Elizabét slow back down to a canter.

Of course, Kat was wrong, too. Maybe she wasn't wrong about them, but she was wrong even to consider compromising on her beautiful script. He couldn't stand the thought of anyone making changes or giving notes to make it more commercial. Reading it had been like having his *abuelita* back in the room with him again. He could feel her warm affection and her humor, the way she didn't give a damn about what was expected of her. It reminded him of all the things she had worked so hard to teach him and Jandro, of her fervent wish that the brothers grow up to live passionate and extraordinary lives.

When they were very young, they would trail ride with her at their *campo* in Argentina, and she would tell them stories about the way she and their grandfather had courted. How, even though their families disapproved of the match, and *Abuelo*'s family had even threatened to disinherit him, they never wavered in their affection. They never backed down. "Your *abuelo* and I, we felt no fear," she'd say, smiling at the memory. "We were meant to be together, it was *destino*, and no one could stand in the way of something so strong."

Sebastian took the pony up to a gallop again, feeling the horse flying under him.

When he was reading that script, he had to admit that there were moments when he thought that maybe the words were just a little bit about *them*, too—him and Kat. That just maybe what his *abuelita* had described—that kind of destiny—was showing itself to be between the two of them as well. Certainly, he'd never felt this way about any woman before, never felt this aching desire that pulsed through him even as he held her in his arms, even as he took her...hell, even after he found his release. He felt like he could have her a million times over and never stop wanting her.

And it wasn't just sex. It was her laugh, and her wit, her generosity. It was the way she cut right to the heart of things. Everything simply made more sense when he was with her.

With her, he saw himself in a new way. He thought he was a stronger, better man when he was in her arms. Before he had met her, the furthest into the future he was willing to think about was what bar or club he would go to that night, and what girl he might go home with after. But with Kat, suddenly he found himself thinking about things not just days ahead, but *years*.

He shook his head, sneering at himself. What was the point of belaboring it? He had been wrong about so much; he was surely wrong about all this as well. She obviously thought him as insubstantial as Alejandro did.

He slowed the horse to a walk, cooling her off. His *abuela* had also taught him to ride it out when things were bad, that time on a horse could work magic, that it could change everything. But as the horse slowed beneath him, he felt a numb, hollow feeling in his chest rise up once more.

He bent to Elizabét's neck, resting his cheek against her velvety coat, and sighed, still waiting for the magic spell to kick in.

Chapter Twenty-eight

Kat sat with her father over dinner. The rehabilitation center seemed quiet tonight. Or perhaps it was just them. Her mother had pleaded a headache and sent Kat alone, her father seemed tired, and Kat herself couldn't seem to find the heart to keep even a polite conversation going.

The other patients sat at the tables around them. Some of them obviously had family visiting, though few had daily visitors like Kat's dad did. Others—especially the folks who were here long-term—had made friends within the facility. In fact, her father had recently told Kat a rather scandalous story of a couple of married patients who had met during water aerobics and struck up a hot affair.

But Kat felt bad about the people who ate alone, the ones who never seemed to have anyone, who passed their time with a book propped up in front of their plate or who quickly bolted their meal and then hurried back to their rooms. Or worse yet, thought Kat as she watched a sweet-faced older woman picking at her food, the ones who just kind of stared off into space until dinner was over.

Sometimes her family invited people to their table. But tonight it was just Kat and her father.

"Looks like a nice night," her father said.

Kat looked out the window and nodded in agreement. "Yes, not too humid."

The dining hall overlooked the gardens, and usually Kat enjoyed the view—a brightly colored hodgepodge of tropical and native plants, palms and bromeliads, and oversized aloe—but tonight, she couldn't seem to focus.

"This is delicious," said her father, forking up another bite of chicken. "Y'all are spoiling me."

She nodded again and smiled distractedly, toying with her food.

"How's the script going?"

"Oh, well, Honey loved it."

"That's good."

"Yeah, she's slipping it to some people already. I'm really excited."

He scratched his head. "*Hmph*. You don't look too excited to me."

She shook her head. "I am. I swear. I just..."

"You just what?"

"I just keep thinking about...Well, the woman I wrote the script about, Victoria Del Campo? She kind of has me thinking about the idea of destiny."

"Destiny? What kind of destiny?"

She looked up at the ceiling for a moment, considering. "Like, how maybe there is one great thing a person is meant to do, a path you're supposed to take, and it's your life's work to find that path."

He nodded. "Okay."

"And sometimes it's easy to find that path. Like, it's obvious. But sometimes you really have to search."

"I can buy that." He ate another bite of chicken.

She hesitated, looking at her hands. "And so there's just one person you're supposed to find, too, right?"

He laughed. "Aha. I knew it. Boy trouble."

She felt herself blush. "No," she protested. "I'm just talking philosophically, you know? Theoretically."

He shook his head. "Okay, okay. So are you asking me if I think that each person on this earth is meant to walk only one path and find only one great love?"

"Yes. More or less."

He cocked his head, thinking. "Well, I don't know. I mean, we can't all be artists or geniuses, right? We're not all going to cure cancer."

"No, but someone is, and what if that person missed their chance to go into medicine?"

"But isn't the whole point of destiny that it's inevitable?"

She frowned. "Well, I guess that's how it's supposed to work. But do you think that sometimes we miss our calling?"

He took a sip of milk. "You know, honey, I don't know about this on a big old macrolevel, but I do know that I feel pretty strongly that I was put on this earth to be a husband to your mother and a father to you. And I guess there might be another woman out there who I could have loved, and maybe we would have had different children together, and I'm sure I would have felt like their daddy, but"—he smiled—"I can't help but think that if that had happened, I would have always felt like there was just . . . something missing, I guess. Something not quite right. A little itch, you know? And maybe I would have listened to that and found another path to your mama and you."

Kat laughed. "Your poor abandoned theoretical wife and kids, Dad!"

He laughed with her.

"But how about work? Does it happen the same way?" she asked.

"Well, it could, I guess. Though I can't say it's particularly exciting to be predestined to be a handyman."

"But you can fix anything. Not many people can do that. That's a gift."

He smiled, pleased. "I suppose it is."

* * *

Pilar and Georgia had gone out to see a movie together, leaving the brothers alone in the house with the baby. Sebastian sat on the terrace with Jandro and Tomás, having dinner.

It was a beautiful night, warm and balmy but not too humid. The sun was just setting, casting pink and gold rays into the dusk, but Sebastian couldn't enjoy the view. He had been restless all day and then started drinking early. A martini. And then, before he knew it, another two.

Now he was having red wine, and he had a splitting headache and was pretty near drunk. He picked up his fork and then put it back down. He looked at his brother.

"Do you remember trail riding with *Abuelita*?"

Alejandro looked surprised. He fed a small bite of pasta to Tomás. "Trail riding?"

"Yes, at *el campo*."

Alejandro knit his brow. "*Sí*, of course."

Sebastian picked his wine back up and drained it. "Do you remember when she told us that a little time on a pony could solve practically anything?"

Alejandro smiled fondly. "Yes, she said that all the time."

"It didn't, though."

"What didn't?"

"Time on the ponies. It didn't solve everything." He poured himself another glass of wine.

Alejandro shook his head. "What do you mean?"

Seb drank. "I mean, we could ride all day long and *Papá* was still off screwing the help."

Alejandro snorted. "True."

"And you rode and rode and that didn't make Olivia's death any easier."

Alejandro frowned. "I don't see what that has—"

He interrupted. "And *Mamá* rode and *Papá* rode and that didn't stop them from fighting all the way through our childhoods."

"What's your point?" said Alejandro.

"My point is"—Sebastian could hear the slur in his own voice—"my point is that I'm beginning to think that, despite what I was raised to believe, there is nothing so very magic about the ponies. You might win games on them, but that doesn't mean they can do anything else besides eat and shit."

Alejandro shook his head. "Why would you say that? You of all people know better. You love the ponies."

Sebastian shrugged belligerently. "Who says I do?"

The baby made a little squawk as Alejandro wiped his mouth with a cloth napkin. "You're drunk," he said.

"Maybe," agreed Sebastian, "probably. But I still think I'm right. You can ride and ride and you're still going to get off the horse exactly the same as when you get on."

"Not if you're riding the right way."

Sebastian laughed. "Oh! There's a right way?"

Alejandro shook his head. "I'm not going to have this conversation with you right now."

"No, please tell me, *hermano*, what is the 'right way' to ride?"

Alejandro looked at him. "With heart, to begin with. And with discipline."

"Oh, here we go, it's the charity dinner all over again."

"You brought it up, Sebastian."

"And you brought it right round to where you always do"—his voice rose—"to my terrible shortcomings as a player."

"You could be so much better if you just put in a little more effort. You could be great."

Sebastian laughed ruefully. "And how would you feel if I suddenly was, Jandro?"

Alejandro looked at him sharply. "What do you mean?"

Sebastian shrugged. "Never mind. Why talk about it now when we've avoided it our whole lives?"

The baby began to whimper.

Alejandro shook his head and lifted the baby out of the highchair. "I'm not going to let you pick this fight right now. You're drunk, and you're upsetting Tomás."

Sebastian blinked, looking at the unhappy baby. "Yes, of course," he said quickly. He felt like an ass. "I'm sorry."

Alejandro sighed as he walked out of the kitchen. "I'm putting the baby to bed. I suggest you go, too. The women will be home soon, and you won't want them to see you this way."

Chapter Twenty-nine

No party," said Kat as Camelia looked at her expectantly from across the table. "The last thing I need is a party."

Camelia rolled her eyes and stole a fry off Kat's plate. "That's ridiculous. A party is exactly what you need. Get dressed up, drink a lot, dance, flirt—just scrub off all that sad my-boyfriend-just-dumped-me dirt."

"He did not dump me, and he was not my boyfriend."

Camelia snorted. "Girl, in the entire time I have worked for the Del Campos, I have never, not once, seen Sebastian with the same girl twice."

"So?"

"So you guys have been holed up together for, like, a month. I mean, this has to be his record."

"I wasn't just with Sebastian that whole time, you know. I've been working, writing. And helping out with my dad."

"Mmm-hmm," said Camelia, helping herself to another fry.

Kat grabbed her plate away. "Stop eating my fries. Get your own."

Camelia laughed. "You have not changed one bit, Katy Ann."

"What are you talking about?"

"I'm talking about the fact that you still hate sharing your food. I'm talking about your temper. And I'm talking about the way you're so insistent about pretending that something isn't bugging the shit out of you when it very obviously does."

Kat felt her face burn. She pushed the fries back at Camelia. "Fine. Take them."

Camelia shook her head. "Look, I don't blame you even one little bit. If I'd ever even dreamed that I could've held Sebastian's attention for more than one night, I would have been all over him like sauce on pasta."

Kat rolled her eyes. "That's absurd."

Camelia laughed. "No, it's really not. Perhaps, coming from the land of movie stars and billionaires, you have not noticed that Sebastian Del Campo is basically the hottest guy in the entire world."

Kat sighed. "I've noticed."

"Well then, it's okay to cry a little over him slipping free. I know I'd be a puddle of tears. And then I'd put on my hottest dress and go make myself feel better at the awesome party my BFF just invited me to."

Kat looked at her suspiciously. "What kind of party is it, again?"

Camelia shrugged. "You know, just the Wellington usual. No big deal. But it should be fun."

Kat ate a fry. "Okay. Fine. Whatever."

"Yay!"

"But for the record, he did not dump me. I broke up with him."

Camelia nodded. "You just keep telling yourself whatever you need to make it through the night, sister."

* * *

Sebastian lay on the couch, trying to watch a movie, but his mind kept drifting. He turned off the flat screen with an exasperated sigh. It was useless. It seemed that the woman had spoiled everything fun for him. Drinking, movies, probably sex with anyone else but her...

He shook his head. This would not do. He was not going to be a sad, mean, abstinent monk of a man for the rest of his life. He was going out.

He pulled on his jacket and found his mother outside in the garden, trimming roses. Pilar wore an enormous straw hat, which she swore was the reason she had yet to succumb to a face-lift.

"I'm going out, *Mamá*. Maybe late."

Pilar frowned. "But you'll be back before we leave tonight?"

He shook his head. "Leave for what?"

"*La fiesta.* The party Lord Henderson is hosting."

He groaned. "I forgot all about it."

"I told you last week. The whole team needs to be there."

"But I'm not on the team. Tell Jandro to call up Mark Stone."

She snorted in exasperation. "I'm certain he will be there, too. But this is a party for real polo players."

"Where was that snobbery last week when I needed it?"

She waved her hand. "Make sure you have time to change your clothes. It's black tie."

He groaned. "Oh come on, *Mamá*."

She met his eyes. "You need this."

He looked away. "I don't know what you're talking about."

"Don't be coy with me, *hijo*. A mother knows when something is wrong."

He shrugged. "It's nothing, *Mamá*. A tiny bump in the road."

She shook her head. "No. Even before the girl. You and Jandro fighting all the time—"

"Who said anything about a girl? And the fighting is all Alejandro."

"The way you were playing on the field."

"I had one bad game, *Mamá*."

"No. No. You are in trouble. A mother knows."

He sighed in exasperation. "And putting on a tux will somehow save me?"

She considered him for a moment, her green eyes flashing, and then went back to cutting her roses with a shrug. "It would be a beginning."

Chapter Thirty

Kat was dressed and waiting for Camelia when her phone rang. It was her manager, Honey.

"Babe, I've got news about the script."

Kat's heart started to beat faster. She sat down on her bed. "Good or bad?"

"Well...could be either. Okay, so I've got two studios very interested."

Kat punched the air with her fist in glee. "But that's great! Do you think we can get a bidding war going? Do you think we can guarantee that I'll direct?"

"Well, wait a minute, okay? I have two studios very interested but they both have the same questions."

"Which are?"

"Can we change polo to something more relatable—say, football?"

Kat groaned. "Oh, come on."

"And can the lead—Victoria—be switched over to a man, not a woman."

Kat exploded. "What? Are you serious?"

"I told you. Good news. Bad news."

"Well, that's just frigging ridiculous. They're missing the whole damned point if they think—"

"Hey, I know. I know. I already told them there was no way on God's green earth you were going to go for it. But I had to ask. It's my job. Don't worry. This interest is a good sign. And I've leaked it to a small handful of top actresses. All we have to do is get someone attached."

Kat took a deep breath. "Okay. Okay. I know. You're right. Okay. Thanks, Honey."

"My pleasure, babe. I love this one. You know I do. We'll find the right people for it. Don't you worry."

"I'm not," she lied.

She threw herself back onto the bed, closed her eyes, and groaned. Sebastian had been right. They were going to tear this script to pieces.

Her phone beeped with a message from Camelia. She was five minutes away.

Kat didn't care. She didn't want to go out anyway. And she certainly didn't want to go out wearing a formal gown.

When Camelia had said "party," Kat had imagined some club night—not black tie. It was only when Camelia had called the day before to ask Kat if she had a pair of elbow-length gloves that she could borrow that Kat got a clear view of what was expected.

She'd chosen a strapless black satin sheath—an ex-boyfriend had once told her looked like a black calla lily when she wore it. She wore her hair down and wild—her curls springing out in all directions. Sometimes it was easier not to fight Mother Nature. She slid on a pair of six-inch black sandals, and the only jewelry she wore was a pair of teardrop-shaped rubies in her ears. The stones were glass, but she thought they could pass for real in dim light.

Camelia hadn't told her much else about the party except that it was in Palm Beach and had nothing to do with polo, so there was almost zero chance that any of the Del Campos would show up.

The doorbell rang, and she heard the murmur of her mother's voice combined with Camelia's more exuberant one.

She sighed. *Suck it up, Parker*, she thought. *No backing out now.*

* * *

Sebastian mixed himself a rum and Coke. It was something he hadn't tasted since he was a teen, but he thought a little nostalgia might help to work up his enthusiasm. He pulled on his tuxedo jacket, and as he examined himself in the mirror, he had to admit that his mother might have been right. Putting on the old monkey suit did seem to brighten things up a bit.

He plugged his iPod into his speakers and turned up D'Angelo, then stopped it and replaced him with Jay Z. He needed to be bold. He needed to be brash. He needed to get back to the man he'd been before this whole mess happened. The man who didn't give a fuck about anything but having a good time.

He made a plan. He would go to the party to make his mother happy, be sure that Hendy saw that he was there, and then go right back out and have his night on the town. The tuxedo could do double duty tonight. For the party, of course, but after he left, he could unbutton the top button of his shirt, untie the bow tie, and leave it dangling as bait for women in the bars. It was his experience that a little casual nonchalance went a long way when a man was wearing formal wear.

He tied his tie and fastened his cuff links, picked up his drink, and was ready to go.

He met his mother in the hallway.

"Very nice," she said as she smoothed out the lapels on his jacket and fussed with his tie. She was wearing a long black dress with a silver sequined jacket over it and diamonds at her throat, ears, and wrists. "You look *muy guapo*."

As they came down the stairs, she turned her attention to Alejandro, who was waiting for them. "Oh, you look wonderful as well, *hijo*. Is that a new suit?"

Alejandro smiled. "Georgia picked it out."

Pilar turned to her daughter-in-law. "*Ay*, nice work, *chiquita*."

Georgia, who was wearing pink silk and black diamonds, blushed, obviously pleased by Pilar's praise. "Oh, well, he looks good in anything."

"Nobody will even look at me as long as I'm with you, *querida*," said Alejandro to his wife.

"And you look lovely as well, *Mamá*," said Sebastian. "Truly."

Pilar beamed.

"So since we all look *fantástico*, shall we get going, then?" asked Alejandro. "I think we can all take one car if we like."

Sebastian shook his head. No way was he getting caught in Palm Beach without his car. "I'll take my car and meet you guys there."

Pilar shot him a questioning look.

"What? Georgia and Jandro will need to get back early for Tomás. What if I want to stay late? Or what if *you* want to stay late, for that matter, *Mamá*? What if you meet a tall, dark, and mysterious man?"

She snorted, but then grudgingly nodded with a tiny smile on her face.

"Fine, then," said Seb. "I will see you lovely ladies—and my equally handsome *hermano*—at the party in a few minutes."

And before they could answer, he was walking out the door, whistling and feeling unaccountably cheerful.

Chapter Thirty-one

The house felt familiar to Kat. Unlike the old-world glamour of the Del Campo home, this place was pure Rat Pack nostalgia. A sleek, masculine, early sixties ranch so tastefully done that there wasn't even the slightest hint of camp. Half the successful young directors of Hollywood had houses like this—all glass and gleaming, polished stone, filled with expensive plastic and metal midcentury furniture—but they couldn't hope to touch this level of authenticity. If Frank Sinatra himself had strolled up with Ava Gardner hanging off his arm, Kat didn't think she would have batted an eye.

"Who did you say owns this place?" she said to Camelia as they gazed out onto a lanai that overlooked a perfect kidney-shaped pool.

Camelia gripped her arm. "Okay, please, please don't kill me."

"What are you talking about?"

"So, I was at the barn a couple of weeks ago, and I walked in at just the right moment when Hendy was inviting Alejandro to this party—"

"Wait, what?" Kat's heart started to race.

"And grooms never get invited to these things, but Hendy is super polite, so when he saw me and realized I'd overheard them, he got all gentlemanlike and asked me along as well."

"Camelia—"

"And I know it's the last place you want to be, and yes, Sebastian will probably show up, but maybe that's not the worst thing in the world, right? Maybe deep down, you might actually want to see him?"

"Damn it, Camelia!"

Camelia tightened her grip on Kat's arm. "Kat, Skye is getting older. He won't be able to compete in a few more years. And let's face it, I'm getting older, too. There are potential sponsors at these things, Katy Ann. Aging people who still want a little piece of the glory. People who are willing to trade grooming work for training. People who just love horses and might be willing to throw some money at me, you know?"

"So why do you need me?"

"I knew that I'd look like a total moron if I showed up alone and no one would talk to me, so I figured if I brought my friend—who just happens to be a big Hollywood director—"

"God. Come on, Cam."

"I know," she pleaded. "I'm a total asshole. But I had to take the opportunity. The Olympics aren't going to wait for me forever. And I know this is hard for you to understand, but I feel like I owe this to Skye. He deserves to show."

"I'm leaving," muttered Kat, disengaging herself from Camelia's death grip on her arm.

She turned on her heel and headed out the door and then stopped. A dark green Porsche had pulled up to the valet in front of the house.

"Damn it," she swore and then retreated back in through the front door, where she was met by a relieved Camelia.

"I knew you wouldn't let me down," Camelia said happily. "Besides, I'm your ride home."

Kat kept walking. "Trust me, I didn't come back for you," she said. "Now, help me find a place to hide."

* * *

The party didn't look terrible, Sebastian decided, as he checked out the room. Hendy had surprisingly democratic taste in friends for an English lord. There was a good mix—not all horsey people and not all billionaires—and even though Sebastian was technically both, he appreciated the way Hendy liked to mix it up.

The music was good. Hendy had hired a small band to play torch numbers and swing, and the food and liquor would be top notch, of course. Sebastian relaxed as he wound his way through the crowd toward the bar that was set up on the lanai. Maybe he'd stay a little longer than he'd originally planned.

He was ordering himself another rum and Coke (he'd been amused to discover that he still liked the drink when he'd sampled it at home) when he saw Liberty Smith. In a floor-length shimmering dress that looked like molten sapphires had been poured over her curves, the movie star was standing alone by the pool, looking slightly bored.

This didn't surprise Sebastian. He had experienced enough celebrity to know that it was common to be at two extremes—either bombarded by attention and barely able to breathe or, in more rarified situations, completely abandoned because everyone had decided you were unapproachable.

He caught her eye and smiled, lifting his glass in salute. And after a brief moment, she smiled back.

Oof, thought Sebastian, there was a reason this woman's face lit up screens all over the world. She was like a tiny, exquisite piece of art. Her cascading waves of hair shifted from auburn to gold to butter, her skin seemed to emanate a soft peach glow from within, her eyes were huge and heavily lashed and almost violet in their blueness, and her body was unstoppable—all flares and curves and with a waist so small he was sure he could span it with his hands. And yet, in contrast, her smile was one of perfect sweetness and innocence. No wonder she had once been dubbed "the girl you *wish* lived next door."

Sebastian knew her story because everyone knew her story. She'd been raised in poverty by a single father in a small town in South Dakota. Her dad had died when she was a teen, and she had run away from abusive foster parents and hitchhiked her way to L.A., determined to become a star. Then, in the very first audition she had walked into, she'd been cast in the lead role. She was the queen of romantic comedies from then on.

She'd married three times. The first time to another up-and-coming actor whom she divorced after meeting her second husband, the lead singer of a popular rock band, and the third time when she met her current husband, billionaire and financier David Ansley, while she was still married to the rock star.

Her last movie, Sebastian remembered, had been a bomb. No one was really watching those old-fashioned romantic comedies anymore, and there had been a murmuring in the press that maybe she was finally past her prime.

She walked over to him, a trace of that sweet smile still on her lips, and placed her hand on his arm. "You're Sebastian Del Campo, right?" Her voice was soft and girlish and was filled with a shimmer of nascent laughter. "I've seen you play."

* * *

Kat felt sick as she watched Sebastian smile down at Liberty Smith. She had retreated to a table in a dark corner of the patio and blown the candles out around her for good measure. Camelia had left her there to troll the party for sponsors, and Kat had figured that she would wait until the coast was clear and then leave before Sebastian ever knew she'd been there.

But then he'd walked onto the lanai, looking devastatingly handsome in his tuxedo, and Kat's heart had skipped a beat. For a moment, she wondered how she could have been so stupid. Here was this gorgeous, funny, horrendously sexy man, who had only wanted to help her make her dreams come true—and she had insulted him, refused to trust his good intentions, and driven him away. She'd been a fool.

She wanted him back, at least for the night, and she was just working up the nerve to stand up and tell him so when the most famous movie star in the world had walked over, put her hand on Sebastian's arm, and turned her big, dreamy violet eyes up at him.

Kat couldn't hear what they were talking about, but it was easy enough to read between the lines. It was an open secret in Hollywood that Liberty's billion-dollar marriage was not exactly based upon trust and fidelity, and from the way she was smiling up at Sebastian, Kat didn't think they were discussing the weather.

Take your hand off of him, she willed, *just take your hand off of him and walk away. No harm, no foul.*

But instead, Liberty took a step closer and then threw her head back and laughed.

For a moment, Kat almost got to her feet. She fantasized about racing over, inserting herself between them, and pushing the smaller woman into the pool. Then she would take Sebastian's arm and they would march out of this party together, never looking back at the irate movie star bobbing in the water.

She smiled at the image, willing herself to go through with it, willing herself to fight for the man that she had fallen in love with.

Fallen in love.

God. She hadn't realized. She hadn't been able to admit it to herself until this very moment. She loved Sebastian. She was in love with him.

Her smile got wider, and a warmth thrilled through her. She had never felt this way before. She'd been in relationships, she'd been fairly content with other men, she'd even considered making things more permanent once or twice— but it had never been like this. It had never felt like it was...*everything.*

But then, her heart plummeted. Because Liberty finally took her hand off Sebastian's arm, but it was only so she could tuck herself under his other one, and then they turned their backs on Kat and walked out of the party together.

Kat stared, numb, as they disappeared into the crowd. After a moment, there was a hand on her shoulder.

"I saw them," whispered Camelia. She looked truly upset for Kat. "Come on." She pulled Kat to her feet. "Let's go get a drink."

* * *

Kat took another shot of tequila. "You know what?" she slurred to Camelia. "Maybe it doesn't matter that the man I only just now frigging realized that I love left the party with the most beautiful woman in the world. Maybe it was destiny."

Camelia nodded seriously and took another shot herself. "You could be right. Maybe the man you're really meant to be with is at this very party right now. And if that beautiful, beautiful, beautiful movie star hadn't stolen your other man, you would never meet him."

Kat gazed fuzzily around. "You think so? Really? Which one is the guy I'm really supposed to be with?"

Camelia shrugged and drank again. "I dunno. They're all kind of starting to look the same to me at this point."

Kat nodded. "It's a lot of tuxedoes, isn't it? Like a herd of fancy waiters."

"Wait, I take that back," said Camelia, squinting into the distance. "Change of plans. I think I just saw the guy *I* was meant to be with."

"What about finding a sponsor?"

Camelia shrugged. "At this point, I think I'd rather get laid."

Kat flourished her hand in a dramatic gesture of farewell. "By all means, then go, my friend. Go out and find satisfaction! I shall be here. Drinking."

Camelia headed off across the room as Kat turned to order another shot.

"I don't know if that is the best idea, *hija*," said a strangely familiar voice.

Kat turned back around and groaned. Pilar Del Campo,

drinking a martini and dripping with diamonds, stood in front of her with an amused look on her face.

"Oh man," said Kat. "Seriously?"

Pilar laughed. "How about a glass of champagne, at least? I think another shot of tequila might be *el fin* for you."

Kat drunkenly considered this for a moment. "Okay. Based on your jewelry, you look like you probably know about things like champagne, so I'm going to take your advice."

Pilar ordered for her. "A glass of the sparkling rosé for my friend, *por favor*." She held the flute of shimmering pink liquid up to the light and sighed happily before handing it to Kat. "How can one not be joyful looking at such a sight?"

Kat tipped her drink and felt the bubbles sparking on her tongue. "It's good," she agreed.

Pilar sipped her martini. "So," she said, "I think you broke my son's heart."

Kat's head snapped around. "I did what?"

"Sebastian. I think you broke his heart."

Kat thought about this, trying to pierce the fog of alcohol currently dimming her brain, and then shook her head. "No," she said slowly, "I'm fairly certain I did not. And either way, I don't think it's a very good idea for me to be talking to you about your son at this exact moment. Or maybe ever, really."

Pilar nodded and took another sip of her drink. "Fair enough."

They watched the crowd together for a moment.

"It's funny," said Pilar, "but I met my Carlito at a party very much like this."

"Yeah?" said Kat.

"Yes, but it was after a game, so Carlos was still wearing

his uniform. Jodhpurs. They still wore jodhpurs back then. *Muy sexy.* Very tight. Much better than the white jeans they wear now." She sighed. "Did Sebastian mention his father to you at all?"

Kat started to shake her head and then stopped. "Oh, wait, yes, he did. I believe he said he was an asshole."

Pilar's eyes widened, but then a smile tugged at the corners of her mouth. "An apt description, I suppose. He was an asshole. But *ay*, he was so handsome. Maybe even more handsome than my boys."

Kat raised her eyebrows. "I find that hard to imagine."

"It was so good in the beginning. But then, after Alejandro was born, Carlos started cheating. And no matter what I did, he kept cheating. He cheated on me until the day he died."

Kat met her eyes. "I'm sorry."

Pilar shrugged. "Eh, what can one do? We were meant to be."

Kat blinked. "But how can you say that when he made you so unhappy?"

Pilar drank. "Who said that finding your soul mate necessarily means you will be happy, eh?"

Kat laughed.

Pilar leaned back against the bar. "I like you, *hija.*"

Kat smiled. "Pilar?"

"*¿Sí?*"

"Let's say I did do to Sebastian what you said I did?"

"Broke his heart?"

"Yes. That. If I did do that, does that mean you're going to fire my mother?"

Pilar looked shocked. "*Ay*, no. Are you *loca*? I would never fire Corinne. In fact," she said, laughing, "I should probably give her a raise. I think having his heart broken might be good for the boy." She shot a look at Kat. "Don't tell your mother I said that. About the raise, I mean."

Kat laughed. "Sorry. I'm totally going to tell her. Look at those diamonds. You can afford it."

Chapter Thirty-two

Kat woke up the next morning with a pounding headache, a bone-dry mouth, and no idea where she was. She cracked her eyes open and moaned at the bright Florida sun streaming through the window. She felt around with her hands and realized that she was on a futon on someone's bedroom floor. She raised her head, fought back a wave of nausea, and looked around. Blue ribbons. Framed photos of a big chestnut stallion. A whole wall full of rosettes and medals for dressage. A black velvet helmet hanging on a hook against the door.

Ah. It was Camelia's room, and—Kat looked around carefully for signs of other inhabitants and felt a rush of relief—it seemed she was alone.

She slowly sat up in bed, trying to calm the churning in her stomach, and groped in her purse for her phone.

Five missed messages—all from Sebastian.

She didn't know how to feel about this. Part of her was happy to see that he had been in touch at all, but part of her was worried about what he had to say.

The last thing she remembered from the night before was

watching Pilar dance with Lord Henderson and that they were surprisingly sexy together, which made her think of Sebastian, which made her order another shot of tequila.

She groaned. Huge mistake.

She dialed her voice mail and nervously held the phone up to her ear.

"Katarina, call me. It's Seb."

That was it. No more messages after that. Just hang-ups.

She shook her head. She was in no state to call him right now. She had to have some water first, and some coffee, and brush her teeth, and find her clothes, and Camelia. Probably not in that order.

She found her dress, but decided against putting the crumpled satin gown back on, instead rooting through Camelia's closet, wishing her friend were about a foot taller and at least two sizes up. Finally she found a T-shirt dress that she imagined came to Camelia's knees, but barely covered the necessary parts on her, and decided it would have to do. She checked the mirror, attempted to rub some of the smeared mascara from under her eyes, and bundled her insanely wild hair up into a quick bun.

"Cam?" she called as she opened the bedroom door and wandered into the living room.

There was a gasp and a scramble on the floor and Kat suddenly realized she had walked in on Camelia and a man—was that Mark Stone?—in the middle of something she truly did not want to see.

"Agh!" She quickly turned her back to them. "You guys!"

There were giggles and the sounds of people putting on their clothes very quickly.

"Okay, okay, you're safe," said Camelia. "It's all covered up now."

Kat turned around slowly. "I think I've been traumatized for life," she muttered.

Camelia snorted. "You've seen worse."

Kat rolled her eyes and smiled. "Hi, Mark. Fancy meeting you here."

Mark smiled back sheepishly. "It's Kat, right?"

"You guys know each other?" Camelia looked at them both, wide-eyed.

"Met at a polo thing," said Mark. "Listen"—he quickly leaned over and kissed Camelia on the cheek—"I'm going to get out of your hair now and leave you ladies alone, but"—he grinned—"thank you for an amazing evening, and I hope you meant it when you said that I could take you out later tonight."

Camelia smiled and blushed. "Sure. Sure. Of course."

"Okay, great. See you at seven, then."

They silently watched him exit. As soon as the front door shut, Camelia turned to Kat with a huge smile on her face. "Oh my God. I can't believe you knew him! What are the chances? What polo thing?"

Kat blinked. "The charity—Camelia, you know who that is, don't you?"

"Sure. He's the guy I decided to sleep with last night. I mean, I know that his name is Mark. Mark...something. I can't remember."

"Mark Stone."

"Okay. Right. Mark Stone."

"He played at the charity dinner."

Camelia shook her head. "I just came at the end to help put the ponies away. I didn't meet any of the players."

"Mark Stone, the CEO and creator of TechInc."

Camelia's mouth fell open. "Wait. What? He said he did

stuff with computers but I thought he, like, worked at a Genius Bar!"

Kat laughed. "Um, try one of the richest men in the world?"

Camelia sat down heavily on the couch. "Holy shit." She looked over at Kat and shook her head. "I guess he did have a pretty nice car for an Apple store dude." She laughed. "He was really good in bed, Kat. I mean, like *really* good."

Kat sat down next to her and giggled. "Well, I guess you found your sponsor, at least."

* * *

Sebastian was sitting on the front porch of Kat's cottage when Camelia's car pulled up and Kat got out of the passenger side.

"Oh! Hiya, boss!" Camelia yelped out the window at Sebastian. She dropped her voice to just above a whisper. "See ya, Katy Ann. No way am I getting in the middle of this." She threw a bright smile at Sebastian, and her voice rose again. "Gotta go!"

"Camelia!" exclaimed Kat as her friend squealed her tires and took off around the corner.

She turned back to Seb, an embarrassed look on her face. He took in her too-tight and too-short dress, bare feet, wildly messy hair, and the paper bag that carried all her stuff. He smiled. "Rough night?"

Kat blinked. "It was fine. What's up?"

She looked upset, he thought. She wouldn't meet his eyes. He suddenly wondered just what, exactly, she had been doing last night and with whom.

"Well," he said, "I have some news. I met Liberty Smith last night."

Kat's cheeks went red. "Oh?" she said.

He wondered why her voice sounded so cold. "Yes, and I gave her your script."

"You what? Oh my God, Sebastian, how could you? You don't have the right to do that without asking."

He blew out an exasperated breath. "Jesus, Kat, I thought I was doing you a favor."

"You see," said Kat, pacing the porch, "this is exactly what I was talking about before. This is a business, and there are certain ways things are done. There's a process. You can't just give a script to an A-list actress. You have to go through her people. You have to find out if she's even looking to take on anything. You can't harass her that way. She probably thinks we're total amateurs now."

Sebastian felt a flash of annoyance. "I did not harass her, as you so nicely put it. I met her at a party. And she was very pleasant. And we talked for a very long time last night—"

Kat's face fell. "You did?"

"Yes, and she is looking for something exactly like this script. She's tired of doing romantic comedies. She wants a chance to take on something meaty—Oscar bait, she said."

"She said that?"

"Yes, and so I pitched her your script."

Kat wrinkled her nose. "You pitched it?"

"I pitched it. And she was very interested. So I gave her my copy."

"Oh. Well... I guess it wasn't the most professional way to do things, but sometimes I suppose if the right opportunity comes up, you might take advantage of the moment. I'm not getting my hopes up, but I guess we'll see what she thinks, then."

He looked at her. "I already know what she thinks. She stayed up all night reading it and called me this morning."

"Wait, she called you? So—you didn't spend the night with her?"

He shook his head. "No, I didn't—we just..." He stopped himself. "The point is. She loved it. She loved the script. And she wants to play Victoria. And she's leaving for L.A. this afternoon, but she wants to meet with you today before she goes." He looked at his watch. "In about thirty minutes at the Polo Club."

Chapter Thirty-three

Kat pushed at the heavy wooden doors of the club and felt a blast of air-conditioning as she rushed to the maître d'. "I'm meeting someone," she said breathlessly, "but I'm a little late. Liberty Smith?"

The maître d' did an admirable job of keeping his face entirely impassive. "Very good, ma'am," he said, "right this way."

Kat followed him through the hushed room, barely taking in the luxurious surroundings and well-heeled people glancing up at her as she passed. She tugged at her sheath dress, wishing she'd had more time to figure out what to wear and definitely a little more time to shower and fix her hair and makeup. She'd done the best she could, but her head was still pounding, and she didn't think all the concealer in the world could do much for the bags under her eyes. She hoped she smelled okay, at least, and she barely stopped herself from taking a furtive whiff at one of her armpits.

"Kat Parker!" said a breathy voice that Kat felt she had heard a thousand times before, and then she was leaning down to accept a kiss on each cheek from the world-famous lips of Liberty Smith.

Kat sat down, her face ablaze, and looked over at Liberty, who was beaming at her. She was, Kat thought with a little pang of jealousy, even more beautiful in person than she was on-screen. If she had truly been up all night reading Kat's script, she certainly didn't show it. She was wearing a simple A-line dress the exact same color as her wide violet eyes. Her penny-bright hair was pulled back into a complicated braid, and though Kat could have sworn that she wasn't wearing a drop of makeup, her skin was perfect, and she looked a good ten to fifteen years younger than the actual forty-some years that Kat knew her to be.

"I'm so glad you could make it," said Liberty. "I told Sebastian I was certain that you'd be busy. I mean, how could you possibly squeeze me in? But he said he would make it happen. Where is he anyway? Is he coming?"

Kat felt her stomach drop at the sound of Sebastian's name. She took a sip of water to cover up her feelings. "Oh, no, I don't think he realized you were expecting him," she said. "I mean, I could call if you think—"

Liberty waved her off. "No, no. It's you I want to talk to."

Kat nodded. "Thank you. I'm a huge fan, and I'm just so excited that you even read my script."

The waiter approached, and before he could speak, Liberty turned her smile on him. "Can you give us the weensiest amount of time before we order? We just have to do some business first."

He backed up, practically bowing, as he made his way back to the kitchen.

Liberty turned her attention back to Kat. "I loved your script," she breathed. "I loved every word. I cried, like, five times, and I laughed out loud, and of course, I love polo, and I love horses, and I loved, loved, *loved* Victoria. What a role!"

Her face grew cloudy. "But is it out to anyone else right now? Sebastian wasn't totally clear about that."

"Oh," said Kat, thinking fast, "well, my manager slipped it to just a few people, and I think there might be some interest, but—"

"Kat, listen." Liberty leaned over and grabbed Kat's hand. The actress's skin was soft as velvet. Her nails were perfect. And she smelled like what Kat giddily imagined to be white lilies melted together with the most expensive marshmallows in the world. "I'm going to be frank with you. I want that part. I need that part. You know my last movie? *Dance While You Can.* Did you see it?"

Kat shook her head. "No, but—"

"Nobody did," said Liberty, cutting her off. "And that's exactly the problem. Do you know how old I am?"

Forty-two, Kat thought.

"Thirty-seven," whispered Liberty. "I'm thirty-seven."

Kat nodded and kept her face still.

"I'm thirty-seven, and I am fairly certain that my time doing romantic comedies is coming to an end. I mean, at least until I'm like Meryl Streep or Diane Keaton's age and then Nancy Meyers can hire me. But only if I stay relevant, you know? I have to find another version of my career. I can't keep playing the ingénue, I'm too old. But honestly?" She lowered her voice. "I'm not ready to play the fucking mother either. Did you know that Sally Field was only ten years older than Tom Hanks when she played his mother in *Forrest Gump?*"

Kat nodded. There wasn't a woman in Hollywood who didn't know that damning bit of information.

"I won't go there. I don't want to play Tom Hanks's mother. I'm not ready. So I've been looking for something different for my next project. I actually have an enormous amount of freedom in what I can do because David—you know David, right? My husband?—David is willing to finance up to fifty million."

Kat's heart clenched. That was almost twice what she'd imagined her budget to be. She wanted this so bad, she could taste it.

"And *Twenty-five Roses*—oh my God, I love the title, by the way, *so* romantic—*Twenty-five Roses* is exactly what I'm looking for."

"I want to direct it," Kat blurted out. She bit her own tongue. God, no finesse whatsoever. What was wrong with her?

But Liberty just nodded. "Yes, that's what Sebastian told me. That you were attached no matter what. But I loved *Winter's Passing*, and I'm not stupid. I think I have a pretty clear idea of what went wrong with *Red Hawk*. I know you lost final cut. Which wouldn't happen this time. I'd make sure of that. Plus, I've never worked with a woman director before, and I know that's going to be just grand."

Kat blinked. "I'm—I'm speechless, Liberty. I mean, do I have this straight? You're not only willing to star, but you're also willing to produce and finance as well?"

"Absolutely. I am certain that I was meant to play Victoria Del Campo. It's the part I've been waiting for my whole life."

"I think you'd be great," said Kat honestly. "I can totally see you in the role."

"Oh wonderful!" Liberty smiled. "I'm so excited. I know we're going to love working together. Sebastian could not stop saying fabulous things about you. It was almost as if..." She trailed off and scrunched up her nose. "I mean, hell, I'll just ask. Are you two an item?"

Kat's face burned, but she shook her head. "No," she said, and then she forced her voice to sound more definite. "Absolutely not."

"Oh good," said Liberty, "I'm so relieved. I mean, not like I'm interested or anything." She laughed, waving her hands in the air. "Of course, Sebastian is just horrendously gorgeous and charming, but I just meant, it's always better to keep things professional, you understand my drift? We can't have the director sleeping with the producer."

Kat knit her eyebrows. "I'm sorry? Producer?"

"Sebastian, of course. He told me about how he wanted to expand into producing, and I understand why you were hesitant, but look, we wouldn't be sitting here right now if he hadn't set this whole thing up, right? And isn't that exactly what a producer is meant to do?"

Kat bit her lip. "That's true, but—"

"No, no, I won't hear another word. I told him I'd talk you into it. It all makes sense. The story is about his grandmother, and he knows more about polo than practically anyone. He's charming, he's smart, he's got great connections, and"—she winked—"he'll be eye candy on the set. I'm afraid that I have to insist, Kat, my dear."

Kat smiled nervously. Everything Liberty had said about Sebastian was true, but somehow she didn't love hearing her say it. She took a deep breath. "Okay. Fine. I guess I can live with that."

Liberty stood up. "Good lord, look at the time. I've got to go. And we didn't even order yet! Listen, I'll have my people call yours right away and get the ball rolling. I'm so excited about this. I just know we're going to be best friends." She gave Kat a huge hug. "I love you already."

"I think I love you, too!" Kat gushed.

"Oh," Liberty said as she started to stride away, "don't worry about the check. They'll put it on my tab. So just stay and order anything you like, okay, hon? Ciao!"

Kat sat for a moment, alone at the table. She felt somewhere between deliriously giddy and a panic attack.

She was getting her movie made.

She was getting another shot at directing.

She would have final cut.

She had a fifty-million dollar budget.

Liberty frigging Smith was her star.

And Sebastian, the man she was desperately in love with, and with whom she had just made damned sure she couldn't be involved with for the duration of the film, was going to be her producer.

Chapter Thirty-four

Sebastian wasn't sure he liked this bed. He rolled over and tried to pinpoint just what, exactly, was wrong.

It wasn't the mattress or the pillows. Surely the Hills Hotel had the finest bedding available. Plus he was staying in the private Royal Bungalow. So basically he was in the most luxurious part of the most luxurious hotel in L.A. The bedding was much more than adequate.

It wasn't his surroundings. The Pink Château, as loyal clients affectionately called the hotel, was five-star Hollywood glamour at its best. The bungalow was charming, sumptuously furnished, and completely private. He had his own pool, patio, and outdoor shower. Not to mention a fleet of people looking after his every need. He felt like he was wrapped up in an opulent gift box, and he had to admit, being the pleasure hound that he was, he rather enjoyed the sensation.

It wasn't the temperature. Unlike humid Florida, L.A weather was pretty much perfect lately. A long string of bright, sunny days, not a whit over seventy-five degrees, and lush, balmy nights, just breezy and cool enough to sleep with the windows open.

It might simply be the fact that he wasn't sharing it with anyone, he mused. A bed this comfortable in a place this beautiful really cried out to be used for more than just sleeping.

He rolled over again, doing his best to push away certain images—a pair of gray eyes, sparked with desire, gazing into his own; a long, golden leg bent and beckoning; a tan and elegant hand trailing over his skin...

He got up and pulled on his jeans and T-shirt.

And not a moment too soon, for suddenly his patio door crashed open and Liberty Smith, the most beautiful movie star in the world, flounced into the room wearing nothing but the barest hint of a purple bikini.

"I'm bored," she said. "How about a swim?"

He looked at her, taking in the long, silky hair dancing down her shoulders, her sleepy violet eyes, her soft, peachy skin that seemed to glow from within...

"Something wrong with your pool?" he asked.

She collapsed onto his bed. "I don't like its shape," she pouted.

He laughed.

Then she laughed. "I know," she said. "I sound exactly like a prima donna movie star, rejecting her private pool. But it reminds me of this old swimming hole in Sioux Falls that I practically drowned in once. I prefer your pool."

She grinned at him and rolled over on his bed, exposing her round, perfect bottom, which was pretty much bare except for the thin purple string that framed the top of each plump, faultless cheek.

Liberty, thought Sebastian, looked like she was created to exist exactly in these old-school Hollywood surroundings. Here she was, in the same bed that Elizabeth Taylor and

Marilyn Monroe had frequented, and it was easy to imagine her fitting right in to their legendary pantheon.

"I have to leave for the set," he said to her.

Liberty groaned. "No, it's not time yet. We don't have call for another three hours at least. They're filming the stuff with Charlie at the polo field in Santa Barbara this morning."

Sebastian thought of Kat—undoubtedly already at work—and flinched. "That just means you don't need to be there, Libby, but I'm definitely going in."

Liberty sighed. "Fine. Just abandon me here, then. I don't care." She rolled over and pulled his sheets up over her head. "I think I like your bed better, too," she said from under the covers.

He shook his head. "I'm more than happy to trade bunga-lows."

"No, mine was Cary Grant's favorite. I like to imagine his ghost watching me take a shower." She laughed at her own joke. "Ugh, if you're going in now, I'll have to listen to Earl the driver the whole way there."

"We really shouldn't take the same car anyway. You know what the paparazzi would do with pictures like that."

"I don't care," she said. "Let them think whatever they want. It would serve David right. He's off in Belize with some stripper right now anyway." Her voice was muffled by the sheets.

He sighed. "You can use my pool while I'm gone."

"I don't want to swim anymore," she said, still hidden un-der the covers.

"Have you had breakfast? I'll call room service."

She popped her face back out. "Black coffee. One of those gluten-free croissants—how do you think they do that, by the way?—and the fresh fruit plate. But tell them I don't want it for another hour. I'm going to sleep in your bed. And if they knock and I don't answer, just to come back later. I don't want to be woken up."

Sebastian snorted. "Why don't you just call when you're up, then?"

"No, no." She smiled at him. "I like it when you call it in. It shows me you care."

Sebastian shook his head and smiled back at her, but inwardly, he groaned. There was no amount of room service that would ever convince Liberty Smith that anyone really cared about her. He'd learned that by now. She was beautiful, and she was sexy, and she was smart, but she was also the most insecure person he had ever met. She was basically a bottomless pit of need.

"Oh, and a green juice, as well, babe, okay?"

He nodded and hit zero on the phone.

* * *

No matter how many times Kat ran the scene, it didn't look right to her. In her mind's eye, she imagined that first time she had seen a polo match, with Sebastian and his family by her side, on that private field in Wellington. She remembered the fire and the passion in the game, and the way it had made her feel at once stricken and thrilled, barely able to breathe, as the ponies had thundered toward the goal.

She had all the right tools. She had the finest ponies—Sebastian had seen to that. And though her leading man, Charlie Ruiz, wasn't a professional equestrian by any means, he could certainly ride decently enough, and there was a stuntman for those times that she needed anything more. All her extras were pro polo players. Sebastian had hired a whole pack of his Argentine friends, and they played beautifully. But still, it didn't match what she remembered real polo to look like.

"Cut," she called. "Take thirty minutes." She walked over to the playback monitor in video village so she could pinpoint what was going wrong. Sebastian was already there, squinting at the screen.

As always, Kat's heart basically stopped when she saw him, and it took her a few deep, shaky breaths to regain her cool.

It had been nearly three months since she had sat Sebastian down and told him that, though she was grateful for all he had done to get Liberty on board, she was only bringing Sebastian on as her producer because Liberty had insisted, and she really didn't appreciate the way he had forced himself into the job.

His only role was to keep Liberty happy, she told him, to do whatever it took to keep her on board the film. If he could do that, he'd be useful to Kat. Otherwise, he just needed to stay out of her way.

She didn't tell him about the way Liberty had asked whether they were a couple and how she had pretty much lied in reply. She certainly didn't tell him about the way that every part of her absolutely seethed and writhed in agony when she thought of him anywhere near the star.

She couldn't bring herself to tell him any of that. Instead, she had been ungrateful and condescending, and basically opened up the door to him sleeping with Liberty, even though that was absolutely the last thing in the world Kat really wanted.

And Sebastian had just sat there and watched her as she made her ugly little speech and then nodded calmly. Then he took out his wallet and counted out fifteen dollars and handed them to her.

Her tip money back, he said.

It was like a punch to her gut.

And since then, he had been the best producer she'd ever had.

"What do you see?" she asked as she walked toward the monitor.

He leaned in closer, his brow wrinkled in concentration. "It's not there yet," he said.

She sighed. "I know. It just doesn't feel like there's enough—"

"Heart," he supplied. "They don't look like they really care if they win or not."

She blinked. "God, that's exactly right. I couldn't put my finger on it, but you totally hit the bull's-eye."

He smiled ruefully. "I am intimately familiar with the problem."

"What can we do to change it up?"

"Offer them some incentive." He grinned at her. "Tell them that the first one to make a goal gets to take you out to dinner."

She tugged at her hair, self-conscious. "I hardly think that's going to do much to get them going."

He shook his head. "You sell yourself short, *linda*," he said softly.

She tried to pretend that he hadn't just used his old pet name for her. And that hearing it hadn't immediately set off a thousand roaring, painful Triple-X memories in her head.

"Maybe I should offer cash instead," she said.

He laughed.

"Or..." She hesitated.

He looked at her.

"I've been thinking. All this work with horses and I still haven't ever even ridden, you know? Maybe it would help if I had some idea how it felt?"

Chapter Thirty-five

Sebastian turned away from the spotted horse he'd been grooming to watch Kat walk into the ring. She was wearing skin-tight gray riding breeches, over-the-knee black patent leather boots, and a snug white button-down shirt opened just wide enough to show off her long, graceful neck and elegant collarbones. She smoothed the pants self-consciously. "Are they supposed to fit so tight?" she said.

Sebastian looked at the way the pants hugged her every curve and did his best to tamp down the visceral thrill of excitement he felt uncurl inside his belly. "Those are exactly as they should be," he said. He watched appreciatively as she bent to adjust her boot. "I should have taken you riding a long time ago," he said huskily. "The gear suits you."

Kat blushed and hastily stood up.

Sebastian tore his eyes away and cleared his throat. "This is Patches," he said, indicating the brown and white mare. "You'll have to help me tack her up. That's part of riding."

Kat smiled nervously and reached out to pet the horse with a tentative hand. The pony, sensing Kat's fear, shied away and whinnied.

"Oops!" said Kat, taking a step back.

Sebastian smiled. "You'll have to do better than that. Come here." He looked through the tack box, pulling out a currycomb and handing it to Kat. "Start with this."

Kat approached the pony again and lifted her hand. Patches rolled her big brown eyes and showed the whites.

"Hey now, *bebé*," said Sebastian to the horse. "Relax." He looked at Kat. "Scratch her right where her head meets her neck," he said. "That's what she likes best."

Kat slowly reached out and scratched. "Oh!" she said. "She's so much softer than I expected. I thought pony hair would be bristly and hard. But this is like velvet."

Sebastian was startled. "You've never even touched a horse before?" he asked.

"Lots of people have never touched a horse, Sebastian."

"Yes, but you've been actually directing this movie. All these ponies—"

"Well, it's not like I had to groom them all myself. I've just been filming them."

He shook his head. "Okay, yeah. This is important for you to do." He stepped behind and guided her hand with the currycomb, making her sweep over the pony's coat. "Like this."

Standing this close to her, he couldn't help taking in her dark, sugary scent. It made him want to close his eyes and just breathe. Instead, he took a step back and watched the way her body arched as she reached to brush down the pony.

He saw women in riding gear every day, but he had never before realized just how sexy those breeches and boots could really be.

"Poor bald pony," said Kat, combing where the pony's mane had been shaved off to a nub. "I still don't see why you have to take off the mane."

"Because it could get caught in the mallet. Very dangerous. Okay"—he handed her the hard brush—"now this. Short, brisk strokes, and put a little more muscle into it this time."

She leaned into the pony, brushing her down. "They're so much bigger up close," she said. "Is this horse especially big?"

Sebastian shrugged. "She's not tiny."

"I really can't imagine being on top of one. You must feel a million miles off the ground."

He smiled. "You will get used to it."

After they'd finished brushing out the pony, he cinched up the saddle, adjusted the stirrups, and fed her the bit. Then he led her over to the mounting block. He looked at Kat, who had followed him over. She was pale underneath her tan skin.

"Don't worry," he said. "I'm just going to lead you around to begin with. You'll be perfectly safe."

She put on the helmet she had been carrying, nodded as she climbed up the steps, then looked at him.

"Just put your left foot in the stirrup and swing your right leg over," he said.

She shook her head helplessly.

He offered her a hand. She grabbed it, closed her eyes, and mounted the horse.

He laughed. "You're on," he said. "But you should probably open your eyes."

* * *

Kat opened her eyes and looked down. She had been right. She felt like she was a million miles up in the air. But what she hadn't expected to feel was, under the saddle, just how *alive* this animal was. She could feel its warmth against her legs, she could feel it breathe in and out, and when Sebastian started to lead her around the ring, her hands wrapped in the short amount of mane the pony had left, she could feel the distinct sway of its gait. It was like being on a listing ship. She was sure she was going to fall off at any second.

"How are you doing?" asked Seb as he looked over his shoulder and grinned. "Shall I speed her up?"

Kat shook her head. "No. Nope. This is fine."

Seb laughed and then came around the side. "Move back a bit," he said.

And then he swung up in front of her.

She gasped and forgot about the horse for a moment. Her breasts were pressed against Sebastian's back, her crotch was pushed up against his rear, her thighs straddled his. She could feel the warmth of him through every cell of her body and smell the intoxicating mix of ocean and earth that was his scent. She swallowed and realized her throat had gone dry.

"Wrap your arms around me, *linda*," he said. His voice was gruff.

She leaned forward, putting her arms tight around his waist, resting her cheek against his back. She closed her eyes, glad that he couldn't see her face.

He took a deep breath. She felt a tiny tremor move through his body. "I'm going to trot first, okay?"

She nodded. "Yes, okay."

Suddenly the horse was moving and she was gently bouncing in the saddle, and Sebastian rose up out his seat on every other step, rubbing against her...

"Oh," she said. She felt the heat rise in her body.

"I'm moving her into a canter now, okay?"

They sped up, and the bounce turned into a soft rocking,

and every time Sebastian moved forward in the saddle, he brought her with him. Her breath caught in her throat.

"Now a gallop. I'm going through these quickly because you don't want to ride double on a horse for very long. Even a big one like this. Hold tight, *linda*."

He kicked his legs, and the horse picked up speed. The rocking smoothed out, and suddenly Kat felt like she was flying.

"Oh my God," she said. As hot and bothered as she had been, she now pretty much forgot all about Sebastian. All she could feel was the horse striding under her, smoothly eating up the ground as they sailed through the air.

Sebastian turned to look at her over his shoulder and grinned. "You like it?"

She smiled back. "I feel like I'm almost part of the horse somehow, you know?"

He nodded. "That's exactly right. That's just how it should feel."

They took the horse around the ring once, and Kat felt the adrenaline surge through her as Sebastian gave the horse another little kick and the pony went even faster. She wondered what it would be like if it were just her on the pony, how it would feel to control all this power.

Sebastian turned back to her again. He laughed when he saw her face. "You look drunk with pleasure," he said.

Kat grinned. "I kind of am!"

"Okay, I'm going to cool her off now."

They slowed to a trot and then a walk, making the circuit around the ring one more time. Sebastian pulled the horse to a stop, swung down, and then reached up to help Kat off.

Her feet hit the floor, and her legs felt like jelly. She kept her hand in Sebastian's and leaned her cheek against the horse's neck. "That was amazing. Thank you," she breathed. She wasn't sure if she was talking to Sebastian or the pony.

Sebastian took a step closer to her. "Katarina," he said. His voice hitched. She turned away from the pony and looked into his eyes. They were dark with longing.

They stayed locked like that for a moment. Kat wanted only to push away the space between them, to wrap herself around him, to feel the press of his body against her own again. She tilted her face up toward him, hardly breathing.

But then, after a moment, Sebastian closed his eyes, as if to block her out, and when he opened them again, she saw something had changed—they had gone cold. He cleared his throat and took a step back, looking at his watch. "We should go," he said. "We're late for the next scene."

Chapter Thirty-six

Kat got home late that night. The ride with Sebastian had put her behind schedule, and even once they'd started to film again, she had found her concentration had been broken. She couldn't stop thinking about being on that horse. She'd dwelled on the magic of riding in general, which had been a true revelation for her, but the particular power of riding with Sebastian was where her mind kept returning, no matter what was happening on set. At one point, Liberty had called a halt to a scene and stood there, talking to Kat through her headset for a full two minutes before Kat had even realized what had happened.

Tomorrow was a day off, and she was glad of it. After that ride, she needed time away from Sebastian to recover her willpower. She was shaken and distracted, and she felt like she was starving for something, but when she wandered into her kitchen, nothing had any appeal.

She'd been happy to be back in her house, surrounded by her things again. She'd given the friend who had been renting the place a break on two months' rent, plus the cost of moving her to a new house, to make up for the inconvenience of Kat coming back early, but it had been worth it to be home.

After she got the final check for writing *Twenty-five Roses*, she'd immediately sent her parents enough money to cover all her father's hospital bills and then paid off the balance on her mortgage. When she wrote that check, a weight had dropped off her shoulders and left her feeling like she could float. Plus she was still getting paid to direct and had back-end points on the film so, for the first time in a long time, money was not going to be an issue.

She was back home, in her beautiful house, with her beautiful things, doing the work she loved best, in her beautiful, carefully cultivated life. Her destiny was back on track.

She should have been ecstatic. But tonight, all her treasures felt tarnished; nothing in her lovely home offered any real comfort.

She decided to make a cup of tea and draw a bath, hoping that she could soak away her restlessness, but she knew before she finished undressing that even the hottest water would feel tepid. There was no satisfaction to be found.

She bathed anyway and then dried off, bundled her hair up in the towel, and pulled on a crisp white cotton nightgown before climbing into bed with her laptop to go over yesterday's rushes. She couldn't relax, and she knew there was no chance in hell she'd sleep, so she figured she might as well work.

They had filmed a difficult scene yesterday—the moment when a young Victoria watched her husband being thrown off a horse and then died in her arms. The scene was very technical. They'd had a horse trainer in to work with the stallion that they needed to buck and rear on cue. They'd also had a stuntman who specialized in bareback riding to swap in for Charlie when he was thrown off the pony. Added to that were Liberty's reaction shots and then the moment when she ran out to the broken, bloodied body of her husband and held on to him while the lovers whispered their last words to each other.

The rushes had come out beautifully. The horse had done exactly what it had been trained to do, the stuntman had taken the fall safely but made it look fatal, and Liberty and Charlie had acted their hearts out. And even though she'd written the scene herself and seen about half a dozen different versions of it already, Kat teared up right along with Victoria when she parted from her beloved.

She sighed, happy that she had what she needed from the scene, and she reached to fast forward to the next part, but just then an outtake came on, one where Sebastian, who had been helping with the horse, was caught on camera. She had noticed that her director of photography, a steady and taciturn woman named Mary, made a quiet habit of film-ing Sebastian whenever she could. And Kat couldn't say she blamed her in the least.

She paused the video and zoomed in.

God, she thought, if this man ever decided he needed yet another career, there was no doubt he could make a killing in front of the camera as well. Sebastian was leading the horse, looking over his shoulder and laughing at something offscreen. The sun was in his eyes so he was just barely squinting, his amazing smile was in full bloom, and the arm that led the pony was flexed and taut. It reminded Kat of the way he'd turned and looked at her on the horse today, asking her if she was ready to go faster.

She felt a warmth rise to her cheeks thinking of it, and then, looking back at the screen, she felt the warmth travel downward as well. She pressed Play, watching him turn and walk away from the camera, and felt her breath catch in her throat. She rewound the image, absently sliding her hand along her bare thigh as she looked at Sebastian's laughing green eyes, the way his black T-shirt and faded blue jeans fit him in all the right ways, the way he moved with such effortless grace. She touched herself and was not surprised to find that she was soaked.

She closed her eyes, wanting to continue down this path, and yet not. All the desire she'd felt while riding with him came rushing back at her, only magnified by the postponement of her satisfaction. She looked at the image of him again and felt herself shaken by her longing.

But at the same time, she was clutched by an intense regret. Because what if sitting in her beautiful house, alone in bed, watching him on the screen like some far-off Hollywood deity, was the most she could ever hope to have from him? What if this was the closest she would ever get to him again?

She shut the computer with a click and reached for her phone. Before she could think twice, she dialed his number.

Chapter Thirty-seven

Sebastian felt his phone buzz in his pocket, but kept his eyes on the road. He'd check messages later. Right now he was concentrating on simply making sure that he and Liberty got out of this night intact.

He hadn't wanted to go out. His plan had been to go back to the hotel, take a long, cool swim, and then, he had to admit, he was going to lie in bed, close his eyes, and play back every second of his ride with Kat that afternoon. And whatever his hands did while he was doing that, he would not hold himself responsible for.

It had been sweet torture, seeing her in those clothes, feeling her pressed up against him as they rode, smelling her scent, becoming aware of the unmistakable quickening of her desire. She had wanted him, he was sure of it, and her hunger had only fed his own.

And then, when they hit a gallop and her desire had turned into an intense joy, when he had watched her almost instantly fall in love with riding—that had only made it worse. It had reminded him, once again, what a remarkable woman she was, and just how desperately he missed her.

He felt haunted. He couldn't wait to leave the set. Once

he got back to the hotel, he dove right into his pool, then he took advantage of his outdoor shower, and slipped back inside his room wearing nothing but a towel.

He had just lain back on the bed, imagining the way her breasts felt pressed against his back, the way her arms had clenched around his waist, the way her breath had panted, warm and unsteady, against his ear, when Liberty had burst into his room wearing a long red wig, a trench coat, and a pair of enormous sunglasses.

"Put on some clothes," she'd declared. "We're going out!"

He'd instantly refused. The last thing he wanted was to abet Liberty in whatever strange scheme she had obviously concocted against her own boredom. He wanted to stay in bed, think of Kat, and be as satisfied as he could possibly get without actually having her in his arms.

"If you don't go out with me, I'll just go out alone, and if I go out alone, you will be directly responsible for whatever might happen to me, Sebastian. Now, not that I couldn't just stand here all night and ogle you in that towel, but you need to put on some clothes, make yourself pretty, and call for your car because I want to go out, and you're driving."

He had groaned and protested, but her threat had worked. She refused to take her bodyguard, so someone had to make sure that she came out of things alive.

And now they were in the car, and Liberty, still wearing what she insisted was a disguise that no one would ever recognize her in (though Sebastian thought that she looked exactly like herself, except with long red hair and sunglasses) was directing him to an East Hollywood strip joint with the somewhat terrifying name of Jumbo's Clown Room.

He had thought about refusing to go. Strip clubs were not

his thing. But he knew that there was no use in refusing Liberty. The only way to get through this night would be to take a deep breath, put his head down, and hope that she didn't get them both arrested.

"Park here," she demanded. "It's just up the block."

He pulled the car along the sidewalk, wondering about the wisdom of leaving a Porsche Panamera parked on a street in East Hollywood. But it was just a rental so he supposed it would be all right.

The bouncer let them in without a second glance at Liberty, which was a hopeful sign. Perhaps they would get in and out without any trouble after all.

The club was very *red* inside. Red lights, red walls, shiny red stage floor. The women who were dancing were lithe, pretty, very flexible, and looked, to Sebastian's jaded eye, bored out of their minds.

"Whoooooooo!" screamed Liberty as she sat down at a table right next to the stage. A blond Asian woman with pierced nipples and a pair of black panties with a ruffled butt danced on over and gyrated right at eye level.

"Sebastian," hissed Liberty, "pay the woman!"

Sebastian rolled his eyes but took out a twenty and carefully tucked it into the side of her underwear. The blonde nodded at him and smiled, and swiveled back to the other side of the stage.

"That's not how you do it!" yelled Liberty. "Watch me!"

And she pulled out a hundred-dollar bill from her pocket—Sebastian realized, with dread, that she had a thick roll of them in there—and stuck it between her teeth and gestured for the blonde to dance back on over.

Seeing the cash, the stripper moved quite a bit faster this time and happily stood still as Liberty managed to stuff the bill down the front of her panties with nothing but her mouth and a wink.

It was the wink that did it. Suddenly the dancer's eyes got huge, like she had just seen a miracle take place right in front of her. Her mouth fell open, and she choked out, "Oh my God, you're Liberty Smith!"

Liberty grinned and held a finger up to her mouth. "Our little secret, right, honey?" she teased.

The blonde blinked rapidly and then nodded, her hips suddenly swiveling twice as fast. She showed zero intention of dancing anywhere else but right there in front of Liberty's face.

Liberty pulled out another hundred, and this time used her hands to get it where she wanted it to go. The stripper grinned and almost clapped, and then leaned down and said, "Are you, like, researching a role? Are you playing a dancer in your next movie?"

Sebastian laughed when he saw how completely delighted Liberty looked by this idea.

She turned to him. "What do you think, Seb? Should I play a stripper next?"

He shook his head and smiled. "I'm sure you would be excellent," he said diplomatically.

The stripper leaned down again "Do you want to come up and dance with me?" she said to Liberty.

Sebastian reacted quickly but not quickly enough. "I think that is a very bad idea," he said, trying to grab Liberty's arm, but she slipped out of his grip, leaving her empty coat in his hands and revealing that this was her plan all along. All she was wearing was a purple G-string, a pair of sparkling gold pasties, and a pair of spike heels so high that Sebastian worried she'd break her ankle.

She threw her sunglasses down at him. "Woooo!" she yelled, and wrapped herself around the pole.

Sebastian had to admit that the woman looked like she knew what she was doing. She was up, and then she was down, and then she was doing splits (a moment when Sebastian was visited with the undeniable urge to stare at the ceiling until it was over), and then she was completely upside down, her long red locks swinging in the breeze, until the other stripper made the fatal mistake of stepping on Liberty's wig and pulling the whole thing off her head.

If people hadn't suspected her before, there was no ignoring her now. Liberty's long blond mane of hair came tumbling down and suddenly there was no mistaking the fact that the world's most famous movie star was hanging upside down, nearly naked, on a red, red stage in an East Hollywood strip joint.

"Holy shit!" came a shout from the guy sitting at the table next to Sebastian. "Holy frigging shit!"

Sebastian stood up. "Okay, Libby," he said, "time to go."

She grinned at him and did an upside-down split in the air.

"For God's sake, Liberty. Everyone knows who you are. This isn't safe."

"Wait, isn't that—" came another shout.

"Liberty," said Sebastian sharply. "We have to move. Now!"

Liberty shook her head and laughed.

A crowd was starting to gather. Sebastian tried one more time.

"Liberty, please, this is dangerous."

Liberty just rolled her eyes and spun.

That was it. Sebastian was up on the stage in an instant,

pulling Liberty off the pole and wrapping her in her jacket.

The crowd booed, and the mood immediately shifted from amazed to ugly.

"Hey!" Liberty yelled, and struggled against him. "I'm not done!"

"We're going," he gritted at her. "Now."

Suddenly there was a surge of revolt from the audience. Men were starting to climb up on the stage with them, yelling at him to let her dance.

Swearing, Sebastian threw her over his shoulder and bowled through the crowd. Hands reached out to grab them and bodies crowded close, but he made it out the door and slammed it behind him. "You have a crowd control problem," he panted at the bouncer as he put Liberty on the ground and then grabbed her hand and pulled her toward the car.

Liberty was cackling wildly, completely entertained by the whole spectacle. "Wasn't that fun?" she yelled as they made it to the car and slid inside. "Wasn't that the best?"

Sebastian hit the gas just as a crowd of men and strippers from the club surged toward the car.

"No," said Sebastian, running a yellow light in an attempt to get away. "That was not."

"*Pffft.*" Liberty blew a raspberry and made the thumbs-down sign. "You wouldn't know fun if it bit you in the ass, Sebastian. Let's go get a drink somewhere else. I'll keep my coat on, I promise."

Sebastian sighed in frustration. It was obviously going to be a long night.

* * *

Much later on, after Sebastian had finally managed to convince Liberty that she didn't need yet another flight of tequila shots, and that they should just go back to the hotel, Sebastian lay in his bed, staring at his phone in disbelief and anger.

Kat had called hours ago. But left no message. Her name blinked on the screen like a missed opportunity.

Why hadn't he checked to see who was calling?

He looked at the clock. It was really much too late to call her back now, but he started to dial her number anyway.

Halfway through, he stopped. Surely she had just been calling about work? How weird would he seem to return her call at 3:30 a.m.?

He considered texting her, but since she hadn't left a message, he didn't want to press.

Sighing, he put the phone facedown on his bedside table and closed his eyes. Immediately the vision of Kat—her gray eyes wide, her high cheekbones flushed red, the white button-down shirt she'd been wearing this afternoon opened maybe just one more button than was strictly decent—swam into his mind.

He let his hands wander as his mind filled with memories painful and sweet. The ache of what he couldn't have mingling with the pleasure of his recollections.

Chapter Thirty-eight

Honey came over the next afternoon with a bag of takeout sushi and a bottle of pinot grigio. It was meant to be a catch-up session between friends, but it was also, Honey informed Kat, a business meeting as well. Since word had gotten out about Kat's deal with Liberty, Honey's phone had been ringing off the hook with offers. Especially from actresses of a certain age, each of whom were dying to work with Kat.

"I'm so glad you're back, babe," said Honey as the friends sat out by the pool and poured the wine.

Honey was wearing one of her less extravagant outfits—just a leopard print wiggle dress and green gladiator sandals laced up to her knees. Her slick cap of hair was pretty close to its natural red, too, not its usual bright blue or screaming pink.

It was practically buttoned down for her, thought Kat with a little smile.

Honey pulled out a list of offers but Kat pushed it aside. "Let's just eat and catch up first, Hon. I don't think I can focus just yet."

Honey nodded. "Okay. So how are things back at home? Your daddy's all better?"

Kat reached for a tuna hand roll. "About ninety-nine percent." She smiled. "The doctors said they've never seen a patient with such determination to get home."

Honey laughed. "I guess stubborn runs in your family."

"Guess so," agreed Kat. "It was so good to see them, though. I told them, when I finish this film, I'm going to take a week and fly them out here, and we're all going to Disneyland together."

Honey laughed and helped herself to some *hijiki*. "And the film's going well?"

"Yeah," said Kat. "I mean, aside from this one polo scene that I just can't seem to get right. It's driving me nuts."

"How's Liberty?"

Kat frowned. "She's...she's not what I expected. I mean, her acting is great. People are going to be amazed when they see her in this. She has totally made Victoria her own. And man, does the camera love her. She just lights it up. I've never seen anything like it."

"But?"

"But...she needs reassurance after every single scene. Doesn't matter how big or how little. You gotta make her believe she was brilliant or she'll freak out and insist on doing it over and over again."

Honey snared some eel with her chopsticks. "She's an actress," she replied, and shrugged.

"Yeah, but it goes way beyond that. It's like there's this giant hole in her that can't be filled."

"*Hmph*," said Honey. "Though I guess Sebastian Del Campo is trying pretty hard to do it."

Kat looked at her sharply. She hadn't told Honey about her time with Sebastian. "What have you heard?"

Honey shrugged. "Oh, you know. Rumors are flying.

Abutting bungalows at the Hills Hotel, her husband's out of the country, and I saw the strangest blind item this morning that I swear was about Liberty and Sebastian at Jumbo's Clown Room..."

Kat frowned. "I'm sure Liberty wouldn't be so unprofessional."

Honey laughed. "Oh, come on, have you seen the guy? I'm gayer than a triple rainbow, and I'd do him in a hot second."

Kat felt something hot and bitter rise in her chest.

Honey picked up her wineglass and took a sip. "Plus," she said, "I realized the other day that Liberty and David Ansley just hit their ten-year wedding anniversary, and you know what that means."

"What does it mean?"

Honey raised an eyebrow. "It means that Liberty can finally throw that hair-plugged serial cheater to the wolves and take on someone young and hot. It means, thanks to California's most excellent divorce laws, that the woman is entitled to half of thirty-eight billion dollars."

Kat rubbed her finger over the brim of her glass. "I'm sure they have a prenup."

"No," hooted Honey, "nope. She wouldn't marry him unless he took it off the table, and apparently he was too enchanted by her magical pussy to hold out." She took another gulp of wine. "I mean, I get it. Can you imagine having someone as beautiful as Liberty Smith in your bed? I think I might be willing to pay nineteen billion dollars, too."

Kat's lips thinned. "I don't see what this has to do with Sebastian."

"Are you blind? Everyone knows that Liberty Smith can't stand being single. She'll be looking for number four ASAP, and she'll want to trade up. Liberty Del Campo has an awfully nice ring to it, right?"

Kat shoved away her plate, suddenly not hungry.

Honey cocked her head questioningly. "Wait a minute. Why'd you stop eating? I've never seen you put down a hand roll halfway through."

Kat took a gulp of wine and then slammed down her glass a little harder than she'd intended. "Is it so wrong to want to protect the movie? It's never good when the talent gets mixed up with the money. Liberty herself told me that. Besides, I can't believe that Sebastian would be interested in a woman who can't even put on her own pants without being praised for what an amazing job she just did."

Honey's eyebrows shot up. "Whoa. You like Sebastian."

Tears sprang into Kat's eyes. She turned away. "I don't," she said shakily.

"You do! I can tell. You like him."

She felt her face flush. She couldn't meet Honey's eyes. "I don't. I don't like him. I don't like him, Honey." She sounded hysterical, even to herself.

"Oh my God," whispered Honey. Her face was stricken. "You don't like him, you *love* him. Holy shit, Kat."

A sob tore itself from Kat's throat. She covered her face with her hands.

"Oh, babe," said Honey as she patted Kat's arm. "How long has this been going on? And what are you going to do about it?"

Kat shook her head. "Nothing. There's nothing to do. I screwed up, Honey," she said. "I screwed it all up so bad."

Chapter Thirty-nine

Sebastian had hired his half sister, Antonia, to work as a farrier on the set. She hadn't wanted to come. Normally, he could scarcely pry her from her job blacksmithing at the Del Campo barns. But since Pilar couldn't stand being around her late husband's bastard child and frequently gave Noni a hard time, Sebastian felt that his little sister might like a break from both his mother and the farm. So he convinced her that he was in desperate need of her help in California.

As it turned out, she had, in fact, been a great help around the set, and Seb had tried to talk her into staying longer. But she was flying back to Florida that night. She said Hollywood horses didn't need her. She wanted to get back to the Del Campo ponies, where she belonged.

Seb found her in a stall, her long platinum blond hair falling over her face, examining the front hoof of one of the ponies. Sebastian was still feeling conflicted about everything that had happened in the past couple of days, and he wanted to talk to his quiet, thoughtful sister before she left for home again. She almost always had good advice to give.

"Good morning, *niña*," he said.

Noni turned her coal black eyes up at him and snorted.

"What have you been doing? You look like you fell off a horse and were dragged across the pitch."

He smiled ruefully. "I'd prefer a pony to a movie star anytime. It's been a long couple of days."

She laughed. "Liberty again, eh?"

He shook his head. "She gets bored, and then she gets into trouble."

Noni turned her attention back to the horse, using a small knife to pry out a chunk of mud from the pony's hoof. "Oh, to have the time to be bored. Or in trouble."

He laughed again and then was silent, trying to sort out what he wanted to ask her.

She seemed to sense his hesitation. "Take her head, will you?" she said, indicating the pony. "I think she's a biter."

He grabbed hold of the horse's reins, grateful to be given something to do. "So," he said, trying to sound casual, "have you spent much time with Kat?"

Noni looked up at him. Her large, dark eyes sparked with amusement. "Um, not like you have, I would imagine."

Sebastian felt his cheeks flush. "That's over," he said.

She lifted an eyebrow. "Is it?"

"Yes. But maybe I don't want it to be," he admitted.

"Oh?" she said.

"I don't know what to do."

"You don't?"

He laughed. "You're not helping a bit."

She grinned. "Seb, I am the last person in the world to give romantic advice. I haven't even had a boyfriend since I was in Germany, and believe me, that was an unmitigated disaster."

He blinked, surprised. Noni almost never talked about anything that had happened to her before she started working for the Del Campos. He knew practically nothing about what her life had been like before their father had died and the Del Campo family had found out that he had left part of his fortune to a grown daughter that they'd never even known existed. But it always seemed obvious to Seb that his little sister had lived through some pretty dark times.

"Do you love her?" she asked him, interrupting his chain of thought.

"Love her? I—I don't know," he stammered. "What do you mean?"

She shook her head at him. "I mean, do you love her? Pretty simple question."

He was quiet for a moment. "Yes," he said softly. "Yes, I love her."

"Well, have you told her that? Because I think that's what you're supposed to do."

"But that wouldn't be professional."

She laughed. "Um, this is the first girl I've ever seen you date longer than a week, Seb. I'd say the hell with being professional."

He smiled. "*Niña*, can I ask you a question?"

She lifted an eyebrow. "Why stop now?"

"Do you believe in destiny?"

His sister's pretty, laughing face suddenly clouded over. "Like, destiny in love? Like soul mates?"

"Yes. Like that."

She ducked her head back down over the horse's hoof, avoiding his eyes. "I used to," she said. "I thought I did."

"But not anymore?"

She looked back up at him, and her dark eyes were fierce with feeling. "All I have to say to you, Sebastian, is that if you think you've found someone you love like that, you better do your damnedest not to let her go."

Chapter Forty

Liberty was a decent rider but lacked the kind of finesse that Kat felt Victoria should have, so Kat flew in Camelia for a couple of days to give the actress some pointers. No one was more elegant and controlled than Camelia in the saddle. Kat hoped that some of her grace would rub off on her star.

The two women had circled each other warily at first. Camelia still hadn't forgiven Liberty for absconding with Sebastian at Hendy's party (even though Kat had assured her that nothing had actually happened between them), and Liberty, of course, was loath to admit that anyone could be better than her at just about anything.

Kat watched them on their ponies in the covered ring and, noticing their stiff postures and unhappy faces, sighed, wondering if she had just set the film back another day by bringing these two together.

"You think this will work?" Sebastian's voice teased her ears as he walked up behind her.

Kat closed her eyes for a moment, trying to gain some control. A day away from him had not mellowed the tension at all. She felt, if anything, even more fraught with longing, and her admission to Honey had shaken her to the core.

She'd been doing her best to avoid him all morning, and he seemed to be doing the same thing. If one of them walked into a room, the other one left. If one of them was needed in one direction, the other headed off the opposite way. It had started to feel foolish, but Kat kept it up, afraid of just what might happen if she didn't.

But apparently Sebastian had grown tired of the game because here he was for no particular reason except, apparently, to stand too close to Kat and drive her wild.

"I think they will either become the best of friends or try to trample each other to death. I haven't decided which yet," she said, still not daring to actually turn around and look at him.

He laughed.

They watched the women on their ponies. At first, Liberty, dressed in head-to-toe denim and riding a little bay, studiously ignored the younger woman, but then Camelia, in her red tank top and black riding breeches, demonstrated a graceful way to do a two-point corner while cantering, and Kat saw that the movie star started to look interested in spite of herself.

When Liberty kicked her pony into a canter and began to imitate Camelia's smooth posting, Kat smiled, feeling the battle was won.

"*Bueno*, there we go," said Sebastian.

"Thank God," said Kat.

The women moved into a gallop, whooping as they raced around the ring together.

Kat laughed, watching them clown.

Sebastian cleared his throat. "Katarina." Kat thought that his voice sounded almost purposefully casual. "I noticed that you called me the other night—"

"Oh," interrupted Kat, her face going up in flames, "that

was nothing. Just a question about work, but I figured it out." She made herself turn around and meet his eyes for a moment.

He looked...disappointed, she realized. Her heart bounced in her chest.

She took a deep breath. "Actually, Seb, that's not true. I—" But before she could come clean, there was a wail from the ring.

She turned around to see Liberty flat on her ass, her horse racing around the ring without her, and Camelia looking worried as she rode over to see to the star.

"Oh no!" Kat ran out to the ring with Sebastian right behind her. "Are you okay?"

Liberty looked ready to spit nails as she glared up at everyone from under her helmet. "I'm fine," she seethed. "Someone go get that pony so I can beat it to death."

Camelia laughed and went to round up the pony.

Sebastian bent to help Liberty up, and Kat couldn't help noticing the tender solicitude he showed her. "Are you sure you're okay, *querida*?" he said quietly.

Liberty took his hand and allowed herself to be pulled up. "I'm going to have a bruise as big as Arkansas on my ass," she grumbled. "It's not going to be pretty."

Sebastian chuckled. "Well, perhaps that will keep you out of a certain kind of establishment. Or at least off a certain kind of stage."

Kat wondered just what he meant as she felt a white-hot arrow of jealousy move through her. Sebastian's arm was still around Liberty's shoulder as he helped brush the dirt off her back.

Liberty glanced over at her and smiled like the cat who got the cream. "Sorry, Madam Director, inside joke."

Kat blinked and tried to smile. "Have you got this?" she

said to Sebastian, indicating the horses. She knew that her voice sounded strained and high-pitched.

The smile on Sebastian's face faded. "Katarina, I—"

She turned around. She didn't want to look at them together anymore. "Great. Good. I'm going to go check on the next shot."

She felt their eyes watching her as she marched away, and she felt like a fool.

Chapter Forty-one

Let's go out somewhere fun," said Camelia as she sat, her feet dangling in Kat's pool. "I'm leaving tomorrow. Let's party."

Kat, who was lying on a chaise lounge and pretending to make notes on her script, shook her head. She was still in a terrible mood after seeing Sebastian and Liberty together. "I have a six a.m. call tomorrow morning," she said. "I just want to get some pizza and go to bed early."

Camelia made a sound of irritation and splashed some water at her with her foot. "Don't be such a loser," she said. "I've never been to L.A. before, and so far the only thing I've seen is a view of Liberty Smith's bruised ass. Oh my God, by the way, did you see it?"

"The bruise? Yeah, it was bad."

"No, her ass! I mean, I always thought I had a pretty nice keister but hers is like a national treasure. I've never seen anything so perfect."

Kat threw down her script. "This is not making me feel any better, Camelia."

Camelia laughed. "Oh, come on. You don't really think those two are up to anything, do you? Liberty is a married woman."

"I doubt that would stop either of them, honestly."

Camelia stopped laughing. "Hon, you're not really upset, are you? I thought you were over and done with Seb."

Kat shook her head. "No. You're right. It's stupid. Come on, I've actually got tickets to this thing I forgot about. And you've only got one night in L.A."

* * *

Kat watched Camelia happily ransack her closet looking for a dress that wouldn't drag on the floor when she put it on.

"Oh my God, Katy Ann! Look at these clothes! I mean, jeez, actually, look at your whole place. It's a long way from Wellington, right?"

"What are you talking about?" she said, amused by her friend's exuberance. "Wellington has way more fancy stuff than this."

"Yeah, but *we* didn't, you know? We wore, like, dresses over jeans and lived in glorified trailers."

"Everyone wore dresses over jeans back then, and maybe you lived in a glorified trailer, but I lived in a perfectly re-spectable ranch house." Kat laughed. "You know how much my parents' place would go for in L.A.? Stick it in Eagle Rock and you'd get a couple million for it."

Camelia pulled off her tank top and pulled on a dress to see how it fit.

"Dress over jeans," pointed out Kat, smiling. "Doesn't look too bad that way, actually. Maybe we can reignite the trend."

Camelia twisted to see herself in the mirror. "Do you ever get sick of it?" she asked. "I mean, being around all these rich people?"

Kat squirmed, wondering if Camelia had any idea how much money she was getting paid to make this movie. "Um. We grew up in Wellington. It's been that way our whole lives. And excuse me, but are you not currently dating one of the richest men in the world?"

"I know," said Camelia, peeling off the dress, "and it feels very weird. When you're around people who take having money for granted, it's very easy to start feeling like you should just have it, too." She laughed. "And it's Mark's money, not mine. I mean, I try to be careful about it. I don't want him to pay for everything, but sometimes I'll catch myself thinking something like, 'Well, gee, my truck needs new brakes, and I am broke and he has more money than God, so why shouldn't he just buy me a new one?'"

"And he probably would."

"I know! That's the thing! He totally would. He'd love to. But I don't want that. That's not how I was raised. I was raised to work for what I need."

"But you were looking for a sponsor for your training."

She went into the closet. "That's different," she called back. "That's like you getting funding to make a movie. Plus, it's for Skye. I'll do whatever I need to for Skye."

Kat flopped down on her bed. "You're so weird about that horse."

Camelia stuck her head back out of the closet. "Hey, don't say anything about the horse. The horse is untouchable. Just because you don't understand horse love—"

"I might be getting there," said Kat softly to herself. She raised her voice. "No, I get it. It's probably better that Sebastian and I didn't work out. I'm not sure I could ever really fit in with a family like the Del Campos. Eventually it would

have been weird. He is actually much better off with someone like Liberty."

Camelia made an exasperated sound. "He's not with Liberty."

"It's only a matter of time."

"Yeah, okay, let's call the paparazzi and inform them."

Kat rolled her eyes. "Come on, pick something and let's
go. We're going to be late."

* * *

"This is amazing," said Camelia happily as they settled on
the bleachers in the Hollywood Bowl.

The Bowl was one of Kat's favorite things about L.A.
A huge, open-air amphitheater, the band shell was actually
carved into the rocky hillside behind it. And because the
crowds were allowed to bring their own wine and picnics,
there was always a festive quality to the concerts—like a giant dinner party with entertainment added in.

Kat passed Camelia a cashmere throw, popped open their
takeout containers of Korean barbecue, and poured the rosé.

"Heaven," said Camelia, "wine and dinner and a movie
and the Philharmonic playing the soundtrack live, all under
the stars?"

"Not just any movie," Kat reminded her. "It's *Doctor
Zhivago*. This will be amazing."

Camelia looked at her. "I remember you being more of a
Breakfast Club kind of girl."

Kat shrugged. "Film school got to me, I guess."

That was a lie. She had, of course, bought the tickets
thinking of Sebastian but she couldn't bring herself to tell
Camelia this. It had been before he had even arrived in town,

but after the disastrous way she had scolded him about being a producer. She'd seen the event listed online and clicked on "Buy" before she had time to think twice.

At first, she'd just intended on giving him the tickets as sort of a peace offering—and assumed he'd take someone else. But then, after things seemed to warm up between them again, she had started thinking they could go together as friends. And if his definition of "friends" just happened to include sitting very, very close together, sharing a blanket, watching a romantic movie, sipping wine, and eventually giving in to the irresistible alchemy between them and fondling her under the stars, she would not have complained a bit.

"Refill," said Camelia, thrusting her cup under Kat's nose.

Kat refilled the glass as the orchestra struck up the score. Camelia grinned and dug her elbow into Kat's side. "Isn't this better than pizza and an early night?" she whispered.

Kat laughed. "I guess."

Camelia gave her a quick hug. "Thank you for bringing me. I'm so glad we're back in touch again."

Kat smiled as she settled back to watch the movie, but couldn't help feeling a small pang of loss as the opening sequence began, imagining what might have been.

* * *

Despite Sebastian's worries about the paparazzi, especially after the all the blind items about the strip club that had bubbled up in the last couple of days, Liberty insisted that he drive her back to the hotel that night. She claimed that her butt still hurt and that his car was more comfortable than hers, plus she couldn't take another hour listening to her driver clumsily hint around about the screenplay he was writing.

So instead, Sebastian had to listen to a never-ending monologue about the faults and defects of Liberty's marriage.

"I mean, it was good at first, you know? Okay, I'll admit it wasn't burning hot like it was with Otto. But how can anyone compete with a rock star, right? When he wasn't drunk or stoned, at least. Anyway, with David, I thought I was getting security. I figured there were no groupies in high finance. Ha! That's how stupid I was."

Sebastian rolled down his window and tried to block her out with the warm night air and the smell of jacarandas.

"Oh, babe, can you roll that back up? It's going to ruin my blowout."

He rolled it back up.

"Anyway, at first he couldn't get enough of me. It's all we did. Screwed like bunnies day and night. And I know he doesn't look like much when you first meet him, but you should see the guy naked. He's hung like—"

"¡*Mira!*" interrupted Sebastian. "Isn't that the food truck that Charlie was telling us about? Are you hungry?"

Liberty looked at him, amused. "I could eat."

Sebastian pulled into a spot on the street. "What do you want?" he asked. "Charlie said the sandwiches are the best."

"Oh," said Liberty casually, "a sandwich sounds good. I'll get out and take a look."

Sebastian looked at her sharply. "Here? There is quite a crowd, Liberty. And you left your bodyguard at home. Again."

She gave him a sweet smile. "That's because I know you can handle it."

Sebastian swore to himself as he got out of the car. He

could already see people starting to stare as Liberty opened her door. It didn't help that she was wearing the tiniest pair of cutoffs and a tank top with no bra, or that she did a slow and leisurely stretch on the sidewalk after she got out of the car.

"Oh, for God's sake," he muttered, following her to the truck. "Here we go again."

The long line at the counter simply parted as she walked up. People took one glance at her and got a glazed look on their faces as if they were staring into the face of the sun.

Liberty looked up into the truck and batted her eyes.

The guy behind the counter gaped. "Oh my God," he said. "Oh my fucking God."

Liberty smiled a slow, slinky grin. "Hmm," she said, "so what's good here?"

The crowd around her stirred. It was as if, by hearing her voice, it suddenly became real.

"That's Liberty Smith," hissed someone behind Sebastian. "That's Liberty frigging Smith!"

"Who's the guy?" wondered someone else. "That's not her husband."

Phones were being taken out; pictures were being taken. Sebastian tried to distance himself.

The first person who got up the nerve to approach her was a muscle-bound man twice Sebastian's size. "Hey Libby," he said, "you all alone tonight?"

Liberty raised an eyebrow. "Do I look like I'm alone?" she said warmly, waving a hand at Sebastian.

The guy barely looked Sebastian's way. "Close enough."

Sebastian sighed. This was only going to get worse.

"Hey, Libby," said a woman this time, "I loved you in *She Never Sleeps*. Can I get an autograph?"

Another woman excitedly pushed her baby toward Liberty. "Oh my gosh, Liberty, you're not going to believe this, but I named my daughter after you!"

"That's nothing, Libby!" said the food truck guy. "I named a sandwich after you!"

Suddenly the crowd was surging forward, grabbing at her, and the look on Liberty's face quickly went from delighted to terrified.

"Sebastian?" she said. Her voice wavered.

He closed his eyes for a moment, took a deep breath, and then plunged in. "Okay, *basta ya*," he barked as he flung his elbows left and right. "Out of the way! Back off!"

But this time, the crowd pressed around him. He could barely move.

"Sebastian!" cried out Liberty. He could no longer see her through the crush of people.

He fought harder, pushing his way toward her. "Liberty?" he yelled. She didn't answer. He struggled desperately, tearing at the bodies in his way.

There was a scream. He hurled himself forward, panicked, trying to reach her. "Liberty! Liberty!"

People pressed in from all sides. He felt himself losing his balance, being lifted off his feet. He grabbed at the shoulder of the person in front of him. The enormous man who had first approached Liberty turned, snarling. "I saw her first," he growled.

He looked like some savage junkyard dog, guarding his turf.

"For God's sake, *hombre*, she's a woman, not a bone." Sebastian shoved at the man's massive chest. "Let me help her."

And a giant fist coming at his face was the last thing Sebastian saw.

Chapter Forty-two

Kat sat next to the hospital bed, holding Sebastian's hand. She never would have dared to touch him if he'd been conscious, but she couldn't help herself when she saw him, his black eye reminding her so poignantly of their first date and their time on the beach.

He had a "light concussion" was how the doctor had put it. Once Sebastian woke up, he could go home as long as he had someone wake him up every two hours and check to make sure it wasn't getting any worse.

He groaned and opened his eyes a slit. She squeezed his hand and felt her heart beat faster. "Sebastian?" she said.

"Liberty?" he croaked.

She dropped his hand like it burned. "No," she said. "It's Kat."

The ghost of a smile drifted over his face. "Kat," he breathed. Then he bolted upright, grabbing at her arm. "Kat!" he said. "*¿Kat, a donde está Liberty? ¿Que pasó?*"

"*Shh, shh,*" she said, trying to gently push him back down. "She's fine. The food truck driver pulled her up over the counter and then locked up the truck. He called the police, and they got her out of there."

He dropped back like a stone. "Oh, thank God."

She itched to brush the hair back from his eyes, but stilled her hand. "Liberty said she could see you fighting your way through, but you couldn't hear her say she was okay. She said you were very brave."

He closed his eyes. "It was crazy."

"You've got a mild concussion. And a black eye."

He touched his eye and flinched. "This is getting embarrassing. You must think I can't ever win a fight."

She laughed. "Well, the odds were hardly in your favor. What in the world possessed you two to go out without her bodyguards anyway?"

He smiled grimly. "She wanted a sandwich, and she wouldn't take no for an answer."

Kat sighed. "Sounds familiar," she said. "Anyway, I called your mom, and she and Alejandro and his family are flying out first thing tomorrow. I told them that the hospital said you'd probably be fine by then, but she insisted."

He chuckled. "I don't imagine you could keep her away."

"The doctor said you can go back to the hotel now, though, if you feel up to it. But you need someone to wake you up every two hours and make sure your concussion isn't getting any worse. I thought maybe Liberty—"

He grabbed her arm. "No way," he said. "I'll be dead by morning."

Kat snorted. "So then maybe someone at the hotel could—"

He looked into her eyes. "Can you do it, *linda*? I mean, I know it's a lot to ask but—"

"Of course I can," she said quickly, "I just need to call Camelia and let her know I won't be home tonight. I didn't know if you'd want me to—"

His voice was soft. "I want you to."

* * *

His head was killing him, but it was worth it, he thought, to get Kat into the bungalow. She had guided him into her car and strapped him in, even though he assured her that he was not that helpless. Then she had rolled down the windows, turned on some soft music, and driven him carefully back to the hotel. They hadn't talked much at all, and he'd been content to lean his head back and rest, but every so often, he caught her looking at him out of the corner of her eye with a worried expression that made him smile.

She was fussing over him now, getting him a glass of water and making sure he took his pain meds. Asking him if he wanted anything to eat.

"Just sleep, I think," he said.

"Of course," she said. "You must be exhausted. Do you need help getting undressed?"

For a moment he considered saying yes, just to see what she'd do, but then he regretfully shook his head. "No, I can do it. But I only have the one bed here, Katarina, so perhaps I will sleep on the couch and you can—"

"Don't be ridiculous," she said. "I'll sleep on the couch. You need the bed."

He sighed. "Katarina," he said. "I would very much like to be a gentleman and argue with you until I got my way, but I am so tired. And my head hurts so much, and I promise you, there is virtually no possibility of anything untoward happening between us if you'd just—"

"Fine," she said quickly. "It's fine. It's a big bed."

"*Bueno*," he said with relief.

He loaned her the top part of his pajamas to sleep in, and

while she modestly went into his bathroom to change, he slipped into the bottoms and climbed into the bed.

When she emerged from the bathroom, her hair down and her long legs bare, he felt a leap in his groin that made him squeeze his eyes shut for a moment, his headache forgotten.

She rushed over to him, concerned, and laid a hand on his forehead. "Are you okay?"

"Fine," he croaked, afraid to open his eyes. Her warm, gentle hand on his face was not helping. It didn't matter where she touched him; he felt it all through his body like a fire. "I'm fine."

She peered at him worriedly and then went around to her side of the bed and slipped under the covers. "I've set my phone to go off every two hours so I can check on you," she said.

He nodded, keeping himself very still. He could smell her burnt-sugar smell, feel the heat coming off her body, and it was driving him wild. She snuggled down into the bed. "Wow," she said happily, "this bed is amazing."

Now it is, he thought.

She turned on her side facing him. "Okay if I turn out the light?" she asked.

He nodded, though he wished he could watch her face all night.

She turned out the light, and they were immersed in darkness. He could hear her breathe.

He couldn't help himself. He reached for her hand among the shadows of the bed and brought it to his lips. "*Muchas gracias, linda,*" he said as he kissed the tips of her fingers. "Thank you for everything."

She was silent for a moment, and he wondered if she had

already slipped into sleep, but then she gently pulled her hand from his and said, "It was nothing, really, Seb. I would do it for anyone."

And he sighed into the darkness and hoped that it wasn't true.

Chapter Forty-three

When Kat opened her eyes the next morning and saw Sebastian's sleeping face a mere few inches from her own, she felt a rush of wild hope.

She had woken him up diligently every two hours the night before, making him sit up in bed, and repeat phrases, and touch his nose, and tell her who the current president of the United States was, until she was satisfied that nothing alarming was going on and they could safely go back to sleep. And now it was morning. He had made it through the night just fine. And Kat realized that this was the first time she had ever actually slept with Sebastian all the way through the night.

She smiled and hugged herself. Something, she thought, felt different between them. Something had changed.

She turned to look at him and drank in his face. With his long, dark lashes; his generous, pouting lips; and the angry purple bruise under one eye, he looked like an archangel who had just walked out of a bar fight. It was all she could do not to snuggle up against him and wake him up in a much pleasanter way than her constant harassment the night before.

He shifted in his sleep, moving toward her. She held her

breath as his hand brushed her arm and then settled on the dip of her waist. He sighed, and a tiny smile played upon his lips.

His hand was heavy with sleep, and she could feel the heat of his skin through her pajamas. She smelled his sea and musk smell and felt herself go slick and wet. She inched herself a little closer, not allowing herself to touch him fully, but getting inches away from his bare chest. Her entire body burned for him.

She was just reaching out to stroke his shoulder when the patio door crashed open.

"My hero!" yelled Liberty as she launched herself onto the bed, right on top of Kat.

Everything happened all at once. Kat screamed, Liberty swore, and Sebastian woke up with a startled cry and looked confused and horrified to see the two women scrabbling around in the bed next to him. "*¿Que?*" he said. "What's going on?"

"What in the hell," said Liberty, "is Kat doing in your bed?"

"What is *she* doing here?" yelped Kat.

Just then, there was a rattling at the bedroom door and Pilar, Alejandro, and Georgia carrying baby Tomás all burst in along with a hotel porter.

Georgia took one look, laughed, and then turned around and carried the baby back out.

Pilar took in the sight of Sebastian flanked by two barely dressed women in his bed and arched an imperious brow. "*Ay, niño,*" she said, "you do not look very sick to me."

Alejandro just sighed and shook his head. "You never change, *hermano*, do you?"

Chapter Forty-four

Things were sorted out fairly quickly. Liberty, mollified to find out that Kat's presence in Sebastian's bed was a medical necessity, went back to her bungalow through the patio door. Kat gathered up her clothes, changed in the bathroom, and gave a hurried and embarrassed good-bye to everyone as she went out the front. Pilar and Georgia and the baby followed the porter back to the lobby to sort out the reservations for their rooms, and Alejandro sat down in the bungalow great room and waited placidly for Sebastian to explain how he had ended up with yet another black eye.

"Being a producer sounds more dangerous than playing polo," said Alejandro wryly after hearing Sebastian's account of the strip club and then the sandwich truck.

"Well, at least I didn't break my arm again," said Sebastian, flexing his now cast-free wrist.

"Ah, *sí*, I've been meaning to ask. When did *el doctor* say you'd be able to play again? Because the summer is about to start and La Victoria has been asked to open the season at Southampton Hunt and Polo before we go to London."

Sebastian stared at his brother. "I can't possibly play. The movie has another month of filming, and after that, there is the editing and sound and all of the post-production—it will be six months at least."

Alejandro stood up and paced the room. "Don't be ridiculous. Your wrist is healed. You should be training. It's time to stop messing around and come back. The team needs you."

Sebastian shook his head. "I have a job, Jandro."

"As far as I can see, that job merely consists of you keeping some pretty actress entertained while you waste your time in Hollywood. We've been patient, Sebastian, but you have a family and a team who have both been waiting for you."

Sebastian stood up and stepped in Alejandro's way. "You know absolutely nothing about what I'm doing here," he said vehemently. "This is harder work than I have ever done, and I happen to be damned good at it, too."

Alejandro ran his hands through his hair in frustration. "Sebastian, you have the kind of gift that comes along maybe once in a generation. People would kill to have your natural ability."

"That doesn't mean I don't have a choice."

"It's your legacy."

"It's my family history, not my inescapable fate."

"You were born to play, Sebastian."

"Last I checked, I was born free."

"You are a Del Campo!" roared Alejandro, giving Sebastian's shoulder a push.

Sebastian got right up into his brother's face. "You sound just like *Papá*," he snarled. "You act like the movies are somehow beneath us, but what is polo but just a stupid game, Jandro? Nothing more."

Alejandro stared at him, stricken. Then turned away. "Polo," he said heavily, "is your family. It is your blood. And it will save you in the end, Sebastian, if only you'd let it."

Sebastian didn't answer, and after a moment, Alejandro left the bungalow.

Chapter Forty-five

Kat sighed happily as the waiter placed a hot, foamy bowl of latté down in front of her. She inhaled the warm, sweet aroma and closed her eyes. There were some things that L.A. did very well indeed. Maybe it wasn't peach cobbler, but it would do just fine.

She tasted the coffee. "Ah," she moaned to herself, "mother's milk."

"You never change, do you, kid?" said an amused voice.

Kat looked up into the smiling face of Jack Hayes and choked. "Jack," she gasped.

"In the flesh," he said, and then poked ruefully at his belly. "Not much of it, though. They've got me on a starvation diet for this next role I'm doing. I play—get this—a starving guy."

Kat laughed.

"Are you meeting someone, Katy?"

"Um, no, actually," she said.

"Can I join you?"

She nodded, suddenly feeling a little shy as he sat down.

Her ex was as good looking as ever, she thought as she watched him study the menu. Blond hair, blue eyes, boyish, and sweet, but with the most devilishly wicked smile. He had a subtle scar off the corner of his upper lip that made his mouth seem just the smallest bit lopsided. That scar was regularly heralded in the press as the "most kiss-able" thing about him.

"Lemon water," he told the hovering waiter. "Lemon water and the kale salad. Hold the nuts. Hold the cheese. Dressing on the side."

Kat lifted an eyebrow. "Wow. You really are suffering for your art."

He groaned as the waiter hurried away. "No one should live like this, Katy. At this point, I'm more cow than man. I just chew my cud all the goddamned day."

She laughed. "Lucky for me, I'm behind the camera."

"Speaking of which, I heard that you're directing the new Liberty Smith?"

"Yup. We're about three-quarters through."

"Nice. Is she as good as the rumors say?"

"What have you heard?"

"I've heard that you're getting the kind of performance out of her that will add another ten years to her career, at least."

Kat blushed and smiled into her coffee cup. "Well, that's pretty strong praise, but I won't take all the credit. She's a very talented actress."

"Oh, come on. I, for one, have personal experience with the way your directing can change an actor's life."

She laughed. "Yeah, as if *Red Hawk* did anyone any favors."

He looked at her seriously. "It was my breakout role, Katy. And that was all you."

She smiled, but waved him off. "Anyway."

"Anyway. So Liberty's still looking good? Her tits holding their own against time and gravity?"

Kat frowned. "For Christ's sake, you're older than her, Jack. How are *your* tits doing?"

He grinned ruefully. "Fair enough." He sipped his water. "So what's after this? Got it all lined up?"

She shrugged. "We're considering a few different things."

"We? Oh, you mean you and Honey. Man, you're still with her?"

Kat stiffened. "Of course I am. She was just about the only person returning my calls these last couple years."

He had the grace to look abashed. "Yeah," he murmured. "Sorry about that."

She sipped her coffee. It had gone lukewarm. "I didn't mean you in particular."

"I know. I just..." He looked down. "Well, I should've picked up the phone. I know I owe you."

She shook her head. "We broke up almost ten years ago, Jack. You don't owe me anything."

"Well," he said, "about that..."

"We really do not need to rehash," said Kat quickly.

"I know, but I guess I just want to apologize. It's been bothering me for years. And maybe to explain myself. You threw me out so fast, I never had a chance to tell you my side of things."

She snorted. "There was another side of things besides me finding you in bed with Magda, my Pilates instructor?"

He looked at her for a moment, then shook his head. "It was that or give you a ring."

"What?"

He laughed. "I was crazy about you, Katy. I mean, really gone. I'd never felt that way about anyone before. But I knew it wasn't mutual."

Jack, I—"

He held up his hand. "No, it's okay. You don't have to lie. It's been ten years, right?"

She nodded. "Right."

"Anyway, I knew you weren't on the same page as me. I was thinking wedding and babies and a ranch in Ojai, and you were thinking about your next script. I knew that your main focus was your work, and I didn't see that changing anytime soon."

"But—"

"Hey, I'm not blaming you for it. Seriously. I know as well as anyone that to get anywhere in this town you have to work your ass off. And you worked harder than anyone I ever met."

"I wanted it."

He nodded. "You did. And I wanted you. I mean, at least I wanted a version of you. One that maybe didn't actually exist. So you see, when I found myself standing in front of Harry Winston's trying to figure out whether you'd like a pear-shaped diamond or a marquise cut—"

"Ugh. Neither."

He laughed. "I suddenly had this realization that I was never going to get what I wanted from you. And that I needed to break it off."

"So you slept with my Pilates instructor."

"I was a coward back then. It seemed like the easiest way."

"You could have just said something. That would've probably worked as well."

He nodded and sipped his drink. "I know. Anyway, I'm sorry. I'm sorry I was such an asshole."

She snorted and smiled. "You really were."

He chuckled and toasted her with his cup of water.

"You know," said Kat, "I appreciate you telling me all that, but somehow it doesn't make me feel much better."

He lifted his eyebrows. "Really?"

"Frankly, I think I'm still working through some of the same old stuff."

"Yeah? You got another man you're driving away with your late nights and insane work ethic?"

She shook her head. "Something like that."

Chapter Forty-six

Sebastian brought his family onto the set the next day. He and Alejandro were still keeping their distance, but his mother and Georgia insisted that they wanted to see some movie stars. They were filming at the Santa Barbara Polo Club again, so he figured it was as good a time as any to show them around.

Liberty found them right away. She was in costume as Victoria. Her hair was set in pin curls, and she was wearing old-fashioned riding gear. As were all the extras.

Pilar looked around, smiling. "*Ay*, the old riding clothes were *mucho más elegante*." She turned to her sons. "You boys should really wear jodhpurs. So attractive. Those jeans you all wear now are just not the same."

Alejandro shot a look at Sebastian and they cracked up. "*Mamá* and her jodhpurs," snorted Alejandro.

"She'll never let them go," Sebastian said, laughing, glad for the brief thaw between them.

"So," said Liberty a little impatiently, "are you going to introduce me to your family, Sebastian?"

"Well, since they already met you in my bed—"

"Oh hush," said Liberty, smacking him on the arm. "I'm Liberty, you guys."

"And this is *mi mamá*, Pilar Del Campo; my brother, Alejandro; his wife, Georgia; and this little guy is Tomás."

"*Encantado, señora*," said Alejandro as he took Liberty's outstretched hand.

Liberty's violet eyes bugged a little as she looked up at Alejandro. "Good lord, Sebastian, I thought you were the most handsome man in the world, but your brother—"

"Uh-oh," said Georgia good-naturedly. "Have a heart, lady. I cannot compete with you on any level."

Liberty laughed and released Alejandro's hand. "Oh, don't worry." She winked at Georgia. "I know a man in love when I see one. I never bother with a guy whose heart is elsewhere."

Alejandro smiled at his wife and kissed the top of her head.

"Anyway," said Liberty, "I hope you all are proud of Sebastian here. It turns out he's not only an amazing producer, but he's a hero, too. I don't know if he told you how he saved my life the other night."

Sebastian laughed. "I do believe the sandwich guy did all the saving, Libby. I just got punched in the face."

"Well, you would have saved me!"

"If I had not been knocked out? *Sí*, maybe."

She reached over and kissed him on the cheek. "I think you were very brave."

Sebastian smiled at her, amused. "*Gracias*, darling." He looked around. "Where's Kat?"

Liberty shrugged. "Talking with Charlie, last I saw her."

The costume designer flagged down Liberty from across the room.

"Oh, gotta go get fitted. So nice meeting you all. How

long are you here for? I'd love to take you all out for dinner."

Pilar smiled. "That would be lovely, dear."

As soon as Liberty was out of ear shot, Pilar turned to Sebastian. "You know she's married, don't you?" she said.

Sebastian laughed. "Oh, believe me, I am well aware, *Mamá.*"

She shrugged delicately. "As long as you know, *hijo*, because"—she looked at Liberty getting her costume measured—"*la doña* over there seems to have forgotten."

Sebastian got them settled with headsets so they could listen in on the next scene. There would be a short one with just Liberty and Charlie, her costar, and then, Sebastian saw, looking at the shot list, Kat would be shooting the polo match yet again.

He found her in her trailer. The door was open, and he could see her hunched over the script, making notes. He smiled at the way her wild black curls were haphazardly held together on top of her head with a pencil. She was wearing a T-shirt and jeans, and her tennis shoe–encased foot tapped out a nervous dance.

"Again with the polo game?" he asked her as he came in through the door. "Didn't offer them enough of an incentive last time?"

She shot him a quick smile before looking back down at the page and sighing. "I just want..." she said. "Do you remember the first time you saw a polo game, Sebastian?"

He chuckled. "I was probably still an infant."

Her foot tapped faster. "No, that's not what I mean, then. I mean, do you remember the first time you really fell in love with polo?"

He thought for a moment, and then smiled. "*Sí*," he said. "I do. In Argentina. I was nine. Old enough to have been riding for some time, but still too young to have started really training for the game yet, *sabes?*"

She looked up and met his eyes.

"And I remember this because Alejandro had just started playing on the family team, and my father, Carlos, he was still playing, and actually"—his grin got wider—"*mi abuelita* was playing as well."

Her foot stilled.

"It wasn't high goal polo. It must have been an exhibition game if *Abuelita* was playing, too, but I remember realizing that three generations of my family were on the field—and *mi mamá* telling me to watch carefully because we might not see it again." He smiled at the memory. "*Mamá* was so young and beautiful back then."

"She's beautiful now," said Kat softly.

"*Sí*, of course, but you know, sometimes when you think of your parents and realize that they were practically younger then than you are now?"

She nodded.

"So it was with *mis padres*. And Alejandro was just a boy really, maybe seventeen, and *Abuelita* was a fierce, strong *dama* who could still keep up with the best of them."

He looked off in the distance—he could see it all happening.

"The crowds are different in Argentina, you know? Here people sort of politely appreciate polo, but there, they *live* it. They go *loco* over it. And it's not just the rich who watch, *sabes?* It's everyone." He smiled. "Jandro always says that, if he could have one thing, he would make Americans see polo like the Argentines do."

She smiled.

"So I don't really remember too much about the game. La

Victoria won, I know that. And *Abuelita* scored three goals, and *Papá* probably scored at least half a dozen, because he always did, and Jandro scored one. I remember that. It was his first game goal actually.

"But what I really remember was watching the ponies fly by, and the look of joy on my family's faces as they rode, and just being filled with this...*anhelo*, you know?" He paused for a moment, translating in his head. "Longing—yearning—is what that word means. *Anhelo* so deep that I could hardly breathe.

"And this part is silly." He looked away, a little embarrassed. "Remember, I was still just a small boy, but I started to cry. And I buried my face in my mother's shoulder, and she asked what was wrong, and I said, 'I just want to fly like that, *Mamá.*'

"And *mi mamá*, she laughed and said, 'Oh, don't you worry, *hijo*, you will.'"

Kat wiped at her eyes and she cleared her throat. "That," she whispered. "I want people to feel *that* when they watch the scene, Sebastian."

Sebastian thought for a moment and then slowly smiled. "I have an idea," he said.

Chapter Forty-seven

Jodhpurs!" crowed Pilar, clapping her hands together. "What did I tell you? ¡*Muy guapo!*"

Alejandro frowned at Sebastian as the makeup artists flitted around them, touching up their faces with powder. "I don't know how you talked me into this."

Sebastian grinned back at his brother. "You're going to be a movie star," he said. "What are you complaining about?"

They were both kitted out in tight sweaters, white jodhpurs, high leather boots, and old-fashioned pith helmets.

"You guys look awesome," said Georgia. "Doesn't Daddy look handsome?" she crooned to Tomás.

Kat carefully sorted through the antique mallets that the prop master had brought over and chose a stick for each of them.

The grooms led out two fresh ponies, one white and one black. "I will take this one," declared Alejandro as he strode over and patted the black pony's neck. "What's her name?"

"*Linda*," said the groom.

Sebastian's head shot up. "No, sorry, that one's mine, *hermano*," he said as he hurried over to the pony.

Alejandro opened his mouth to argue, but Kat broke in, "Sebastian is right," she said. "He should ride that one."

Seb saw that her cheeks were pink, but she looked determined.

Alejandro scowled but went off to attend to the white pony instead.

"You boys ready?" Kat said.

"Absolutely," said Sebastian, and when Alejandro continued to look mutinous, Sebastian leaned over and whispered, "You said you wanted me back on the field, didn't you?"

Alejandro snorted as he swung up on his pony and rode out into the field with the other players.

Sebastian prepared to mount, but Kat caught his arm and smiled up at him. "So, Sebastian," she said softly, "let's see you fly."

* * *

Kat called "Action!"

Squaring off over the coin flip, Sebastian looked his brother in the face and felt his heart beat faster. Kat had told them to just play a normal game. She wasn't worried about who scored a goal or when. She could edit in the story line she needed later. What she wanted was raw footage, real emotion, fireworks. So she had asked each brother to play the number three position against each other on their respective teams.

Number three—*el capitán*. Sebastian flexed his hands nervously. He had never played three on La Victoria. That was always Alejandro's position.

In fact, thought Sebastian, he had not actually played *against* Alejandro since they were boys and their father, Carlos, used to train them together.

When they were very young, they scrimmaged on their back field in Argentina with their *abuelita*, and she encouraged them to play *el picador*—for fun—just hitting the ball around on the field together, fighting over the goals, and paying attention to only the most basic rules of the game for safety's sake. She taught them to play for the sheer joy of playing.

But once Carlos took over their training, it became all about the competition. He did everything he could to pit them against each other and foster a bloodthirsty rivalry, both on and off the field. Both boys were punished badly if either of them made the mistake of not taking things seriously on the pitch.

It had been hard at first, when Sebastian was just beginning. He adored his big brother and loved their informal games on the farm, but now that they played for real, Sebastian was shocked when Jandro grimly and repeatedly beat him into the ground.

But it was even harder later when Sebastian's natural talents started to show through, and he began to win.

Sebastian could still hear his father's voice screaming at Alejandro, see Carlos's red, sweaty face pushed up into his brother's pale and shamed one. "Are you kidding me? You're letting that little boy beat you? Don't be a pussy! What is wrong with you? You're not even trying!"

And so Alejandro tried harder, and Sebastian tried less, wanting to shield his beloved *hermano* from their father's ugly rants and disdain.

And eventually, Alejandro grew up and took over the number three position on the team, and Sebastian didn't ever think to question that.

But deep down, both men knew the truth. Alejandro was

a great player, but he had to fight to stay at a level that Sebastian could achieve just by stepping onto the pitch. And Sebastian automatically held himself back to make sure that he never showed his elder brother up.

Sebastian simply had a gift that Alejandro did not.

The coin was tossed, and the ball pitched in. Alejandro caught it and sent it hurling down the field and then galloped after it. Sebastian paused for a heartbeat, breathless, wondering if his old habits should stand.

But then he glanced over at Kat, watching behind the sideboards, and he thought of her last words to him.

"Let's see you fly."

He gave his pony a little kick, and together they sailed down the pitch after Jandro.

He saw the look of surprise on Jandro's face as Sebastian leaned across and hooked his brother's stick before Alejandro could put the ball through the goal. Then Sebastian wheeled around and caught the ball up with his own mallet and sent it flying through the air in the opposite direction.

He looked carefully at Alejandro as he rode past him, and his heart sank when he saw his brother's bewildered expression. Sebastian took a deep breath, feeling his determination ebb. He started to slow his pony, to hold back like he always did, but then his big brother's eyes met his and narrowed, and he tilted his chin and nodded at Seb with a slow and challenge-filled smile.

Sebastian laughed joyfully and spurred his pony on, soaring down the pitch. He heard Alejandro coming up behind him, the pounding of the white horse's hooves and the ragged grunt of her breath. He sped up, but Alejandro raced his horse until the shoulder of his pony was even with Sebastian's pony. Sebastian gave a quick glance over at his brother, who met his gaze, raised one eyebrow, and grinned just before he abruptly veered over and slammed into Sebastian's horse, sending Seb over the line of the ball, and surging ahead down the field without looking back once.

Sebastian's whole body jerked, and his teeth rattled with the hit. He swore and pulled his pony up short, watching his brother disappear down the field. And then he laughed again before kicking his pony into gear and heading off in pursuit.

* * *

Kat watched the brothers zig and zag through the other player's ponies with her heart in her mouth. At some point, she had stopped seeing the game as a director, depending on her DP to make sure she got the coverage she needed. She was now just watching as a bystander, amazed at what was unfolding on the field.

"They're not really letting anyone else play, are they?" she said to Georgia, who was standing next to her with her mouth hanging open, watching the Del Campos banging into each other all over the field. "Can they do that? Isn't that against the rules?"

"I don't know what they are doing," said Georgia. "I've never seen them play like this."

"I've never seen anyone play like this," added Liberty, who had joined them on the sidelines.

"I have," murmured Pilar. "When they were boys." Her normally placid face broke into a wide grin. "They're playing *un picadito*," she said happily.

* * *

The brothers took turns scoring goal after goal, whooping like crazed children as they raced up and down the field. The other players gave up trying to do much more than offer an assist now and then. Sebastian and Alejandro were both playing like they had ten-goal handicaps, overpowering everyone on the field. No one else had a chance in hell of getting to the ball.

Sebastian scored another goal just as the thirty-second horn sounded. Then the chukka was over, and it was time to get fresh mounts. He'd actually lost count of the score, he realized, as he rode his pony onto the sidelines. He had no idea who was winning.

He switched over to a little roan stallion and then rode back onto the field. Alejandro was on a bay mare that reminded Sebastian of Alejandro's favorite pony at home, Temper.

"How many chukkas do you think she'll let us play?" shouted Alejandro. "This is the most fun I've had on the field in years!" There was a look of delirious joy on his face.

Sebastian blinked. For a moment, he was riding the back field of their old farm, and Alejandro had that exact same look on his face, and he was yelling and giggling and trying to hook the ball away from Sebastian, and their *abuelita* Victoria was right there riding alongside them on her old dappled gray mare, Nube.

He could hear the sound of her voice, rich with laughter. "*¡Vamos, chicos! ¡Rápido! ¡Rápido!*"

He could feel the weight of her arm as she wrapped it around his shoulders, Sebastian on one side and Jandro on the other, after they had put the ponies away and walked back toward the *caballeriza* together.

He could see her merry eyes, dark and crinkled, the soft

gray curls framing her face, her lovely smile gleaming as she beamed down at him, and he felt pure, unfettered love and joy.

And then he blinked, and the teams were getting ready to go again, milling around under the bright California sun. Sebastian closed his eyes and took a deep breath, wondering...

Yes, there it was.

The singular and haunting scent of dried roses.

Chapter Forty-eight

Kat stayed late that night, watching the playback. She'd sent everyone home after the polo game ended. Sebastian and Alejandro had walked off the field with their arms around each other, talking and laughing. She'd never seen Seb look so joyful and at ease.

And now she was in video village, gazing at the monitor, breathless, watching Sebastian on his pony, breaking from the pack, galloping down the pitch...

Flying.

Watching him on that field was like seeing an entirely different side of the man. It was as if the Sebastian she had known up until now had been at rest, in disguise. The person she saw on the field was a revelation. Superman after bursting out of the phone booth.

She watched him pivot on his pony, the powerful way his muscles flexed as he raised his arm to sweep the ball, the intensity on his face as he made the hit. She shifted in her seat, recognizing the same look she had seen in his eyes just as he thrust himself between her thighs. The ferocity, the raw power... She trailed a finger down her own neck, felt her breath start to quicken...

"Is any of it usable?" said a deep voice.

Kat jumped, and turned to see Sebastian standing in the doorway of the tent.

She stared at him for a moment. His hair was damp and pushed back, as if he'd just come from the shower. All the time outside had turned his skin a dark cinnamon gold, which made his beautiful pale green eyes stand out even more. He was wearing faded jeans and a soft white fitted shirt, which she recognized from their first date.

"I know that Jandro and I got a little out of hand this afternoon. I hope it didn't ruin the—"

She interrupted him. "You know, I've never seen you play before."

He blinked. "Well, I don't usually ride quite like that," he said. "Things got a little wild."

He walked over to her and peered into the monitor. She had paused on an image of him bent around the neck of his pony, just about to hit the ball.

He looked so beautiful. Her heart ached. "I feel like a fool," said Kat.

"What? Why?"

She shook her head. "I told you to try something else. I didn't know."

"¿*Que?* What didn't you know?"

"You kept saying that it came easily to you, but I didn't understand what you meant." She swept her hand at the monitor. "It's as if I'd told Mikhail Baryshnikov he should take a break from dancing."

He chuckled. "That's very flattering, but—"

She turned to him. "No. No, it really isn't, Sebastian. This"—she pointed at the monitor—"this is what you were meant to be doing."

He frowned. "And here I thought I was doing okay as a producer."

She stood up and rubbed her forehead, starting to pace. "You're a great producer. That's not what I'm saying."

"Well then—"

She interrupted him. "I thought you were careless," she said as she walked the floor. "I thought you didn't know how to commit to things. I didn't understand. I didn't know." She laughed. "It's like you were an angel, and I met you without your wings."

"For God's sake, Katarina—"

She whirled on him. "What are you even doing here? Why are you wasting your time on this set when you should be with your team, with the ponies? Why are you here?"

His face softened. "I told you why. Because I wanted to help you."

She stared at him for a moment. Then she laughed quietly and turned away. "You really aren't Jack Hayes, are you?"

"The actor? What does he have to do with anything?"

She laughed again. "Nothing."

"*Linda*," he said, "I am here because I believe in this movie. I believe in your talent. You wrote something beautiful. I want to help it get made."

She bit her lip. "God, you've never wanted me to be anyone except exactly who I am," she said wonderingly.

He looked at her, bewildered. "Why would I?"

She crossed the room to where he stood, threw her arms around his neck, and kissed him.

Chapter Forty-nine

They drove separately back to her house, met in her driveway, and climbed the steep stairway up to her hilltop home. Kat led the way, and with every step she took, Sebastian's desire grew. By the time they reached the top, it was all he could do not to lay her down on her front porch and take her right there.

She put the key in the door and bumped at it with her hip. "It always sticks," she apologized, bumping again. Sebastian reached past her and pushed. Hard.

The door flew open.

"So," said Kat nervously, "this is my—"

He stopped her with a kiss. He wouldn't wait. He couldn't. He refused to be tortured any longer. He'd been with her, seeing her, smelling her, near her—without actually having her—for far too long. His desire was liquid heat, pumping through him, filling him with an urgency that simply wouldn't let him take things slow.

She pulled away. "The door," she gasped.

He kicked it shut with his foot.

He kissed her deliriously, running his fingers over her breasts, down the curve of her hips, cradling her rear in his hands, lifting her against him until she wrapped her legs around his back and he held her, suspended, against himself.

"Both hands," he whispered against her mouth, and she smiled, and then he kissed her even harder.

He would never get enough of this, he thought. He would never get enough of her dark sugar smell, the heat and silk of her skin, the weight of her wild black curls as they tumbled down around his neck and over his shoulders. He would never stop wanting to taste her, to feel her, to be inside her.

She slid her legs down his and found the floor again. She fumbled at his jeans. "Now," she breathed. "I need you now."

"Do you have a—"

"I'm on the pill."

He sucked in his breath and grabbed at her waistband, wrenching her jeans and panties down to the floor at the same time that she managed to open his fly and let him spring free. Then he picked her back up again, swung around to brace her against the door, and plunged her down onto his cock, feeling the hot, slick, sweet pulse of her throughout his body.

She wrapped her long legs around his back and groaned. He pulled back and then thrust into her again. It felt so good that he knew he wouldn't be able to hold out for long.

"Katarina," he hissed, "*no puedo*, I can't—"

"Don't," she said. "Just go. Don't stop. I need to feel you come."

A wave of unbearable desire crashed over him at her words. He lost control. He pinned her against the door and thrust into her again and again, feeling her rise to meet his every move, feeling her burning heat and melting softness, feeling the fire roar inside him, raging through him, until he could barely hear or see—but just feel. Until he cried out with the force of his release, surged into her, held her tight, felt the rush and then the explosion, and then felt his body melt into hers, spent, as he collapsed against her.

"I love you," he whispered. "*Te amo*, Katarina."

Before she could answer, he slid down her body to his knees, cradling her behind in his hands and pulling her toward him, kissing her damp curls and then tasting the very core of her, her salty sweetness. She groaned, and her hips jolted. He pulled her back to his mouth, losing himself in her womanly slickness, sucking and licking until she shuddered and cried out, driving herself against his mouth, saying his name as he made her crest and then fall, and then crest again—over and over and over again. Then, when she was almost sobbing with pleasure, he urged her down to the floor with him, pulled off her shirt and bra, tugged his own clothes off, covered her body with his, and slipped into her once more.

It felt like a dream as he slowly moved inside her, holding himself up so he could watch her face. Her skin glistening with perspiration, the deep, ragged sound of her breath as it hissed and caught in her throat. He loved the way she looked at him, her bewitching gray eyes almost stunned with emotion, her luscious mouth parted and damp. He felt the way her body, which had been weak with pleasure when he entered her, slowly started to tense again, the escalation of her desire...

She arched up against him with a moan and ran her fingernails down his back. The feeling seemed to ripple through his body, magnified over a thousand times.

She pulled back. Her silvery gaze met his. "I love you, too," she whispered. "I've missed you so much."

Tears sprang into his eyes. "*Mi amor*," he breathed.

He kissed her forehead, her cheeks, her mouth. He ran his lips down her neck and over her beautiful, full breasts. He tasted the twin points of her coral-colored nipples. He reached down and touched her. She was soaking wet, quivering with passion. He circled his thumb against her, and she gasped, so sensitive that she was immediately sent over the edge yet again, her muscles tightening around him with frantic spasms, a sound of sweet pleasure torn from her throat. "Sebastian," she cried out, "oh God, oh God, I love you."

And then he was over the edge as well, spiraling with her, surging into her. They fell into each other, holding each other tighter and tighter until, at last, they both found their final release and collapsed against each other, consumed and exhausted.

Chapter Fifty

They lay on the floor, Kat's head cradled on Sebastian's shoulder, happily stunned.

"What is this we are we lying on?" Sebastian finally asked.

Kat smiled. "Mexican tile. Very cold. Very hard."

"I am guessing, perhaps, there are more comfortable places in your home?"

"It's not my fault we didn't make it past the entryway."

He pulled her toward him with a growl, kissing her. "*Estoy feliz*," he said, looking into her eyes. "Are you happy?"

A warm thrill shot through her. She closed her eyes and nodded, her cheek pressed against his. "Very," she whispered.

"I'm also hungry."

She laughed. "Me, too."

They got up off the floor and padded naked into Kat's kitchen. Kat looked in the refrigerator while Seb examined her kitchen, picking up her things and then putting them down.

"I'll cook," said Kat, "but first I'm going to put on a robe."

Sebastian pulled her toward him, grabbing her behind with his hands. "Why would you do that?"

She laughed and gave him a quick kiss before pulling away. "Because it's never a good idea to cook naked."

He followed her into her bedroom, retrieving his jeans on the way. She sighed as she looked at him. One of her favorite sights—Sebastian shirtless in jeans.

She slipped on a black silk robe. Sebastian looked curiously around her room. "So this is where you sleep?"

She laughed. "When I can."

He prowled the room, looking at the art on the walls, opening her jewelry boxes, running his hand over the quilt on her bed.

She sat down on the bed and watched him. "What are you doing?" she asked.

"Getting to know your home. Everything in this house is you."

Kat smiled.

"What's this?" he asked, picking up a small crude wooden statue of an elephant.

She laughed. Of all the things he could choose. "It was a prize I won in grade school for best essay."

"What was the essay about?"

"Um, the ancient aqueducts of Rome. Extremely scintillating stuff."

"Why an elephant?"

She laughed. "Why the third degree?"

He put the elephant down, smiling at her, and came to sit on the bed next to her. "There are so many things to know about you," he said, taking her hand and kissing it. "And I want to learn them all." He leaned his forehead against hers. "I want to know about the Roman aqueducts, and why you chose this color green for your walls, and why you have so many pictures and photos of women with cats but no actual cat. You don't have a cat, do you?"

She shook her head. "I always meant to get one."

He nodded. "Good. I like cats."

"A black cat," she said. "They have the hardest time finding homes."

He chuckled. "See, yet another thing I didn't know."

He lay back on her bed, testing it out. "*Cómoda*" he said. "Very comfortable." He ran his hand along the carving on the headboard. "And very pretty."

She looked at him a moment, flashing on all the long, sunny afternoons they had spent alone together in their little bubble of her girlhood room. The way she would sit at her desk and work while he lounged on her bed. The contentment she'd feel every time she turned around to see him there, beautiful and serene, happy just to be with her.

She leaned down and kissed him. "Thank you," she whispered.

He smiled. "For what?"

"For *Twenty-five Roses*. I couldn't have written it without you."

He cocked his head. "Because she is my grandmother?"

"Well, yes, of course. You brought me Victoria. But I meant..." She looked away, suddenly losing her nerve. "I—I just couldn't have done any of this without you."

He smiled and pulled her down next to him. "My pleasure, *linda*."

* * *

They drank red wine and ate pasta carbonara on her patio, gazing out over the lights of the city. Afterward, they stripped off their clothes and dived into the pool together, splashing and playing like children, until Sebastian caught

Kat up in his arms with a gasp, and they twined together, treading water, and kissing under the moonlit sky.

Kat led him out of the pool and into a lounge chair, where she straddled Sebastian and slowly took possession of him. He watched her move over him, her eyes closed, her breath thick with pleasure, the water from the pool still streaming down her body in silvery rivulets, her dark hair clinging to her neck and shoulders in thick, serpentine coils... He wondered what he had done to deserve this moment, to deserve this woman.

They showered together in her blue and green tiled bathroom, rinsing off the chlorine and sweat, and then toweled off and climbed into the soft, warm bed that smelled of her bittersweet scent, and he wrapped her hair around his hands and pressed her to his chest. He fell asleep with the delicate caress of her breath at his neck and the steady pulse of her heart beating against his.

Chapter Fifty-one

They overslept the next morning and hurried to get to the set on time. They took their separate cars, and Kat waited for Sebastian to go in first before she entered. Liberty was already there, getting her makeup done. Kat watched her track Sebastian with her big violet eyes as he crossed the stage.

"Where have you been, Sebastian?" Liberty called sweetly. "I stopped by for a ride this morning, and you were already gone."

Sebastian blinked. "Ah, *lo siento*. I was out last night."

"I guess you were." She sounded nonchalant, but Kat thought she detected a certain strain in her smile.

First up on the shot list was a short scene between Liberty and Charlie. Kat sat down next to her to talk her through it.

"So, in this scene—" she began.

"I'm thinking about a different costume," interrupted Liberty, running her hands down the navy blue watered silk gown she was wearing. "This just doesn't feel like Victoria, you know?"

Kat cocked her head. "Um, how so?"

"I don't know. Would she really wear this color?"

"Well, you picked that color out yourself, as I recall."

"Did I?" Liberty blinked her eyes innocently. "I don't know what I was thinking. I'm pretty sure we need something warmer. A pink or a red maybe?"

Kat tried to contain her impatience. "But that color looks beautiful on you, Libby."

Liberty wrinkled her nose. "We can do better."

If she changed the gown, she'd need a redo on her hair and makeup, too. Kat took a deep breath and tried to keep calm. "Libby, we're running a little late this morning, so maybe—"

"Oh, well," said Liberty, and her voice suddenly lost its friendly tone, "if we're running late, it's only because you and Sebastian decided to roll in at eight thirty."

Kat bit the inside of her cheek, doing her best not to crack. "Okay. If you really want the change . . ."

"I do," said Liberty and turned back to the mirror.

* * *

They were still waiting to start the scene two hours later. Liberty had retreated to her trailer with a dozen different options that wardrobe pulled for her, but according to her, none of them would do.

"I'm just not feeling anything yet," she said to Kat through her closed trailer door. "Do we have anything in a dark green?"

"I thought you wanted a warmer color."

"I do, but you know, just in case."

Kat sighed and silently sent up a little prayer for patience. "I'll have them look for green."

"Or what about orange?" Liberty called out.

Kat rolled her eyes and decided she needed a cup of coffee

before she tracked down the costume designer. Sebastian met her at the craft services table.

"What's going on?" he said. "Where's Liberty?"

Kat shook her head. "She just asked me to find her an orange dress. As if Liberty Smith would be caught dead in orange. I think she suspects something."

"About what?"

Kat shot him an exasperated look. "Us, of course."

Sebastian looked puzzled. "Why would she care about that?"

"Um, aside from her very obvious crush on you?"

Sebastian made a face. "What? No. She is like that with everyone."

Kat laughed. "She's certainly not like that with me."

"No, really, trust me. She is not interested in me that way at all. She just likes attention."

Kat took a cookie from the table. "Whatever you say."

Sebastian frowned. "Do you think I should talk to her?"

"I don't know. Maybe. I'm not getting anywhere with her, and we've already lost the whole morning. I'm not sure how much longer she's going to keep this up."

"On the other hand," said Sebastian, and he took a step closer to Kat, "I think I saw an empty supply closet with enough room for two." He took the cookie from her hand and bit into it. "Perhaps we ought to take advantage of the downtime."

She smiled and swiped the cookie back. "Get your own cookie."

"That is exactly what I am trying to do," he said, laying a hand on her hip.

Someone cleared their throat. "Uh, guys?"

Liberty's pretty young assistant, Nancy, was standing behind them. Sebastian dropped his hand, and Kat jumped back a step.

Nancy looked nervous. "Um, Liberty wanted me to tell you that she's not feeling well and wants to go back to the hotel."

Kat groaned. "Well, there goes the rest of the day."

"And, uh," added Nancy, "she told me to say that she wants Mr. Del Campo to drive her."

Kat shot an *I-told-you-so* look at Sebastian, who shook his head helplessly.

"Just go," said Kat. "I'll do some contingency scenes with Charlie."

Chapter Fifty-two

Liberty seemed perfectly healthy and cheerful as Sebastian idled in the creeping freeway traffic. She fiddled with the radio, squealing when she found a song she liked, loudly singing along without any concern as to the actual notes.

"Liberty," said Sebastian. He turned down the music. "*Liberty.*"

She looked at him, a bright smile on her face. "What?"

"So what type of sick are you? Head? Stomach? Throat?"

Liberty rolled her eyes. "Oh God, come on. I never get sick. I just needed a little holiday." She rolled the car window down and stuck her head out. "Call it an actor's holiday," she said.

She waved at the man in the car next to them, who did a double take. Sebastian saw him mouth, "Oh my God! Liberty Smith!" as the man's window started to roll down.

Sebastian pressed the button to roll the passenger window back up, forcing Liberty's head back into the car, and then hit the child lock.

"Hey!" said Liberty.

"Let's not cause yet another riot," said Sebastian as he nudged his car into the next lane for good measure. "You know, as your producer, I have to point out that it costs a lot of money to lose an entire day of shooting," he said.

Liberty made an unimpressed noise. "I'm a producer, too, you know."

"Then I would think you'd care more."

"Stop being such a spoilsport, Sebastian. I made sure you got a little vacation, too, didn't I?" She grabbed his knee suddenly. "You know what I think we should do? Go to the beach! Let's just stop at the hotel and get our suits and then we can go to Malibu."

Sebastian imagined the havoc that Liberty Smith would cause in one of her tiny bikinis on a public beach. "Are you trying to put me back into *el hospital*?" he muttered.

"What?"

"No, we are not going to the beach. I am taking you to the hotel, and then I am turning right around and going back to set."

"*Gaaah*," groaned Liberty, flopping back in her seat, "you're so boring!"

Sebastian inched forward into the traffic, which had basically come to a total standstill. "I am doing my job," he said.

"I know," said Liberty, shaking her head, "and your job is frigging lame."

* * *

Kat watched as Charlie paced the soundstage, finishing up his monologue. She sighed. They'd already filmed the scene three times. There was really no good reason to film it again.

"Okay, cut!" she shouted. "Set up for the next shot. Everyone else take thirty. Nice work, Charlie," she said as the actor came offstage.

He saluted her. "Anything for you, boss," he said as he headed off toward his trailer.

Kat checked her watch. Sebastian had left two hours before. He should have been back long ago.

As she walked back to her trailer, unbidden images tumbled into her brain and made her catch her breath. Sebastian holding her against the door. The way he looked into her eyes as she moved over him in the moonlight, his wide, chiseled chest naked and still wet from the pool. His head between her legs as he crushed her to his mouth and made her writhe in the most delicious agony...

But then, just as suddenly, the image was replaced with Liberty being held against the door, Liberty hovering over Sebastian in the night, Liberty watching Sebastian with her sleepy violet eyes as he moved his mouth between her legs...

Kat shook it off, chiding herself. It had been less than twenty-four hours since Sebastian had held her in his arms and told her that he loved her, when he had tangled himself around her, keeping her close as she slept through the night. The first thing she'd seen after she'd awoken this morning was his sea green eyes, watching her with a look that she could only be described as grateful amazement.

"*Mi corazón*," he had called her, smoothing back her hair and placing a fervent kiss on her forehead.

My heart.

But still, Kat thought, as she paced her trailer, ignoring the stack of props that she was supposed to be sorting through, she had seen the way Liberty looked at Sebastian. The way her eyes lit up with interest whenever he walked into the room. The way she clung to his arm every day when they headed home for their hotel. The way they had stood together after Liberty fell from the horse...

She heard Honey's voice echoing in her head. *Liberty Del Campo has an awfully nice ring to it, right?*

Stop. Stop. Stop, Kat commanded herself. God. She had never been this jealous before. But then again, she'd never been in direct competition with Liberty flipping Smith, the most beautiful woman in the world.

Perhaps Liberty was difficult and complicated, but that didn't make her any less attractive. She was like Sebastian, really. So exceptional in her beauty and talent that she almost seemed like she was of another species entirely—some higher life form that only the lucky few could claim kin to. They were made for each other in a way. Two creatures extraordinarily beautiful in their form and absolutely singular in their gifts.

If Liberty wanted him, what heterosexual man in the world could possibly turn her away? Hell, if Liberty wanted *anything*, she generally got it. Movie stars were the closest thing this world had to gods walking upon the earth, and Liberty was a queen among those goddesses. What hope did any mortal woman have against her?

Still, Sebastian had never given Kat any reason not to trust him. And last night—what had happened between them last night was the kind of thing that people waited a lifetime to feel. There was something so right about being in Sebastian's arms. As if she had been born to take her place there.

She closed her eyes and took a deep breath, willing her doubts away. Then she sat down at the table and started to sort through the vintage hair combs that wardrobe had sent over for her to approve. Combs with peacock feathers, combs with garnets and diamonds, combs with amethysts the exact color of Liberty's legendary eyes...

She checked her watch. Two and a half hours since he'd walked away...

Chapter Fifty-three

It had been some of the worst traffic Sebastian had ever seen. They had crept along the freeway inch by excruciating inch, taking three hours to get through what normally took thirty minutes. And it was made all the more torturous by Liberty's restless boredom and never-ending complaints. She was hungry. She was thirsty. She wanted a mojito. Her phone was dead. By hour two, Sebastian started fantasizing about throwing open the door and just walking down the freeway, leaving Liberty and the car to fend for themselves.

He'd left his phone at Kat's, he realized. They'd run out in such a hurry that morning that he'd left it on the bathroom counter. Liberty's phone died after the first half hour, and Sebastian cursed when he realized that he'd given his car charger to her a few days before when she had complained that the one in her car didn't work fast enough.

He tried blocking Liberty out, wanting to close his eyes and simply lose himself in memories of the night before. But the first time he had tried this, the jolt of brutal lust he'd felt when Kat's face swam into his imagination, her cheeks flushed pink, her long black curls falling around her shoulders, her silvery gaze filled with a depth of emotion he had never seen in any woman's eyes before, made him realize that he could not take this particular escape while he was trapped in a car with another person. Especially not a person like Liberty Smith, who seemed to have a second sight when it came to knowing whether or not someone was paying her the exact amount of attention she felt was her due.

Finally they reached their exit and headed for Beverly Hills. Liberty popped the visor mirror down and redid her lipstick as he pulled up in front of the hotel to let the valet take his car. Sebastian had never been so happy to see the ornate edifice of the Pink Château. His plan was to get back to his bungalow, call Kat, and convince her to let him pick her up and take her to Capo in Santa Monica. He wanted to share a great meal with her, drink a bottle of champagne, see an ocean view, and afterward, walk the beach in the moonlight just like they had done so many times in Wellington.

Sebastian eagerly tossed the valet his keys and turned to say a hasty good-bye to Liberty, who was being helped out of the car by a bellboy, when he was suddenly blindsided by the flash of multiple cameras and the shouts of "Liberty! Liberty! Who are you with? Where's your husband, Liberty?"

At least a dozen paparazzi were trampling down the driveway toward them, cameras blazing.

Sebastian acted instinctively, grabbing Liberty's arm to pull her inside the lobby, but for some reason, she took his hand and froze, smiling strangely as the press converged around them.

She turned to Sebastian, a little hint of regret in her eyes.

"Sorry," she whispered, and then she threw her arms around his neck and kissed him with everything she had.

* * *

Kat finally decided to pack it up and go home for the night. One of the problems about making a biopic about one woman's life was that, if that one woman wasn't around, there was only so much that could get done.

She'd texted and called Sebastian's phone several times but it just kept going straight to voice mail. She pushed down her worry as she gathered her things and headed to her car. There was surely a reasonable explanation for his absence, she thought, and she'd feel stupid later if she let herself get too worked up about things.

On the way home, she stopped at a little neighborhood takeout place for a salad and some chicken, and then, after hesitating for a moment, doubled her order and asked them to throw in two pieces of lemon pie as well. She already had a nice bottle of pinot grigio chilling in her fridge, she remembered. She wanted to be prepared, just in case.

She got home, put her packages on the kitchen counter, and decided to take a long, hot shower. While she was stripping off her jeans and T-shirt, she spied Sebastian's phone on the bathroom counter. She tried to turn it on, but it was dead. She was ridiculously pleased to have an explanation as to why he hadn't returned her texts or phone messages.

She sang in the shower. Al Green songs. Whitney Houston songs. Early Madonna. Love songs. At the top of her lungs. She used her very best lotion and stood in front of her closet for a full ten minutes, trying to figure out just the right combination of casual and sexy. She had the notion that the way Sebastian saw her in these next few days would be the way she would be fixed in his mind for a lifetime, even when she was wrinkled and sagging. She wanted to be beautiful in his memories.

She finally chose a little black T-back shift dress, and

nothing else. She felt a shiver run down her spine at the thought of Sebastian's hand casually slipping up her dress and discovering that she was completely naked underneath. She bundled up her hair, did a few quick things to her face, dabbed on some perfume, put on a turquoise pendant on a long chain that she thought might look fetching if she was wearing nothing else, and then headed into the living room to wait. She couldn't imagine that he wouldn't be there soon.

After about fifteen minutes, she drifted into the kitchen, opening up the takeout containers and picking at the pie. After another thirty minutes, she ate both pieces.

She jumped guiltily as her phone rang. Then she laughed, looking at the empty cardboard containers. She would just tell him to pick up something sweet on the way over, she thought as she rushed to her phone.

She didn't even check caller ID—she was so sure it was him—but then, it was not.

"Katy Ann?" boomed Camelia's voice. "You'll never guess where I am right now!"

"Camelia?"

"I'm on a beach in Ibiza." Camelia laughed.

"You're what? But didn't you just get home?"

"Mark flew us out for the week on his private jet."

Kat chuckled. "Did you let him buy you a truck, too?"

Camelia snorted. "No. But I figured since he already had the jet, what the hell, right? I've got to find some balance between taking nothing from him and missing Ibiza. Plus he asked me to give him riding lessons so we made an exchange."

"I think he got a good deal actually. Where is he now?"

"Oh God, it's ridiculous. He's down the beach haggling with a guy about a cowrie shell necklace. You know those choker-type things that frat boys wear? He thinks he's going to wear one. But not on my frigging watch."

Kat smiled. "You sound happy, Cam."

Camelia laughed again. "I suppose I am. Go figure. But anyway, I just wanted to call and make sure you were okay. I guess you were right after all. I just saw those gross pictures of Seb and Liberty on my phone. They must be such a pain in the ass to work with right now."

Kat's heart started beating faster. "What pictures?"

"I mean, you totally called it, but I thought the guy could have at least waited until you were done with your movie, right?"

"What pictures, Cam?"

"Oh, the pictures of the two of them in front of the hotel. Totally ick."

Kat turned and popped open her laptop, Googled Liberty's name, and then felt herself go weak in the knees.

"Katy? Are you there?"

Her head swam. "I gotta go, Camelia. I, um—"

"Katy Ann?"

Kat hung up the phone. With a shaking hand, she clicked on one of the images. There they were—wearing the same clothes they'd been wearing today, locked in an embrace that rivaled anything she and Sebastian had been doing the night before.

Her phone rang. She ignored it, clicking on the caption:

Caught! Liberty Smith in a lip lock with Latin boy-toy and polo player, Sebastian Del Campo, as they enter their love nest at the Hills Hotel. A close friend is quoted as saying that these two have been seeing each other since they started filming Smith's upcoming new film, Twenty-five Roses. *Notorious playboy Del Campo is single, but Smith is famously not, of course. No word yet from her husband, billionaire financier David Ansley.*

Kat felt like she couldn't breathe. She clicked on more pictures, hoping to find something that would explain what she was looking at—that would prove that it was just a weird camera angle or a friendly hug, but there was no other way of seeing a photo where Liberty's hand was squarely on Sebastian's ass and her tongue basically down his throat.

Her phone rang again. She didn't even look at it.

She shut the computer with a little click and sank down on a kitchen chair. What had changed, she wondered. What had changed since last night, when right here in this house he had told her loved her, when he had held her with such awe and reverence, when she was sure that whatever was happening between them was the beginning of forever? How could they have gone from that to this?

She stifled a sob. Obviously, Liberty had just crooked her finger and Seb had come running. Or maybe they'd been together all along. She remembered all the rumors that Honey had heard. The private joke they had shared between them after Liberty had fallen. Kat's mouth went dry. Maybe she herself was actually the other woman—which was why Liberty was so furious with them both this morning. Maybe Kat was the fling and Liberty was the girlfriend?

Her phone rang again. She put her head down on the table, hoping to calm the churning in her stomach. It kept ringing so she reached up to look at it, saw that it was Sebastian calling from the hotel, and immediately dashed her phone onto the kitchen floor in response. It broke in half and lay silent as she bent her head and cried.

Chapter Fifty-four

Sebastian slammed down the phone in his room. Where the hell was she? Kat was never without her cell. It was her work lifeline. There was no way she didn't have it.

He prowled through the living room. Goddamn Liberty. The pictures were everywhere now. They'd gone viral. It had been nearly instant—minutes after he'd stood there, totally stunned, as Liberty had groped him for the cameras. He'd been shocked, and then angry, and had wrenched himself away. But the damage had already been done. The first picture popped up online by the time he was back in his bungalow, everyone racing to get the scoop.

He hadn't said anything to Liberty. Just pushed her away and got out of there as fast as he could. His only concern had been Kat. Reaching her before she saw the photos. Because he knew what they would look like. Liberty was, if nothing else, a very good actress.

But obviously, he'd failed. There was no doubt that Kat had already seen them, he thought as her phone went straight to voice mail.

He'd have to drive over to her place. Explain himself in person. He knew it looked bad, but Kat knew Liberty. Surely she would believe him once he told her the whole crazy story.

What the hell had Liberty been trying to do? All current evidence to the contrary, he was still absolutely certain she had no real interest in him. But obviously she had tipped off those reporters. He flashed to her redoing her lipstick just before she got out of the car. She'd been ready to put on a show.

Was she trying to drum up publicity for the movie? Maybe she was just bored and wanted to make trouble. He couldn't begin to guess. But it didn't matter. He needed to find Kat. He couldn't stand to imagine what she was feeling right now.

He was heading out his front door when Liberty came through the gate between their bungalows.

She looked like shit, he thought. Perhaps for the first time ever.

Her face was blotchy and red. Her famous eyes were bloodshot. She was carrying her phone in one hand and blew her nose on a paper towel with the other. She stumbled a little, as if she had been drinking. She looked like an entirely different person from the woman he'd known. She looked defeated.

"We have to talk," she said. "I really fucked up."

"I do not have time to hear what you have to say, Liberty," he said. He tried to get around her.

She stepped in his way, getting up close. She smelled like booze. "Are you going to see Kat?"

He clenched his fists. He wanted to charge right through her. "Let me through, Liberty."

She shook her head. "You have to hear me out first. Kat will need to know."

"Kat will need to know what? That you just kissed me in

front of every *puto* reporter in Hollywood? I am fairly certain she is already more than aware of the fact."

He maneuvered around her and reached for the latch on the gate. She caught his arm.

"No," she said. "Not that. She'll need to know that David just pulled the plug on the movie. He cut off all the funds."

Sebastian could have sworn he felt his heart stop. "What did you just say?"

Liberty started to sniff, and then full-on cry. "I didn't mean for this to happen," she sobbed. "I just wanted to make him jealous. I needed him to see me with you so he could see that someone still wants me. Someone like you. That I'm worth something."

"Liberty, *por favor*, go back. What did you say about the movie?"

"He cut us off," she choked out. "I thought he'd see the pictures and fly back home. I thought he'd fight for me. Instead, he freaked out and started screaming about how I had humiliated him. How he wasn't giving the movie another cent. How I'd made him look like a pussy in front of the whole world. Even though he's fucked a hundred girls since we've been married. Even though I've never, not once, been with anyone else since the day I met him." Her face twisted with pain. "Asshole!" she raged. "He's such an asshole!"

She bent over like she was in agony, sobbing uncontrollably. "I love him so much," she choked. "I love him."

Sebastian caught her as she fell against him. She buried her face in his neck, wailing out her sorrow. He held her as she rocked with heartbreak.

"*Está bien*," he soothed. "It will be okay, *chica*."

She looked up into his face. Tears were coursing down her cheeks, and her nose was running. "I'm sorry," she slurred.

"I'm really sorry, Seb. I know there's something going on with you and Kat. I know there always has been. And I swear, I wasn't trying to mess with that. I'll explain it all to her, I promise. I'll make it right."

And then, as if in slow motion, Liberty's eyes rolled back in her head, and she slid out of his arms, hitting the ground with a thud.

Chapter Fifty-five

Kat was lying on her living room couch with her eyes shut when the doorbell rang.

She ignored it. It had to be Sebastian, and she had zero interest in seeing him.

The doorbell went off again. Then someone knocked. Loud.

"Go to hell!" she yelled without opening her eyes.

"Kat?" It wasn't Sebastian. Kat opened her eyes. "Kat, open this goddamned door or I'm going to come in there and put my foot up your ass."

It was Honey.

"I don't want to talk, Honey," Kat said. "I'll call you later."

"Not an option. Need to talk to you right now. Open the door before I break a window."

Kat exhaled and got up. She heard Honey violently rattle the knob. "Fine!" Kat shouted, flinging open the door. "What the hell is so important?"

"Liberty is in the hospital. She OD'd."

Kat felt the whole room sway. She grasped Honey's arm. "Oh no," she whispered. "God, no. Let's go right now."

* * *

Sebastian was in the waiting room when she and Honey arrived. He had his head in his hands, but he looked up as they came in.

"Katarina," he said, and quickly stood, crossing over to them. "I'm so sorry. I couldn't reach you on your phone."

Kat took a step back. She couldn't look at him, and she certainly didn't want him to touch her. "Where is she?" she said hoarsely. "Where's Liberty?"

"She's with *la doctora*. They pumped her stomach. She took a handful of Prozac, apparently. Chased it with vodka."

Kat flinched. "Why?"

"It's a long story," he said. "But you should see her first. She needs someone, but I was stupid and told them I am not related."

Kat strode over to the front desk. "I'm Liberty Smith's sister," she said to the male nurse behind the counter.

He looked at her and shook his head. "Nice try. Everyone knows that Liberty Smith doesn't have any family."

"I'm her director then," said Kat. "That's almost the same thing."

He pursed his lips and looked at her. "You're Kat Parker?"

She whipped out her wallet. "Here's my ID."

He looked at it and smiled. "I loved *Red Hawk*."

She blinked. "You did?"

He nodded. "You need any extras for the film you're doing now?"

She shook her head. "Only in frigging Hollywood." She turned around. "Honey, hook this guy up with a part, okay? No more than one line." She looked at him. "All right?"

He buzzed open the door. "Room two thirty-seven."

As she walked through the door, she heard Honey say, "You, sir, are an extremely shitty nurse."

* * *

Liberty was alone when Kat walked in. She looked terrible, washed out and fragile, which Kat found almost as shocking as anything else that had happened this day.

Her amethyst eyes fluttered open. *Oh yeah*, thought Kat, *there she is*.

"Kat?" Her voice was hoarse and ragged.

Kat sat down next to the bed and took Liberty's hand. She glanced down at it. It was ice cold, but still soft and perfect. "How are you doing, Libby?" she said softly.

Liberty's eyes filled with tears. "Oh, I'm great," she said, attempting to smile. "Just awesome. And I'm so sorry. Did Sebastian tell you about the movie?"

Kat shook her head. "Don't worry about the movie right now, Libby. You take all the time you need. It will still be there when you're better."

Liberty laughed. She sounded miserable. "No. No, it won't. David cut off the money."

Kat felt her stomach drop, but she kept her face still. "Why?"

"He saw the pictures of me and Sebastian."

Kat clenched her fists and looked away, desperately fighting her absolute rage, resisting the urge to just get up and leave this woman alone in her own mess.

"Hey," said Liberty. "Oh wow, listen, Kat. Seb didn't do anything, okay? That was all me. I wanted to make David jealous. I totally set Sebastian up. I just kissed him for the cameras, okay? Nothing else."

Kat looked at her. Suddenly she felt like she could breathe again. "Really?" she said.

"Absolutely. He was totally grossed out. It's like he was kissing Hitler. He couldn't get out of there fast enough. He almost mowed me over."

Kat couldn't help it. She smiled.

Liberty snorted. "Nice, Kat. Glad I could make you feel better."

Kat bit her lip. "Sorry."

Liberty closed her eyes. "I told you. I don't ever bother with a guy whose heart is elsewhere. And goddamn, is Sebastian's heart elsewhere."

Kat smiled again.

"Quit smiling," said Liberty without opening her eyes.

Chapter Fifty-six

Kat insisted on staying with Liberty at the hospital that night so Sebastian went back out to pick up some necessities for them both. He went to Kat's house first, finding a change of clothes and grabbing her toothbrush and a comb from her bathroom.

He came back into her bedroom and picked up a pillow from her bed. He put his face to it, inhaling the scent that made him think of both sex and . . . home, he realized.

He'd been so relieved when she had come back out after seeing Liberty. She had strode right over to him and wrapped her arms around his neck, holding him tight. It had been obvious that Liberty had kept her promise and explained herself. For the first time since Liberty had kissed him, he had felt his heart stop furiously beating in a panic and slow back down to its normal rate.

They talked briefly about the movie. Kat thought they might be able to have one of the studios step in, but that would probably mean losing creative power. She had assured him that they would figure it out somehow, in any case.

He put the pillow back and patted the bed, certain that he would be back here later.

* * *

Sebastian drove back to the hotel and had the concierge let him into Liberty's bungalow to gather a few of her things. Afterward, he considered going to Alejandro and Georgia's bungalow, but it was late, and he didn't want to chance waking the baby. So he went into the main hotel to find his mother's room and let her know what had happened. He realized he had been unreachable all day, and that she was probably worried.

He knocked on the door to his mother's suite and Alejandro answered. He looked both relieved and pissed when he saw Sebastian. "*Idiota*," he said, "why have you not picked up your phone all day?"

"*Hijo?*" came his mother's voice. "Sebastian?"

"*Sí, Mamá.* It's him." Alejandro stood back to let him in.

Pilar rose from the couch, clutching her green silk dressing gown to her chest. Sebastian was shocked when she flew at him and shoved his shoulder with enough force that he was almost knocked backward.

"*Ay*, boy, you told me you were not seeing that married woman!" she hissed. "We saw *las fotos* on the computer! How could you? How could you do something like that after watching what your father did to me?"

Sebastian blinked. "Liberty is in the hospital," he told her.

From the shocked looks they gave him, he could see that this, at least, was not common knowledge yet.

Good, maybe they could keep it that way.

"But those pictures," his mother stammered weakly. "That's why we were worried—you told me you weren't—"

He sank down onto the couch and closed his eyes for a moment. "We're not, *Mamá*, but it's a long story."

* * *

They listened as he spilled out all that had happened with Liberty that day, and with Kat from the beginning of their time together. The way it had begun, the way it had ended, and then the way it had started again.

His mother looked at him with a smile of satisfaction. "I knew there was something *especial* between you two," she said.

Sebastian wryly raised a brow. "As I recall, you told me I was not allowed to date the housekeeper's daughter."

"No, no. I told you that were not allowed to break her heart," she said. "Which I now know you will not do."

He nodded. "You're right. I won't," he said simply.

"But," said Alejandro, "the movie? David Ansley cut you off?" He scowled. "*Hijo de puta.* I never liked that guy."

"Yes," said Sebastian, rubbing his temple, "halfway through. We'll have to stop production tomorrow until we can figure it out."

"No," said Pilar, "over my dead body."

Alejandro and Sebastian turned their eyes to her, surprised.

She drew herself up, her green eyes glittering. "Carlos was a terrible husband," she said. "A complete *cabrón.*"

"*Mamá.*" Sebastian laughed in protest.

"*Lo siento, hijos*, but he was. He was, perhaps, a better father—"

"Slightly," muttered Alejandro.

"But *Dios mio, cabrón* or not, I loved him. And everything I loved about him—all his good—he got directly from Victoria. She was everything kind, everything fun, everything brave, everything tender about Carlito. And I loved her like she was my own *mamá*." She lifted her chin in defiance. "Perhaps more." She looked at her boys. "I miss her every day."

They nodded.

"Me, too," Sebastian said softly.

"Victoria's story will be told," said Pilar. "I want it told." She looked at Sebastian. "How much money do you need to finish the movie?"

Sebastian blinked. "Well, since we're halfway through, probably about twenty-five million."

Pilar looked at her elder son. "Jandro?"

Alejandro looked thoughtful, running his hands through his hair.

Sebastian felt his heart beat faster. "It would be an investment, Jandro," he said. "You've seen how good it already is. I have no doubt it will make all its money back and more."

"Well, Sebastian, we do not have thirty-eight billion dollars like Ansley," said Alejandro slowly.

Sebastian's hopes plunged. "No, you're right," he said. "Of course. It would be foolish to—"

"But we have enough," Alejandro interrupted. "More than enough." He looked at his brother. "From what I have seen, it will be a very good investment. The movie is going to be great," he said. "*Your* movie is going to be great, Seb."

Sebastian smiled and blinked back the sudden tears in his eyes. "*Hermano*," he choked out.

Alejandro pulled him into a hug. Sebastian gripped his big brother and did his best not to cry.

"*Mis hijos*," said Pilar. "This makes me so happy."

Alejandro stepped back but kept his hands on Sebastian's shoulders. He cleared his throat. "But after the film is done," he said, "you'll come back to the team? And we will trade off on number three?"

It was a question. Not a command.

Sebastian smiled. "*Sí*," he said. "You and *Abuelita* were right. I need the ponies. Just as long as we keep playing *el picador*, okay?"

Alejandro clapped him on the back. "*Claro que sí, hermanito.* Of course."

Chapter Fifty-seven

They brought Liberty back to the hotel and walked her to her bungalow in the dark.

Kat took her hand. "Are you sure you don't want to come stay with me?" she said. "You're more than welcome."

Liberty smiled and shook her head. "I'm okay," she said, "really. I'm done with all the drama. Now I just want revenge. I'm going to go to bed, get a good night's sleep, and then, when I wake up, I'm going to call my lawyer and make sure I take that asshole for every red cent he owes me."

Kat smiled. "Let us know if there's anything we can do to help make that happen."

Liberty hugged her and then Seb. "Thank you," she said, "for everything. I don't know what I would have done without you guys." She looked at Sebastian and grinned devilishly. "I know I should probably say sorry again that I kissed you, but I'm actually not so sure I am. You're still pretty much the best-looking guy I've ever seen, Sebastian."

"Hey," protested Kat, laughing.

Liberty shrugged and smiled at them both. "If only his heart wasn't already taken, eh?"

Sebastian smiled back at Liberty and then looked at Kat and pulled her close, resting his head against hers. "Indeed."

* * *

Kat drove them back to her house, and they went straight to her bedroom. It had been a long couple of days at the hospital, and they were both exhausted.

She sat on the bed and hazily watched Sebastian undress. Even through her fatigue, she couldn't help admiring his sleek, muscular body, the way his muscles clenched and shifted as he stripped off his clothes.

She loved him and the thought sent a tendril of warmth throughout her body. She loved the dark fall of hair over his brow, the way his skin seemed to glow in the soft light of the room, the spark that came into his eyes when they looked up and met hers.

He smiled fondly. "You look so tired, *linda*. I'm going to draw you a bath."

She didn't protest. Nor did she protest, a few moments later, when he came back into the room, smelling faintly of lavender bath salts, and gently pressed her back onto the bed so he could undress her like a sleepy child.

He tenderly lifted her shirt over her head and helped her out of it, then he unhooked her bra and pulled that off. Next, he pulled off her socks, and then he helped her raise her hips and unzipped her jeans so he could tug them down, along with her panties.

She had never felt quite so completely naked before. The usual zinging sexual undercurrent that accompanied this kind of nudity was strangely absent. It was just her and him, and this warm, safe feeling of absolute trust.

He scooped her into his arms.

She laughed. "I can walk, you know."

"I know," he said huskily as he carried her into the bathroom and gently deposited her into the steaming, foamy, sweet-smelling water.

She took his hand, inviting him in.

He smiled and, with his other hand, began to unbutton his shirt.

The water sloshed out of the copper slipper tub and onto the dark blue tile floor as he lowered himself in behind her, straddling his legs on either side of her and bringing her back to rest against his chest. He wrapped his arms around her waist, pulling her even closer, and kissed the top of her head. "*Mi amor*," he whispered.

She closed her eyes and sighed. A long, sweet shudder of release.

They stayed like that for a while, skin to skin, drifting in the soft, warm water.

And then Kat slipped around, pressing her cheek to his neck, holding him close. "I think I finally understand what Victoria meant when she talked about destiny," she whispered.

She looked up to see that Sebastian's eyes glimmered with tears. He smiled at her—that slow, sweet, impish smile she knew and loved so well—and he reached out and touched her cheek, tracing a path on her skin. "I was outside of Eden before I met you, *mi amor*. I was a man who did not know his true place in this world. And now?" He reached over and softly kissed her lips. She felt a deep, electrifying thrill ricochet through her body. "And now I find myself at home."

* * *

They made love slowly and tenderly in the water, their bodies melding into each other, their hearts and souls following. They tangled and entwined together in a way that, both of them were certain, would never fully come undone.

Afterward, they padded through the darkness and climbed into the welcoming bed, burrowing under the covers, barely touching their fingers together, and then her arms crept around his neck, and his hands intertwined in her hair, and they curled up against each other, soul to soul, heart to heart, destiny fulfilled.

Epilogue

Kat paused in the doorway of the club to watch Liberty, in a flowing midnight blue cashmere jumpsuit, working the room like the pro that she was. The star was stopped at every turn, smiling here, flirting there, taking selfies, and signing autographs. Everyone wanted her attention.

Liberty Smith was the talk of the Sundance Film Festival since *Twenty-five Roses* had premiered earlier in the day. The film had been received with a standing ovation and serious buzz. No one could stop chattering about the stunning, transformative performance the actress had pulled off. The Oscar drums were already beating. And not just for Liberty. Honey, dressed in a head-to-toe tiger print with her hair colored to match, was tucked into a corner of the party, working her phone and, Kat knew, fielding the bidding war among all six major studios as they vied for who would get to pay for the honor of distribution.

Over by the bar, the Del Campos, minus Sebastian, held court. Pilar, on Lord Henderson's arm, looked pure Hollywood old school, wearing a full-length black vintage fur cape, which she had confided to Kat had been Victoria's back in the day, and a necklace of emeralds so big that Kat could see them sparkle all the way from across the room. Georgia, in a slinky coral dress draped with a soft pink pashmina shawl, drank a glass of champagne with one hand and held on to little Tomás with the other. Now that he was truly mobile, the two-year-old could not be counted on to stay in one place for longer than a few moments at a time.

Alejandro stood talking to Noni, who was leaning against the bar and wearing a tailored black satin tux jacket and pants that set off her platinum blond hair and arresting raven dark eyes. Kat smiled to see her here, happy to that Sebastian's little sister was out of her blacksmith clothing for once and dressed for a party. On the other side of Noni, wearing a minidress so short that Kat shivered to look at it, was Valentina, Alejandro's daughter, on her break from college and gawking, round-eyed and eager, at all the celebrities in the room.

Alejandro himself, in a cashmere jacket and loosened tie, smiled graciously at well-wishers who stopped by to talk with him. The people who knew him at Sundance were broken into two camps—fans of polo, where, he was, of course, a superstar, and people who had seen the film and noticed the handsome athlete in his scene on the pitch. Even in his small role, Alejandro had generated so much star power that Kat liked to tease that she would cast him as the leading man in her next film.

Camelia, wearing a bright red dress that showed off her lithe curves to perfection, hung on to Mark Stone, the two of them fooling around on the dance floor and laughing together as if no one else were in the room.

Kat's parents were sitting happily at their own table, being entertained by the silver-haired and debonair James Little, one of their all-time favorite actors. James was appearing in Kat's next film, and he seemed more than pleased to have the devoted attention of Corinne and Joe. Kat thrilled to see the way that her father seemed to be fully back to his normal, healthy self as he put his arm around his wife and threw back his head and laughed.

Kat sighed happily, taking in these last few moments before anyone saw her, before the windstorm of attention would be aimed in her direction. Before, she thought with a little thrill of trepidation, her life would irrevocably change yet again.

"*Mi corazón*," a silky, mischievous voice whispered in her ear as strong arms slipped around her waist and held her tight, "are you waiting to make a grand entrance?"

Kat smiled, a thrill of warmth surging through her, and turned to her fiancé.

* * *

Sebastian gazed down at Kat, noting that the antique silver color of her dress echoed the gleam of her steady gray eyes. At her throat was a single diamond, as big as a robin's egg, which his mother had given her when they had announced their engagement. He pushed a glossy black curl away from her face.

She laughed, caught. "I'm a little scared," she admitted.

"Oh?"

She slid her arms up over his shoulders and locked them behind his neck. As her curvy body, sheathed only in a thin layer of silken velvet under her heavy wool coat, nestled up against his, he felt a roar of desire unfurl inside himself.

"Everything is so perfect right now," she said. "I can't imagine being any happier."

She kissed him, her sweet pink lips barely touching his own. He pulled her closer, breathing in her scent.

"I'm almost afraid to go in," she sighed.

"Let's not go in, then," he murmured. "It's still early. We won't be missed just yet. Come with me."

She looked up at him, an irresistible smile dancing over her face. He grabbed her hand and led her out onto a small balcony to the side of the building.

The snow fell in tiny, glittering shards, resting in the curls of Kat's hair and clinging to her black coat like minuscule diamonds. It was after dark, and groups of people below were hurrying from shelter to shelter, heading for film premieres or attending the various celebrity-clogged parties. The only light was the warm yellow glow of the lodge from behind them and a discreet streetlamp illuminating the flakes of snow as they drifted through the air.

They stood far above the street, watching the crowd, listening to the squeak and crunch of ice grinding beneath feet. Sebastian took Kat's hand, and it felt to him as if they were alone in their own little world again, once more in the bubble of their romance, just Kat and Sebastian.

Finally, she spoke. "Seb?"

"Mmm-hmm?" He pulled her back toward him, tucking his hands around her waist and trying to keep her warm.

"You remember when I told you that I couldn't have written *Twenty-five Roses* without you?"

"*Sí,*" he said.

"I meant that. And not just because of Victoria."

"No?" he said as he pulled her even closer.

She paused for a moment. "Do you remember when Victoria wrote about meeting your grandfather? About how she knew, right away, deep down, that he was her great love?

288

Her *amor verdadero*? That, suddenly, everything in her life just slipped into place—because she realized that all she had done, every moment before, every breath she had taken, had simply been leading up to the moment when she met him?"

He tightened his grip around her and nodded.

"I couldn't have understood that, I couldn't have written about that like I did, except that you—being with you—showed me exactly what she meant." She turned toward him. "Do you know what I mean?"

He drew in a deep breath, watching the play of emotions flicker over her face. "*Sí,*" he said. His voice was husky with feeling. "*Sí,* yes, of course I do. Katarina."

She slipped her arms around his neck as he pulled her to him, gripping her tightly. Their gazes locked.

"You are exactly as she described," she whispered. "You are my one. And I am so, so grateful for that. Thank you."

He looked at her, and her cheeks were flushed red with the cold, and her eyes seemed to sparkle in the dark, and the snow glittered like jewels in the dark nimbus of her hair. And as he bent to kiss her, just before the moment that his lips met hers, he could have sworn that he detected the softest, sweetest scent of roses on the winter's night air.

ANTOINETTE BLACK HAS ALWAYS KNOWN WHERE SHE STOOD WITHIN THE DEL CAMPO FAMILY—A BASTARD DAUGHTER. BUT TO STABLEMASTER ENZO RIVAS, AS MUCH AS HIS HEART WANTS HER, NONI WILL ALWAYS BE UNTOUCHABLE, JUST LIKE ANY OF THE FABULOUSLY WEALTHY DEL CAMPOS. WHEN A SECRET FROM HER PAST COMES TO LIGHT, THOUGH, ENZO WILL HAVE TO DECIDE WHETHER TO TAKE HIS CHANCE OR LOSE HER FOREVER.

PLEASE SEE THE NEXT PAGE FOR A PREVIEW OF

Nacho Figueras Presents:
Ride Free

Chapter One

When Sunny started crow hopping, Lorenzo Rivas didn't worry. The big mare had always been hot, and it wasn't out of character for her to occasionally get a little bored and try to test her rider.

But when Sunny started to buck, Enzo knew something was seriously wrong.

The pony kicked out her legs and whinnied fearfully, almost sending Enzo out of the saddle. He dug his heels in, grabbed the reins and battled to pull her head back up. She fought him, flinging her neck down and heaving her back legs into the air.

For a moment, he thought he was going to be thrown, and his body automatically tensed, preparing to hit the ground hard.

It wouldn't have been the first time Enzo lost his seat to an unruly horse. It was part of his job, after all. Nobody trained horses and didn't occasionally get thrown. But that didn't mean he wouldn't fight it.

Sunny came back down onto all four legs again, and Enzo, sensing a split second of opportunity, yanked the reins sharply to the right, forcing the pony's head so far over that her nose touched his knee. She screamed in outrage and spun in a circle, but she was powerless to kick her hind legs from this position.

Enzo kept her in that stance, letting her spin as many

times as she wanted, speaking to her softly in Spanish, until he could feel her temper start to ebb and her muscles soften, one by one, under him.

He relaxed the reins and let the pony's head back up. As they cantered forward, he noticed a large, bald-faced hornet floating away from them.

"Ah. Poor girl," he said, "you got stung."

Sunny snorted complacently as if in agreement, and then reared up, threw Enzo backward into the grass, and bolted, riderless, down the pitch.

Enzo lay there for a moment, the breath knocked out of him, staring at the cloudless Florida sky. It had not been a bad fall, as falls went, and he knew that once he could breathe again, he'd be fine. But he was also pissed, and he knew it would be better to get his temper under control before he chased down the errant horse. It never helped to be mad when dealing with ponies.

"Rivas?" came a distant voice that made him close his eyes and smile ruefully. *Of course* she would find him like this.

"Enzo, are you okay?"

She was closer.

He struggled to a sitting position, still a little winded, but determined not to be on his back when she reached him.

"I'm fine," he said, and then almost fell over again, he was so dizzy. Damn that horse. He bent his head to his knees and closed his eyes.

"You don't look fine. You look like you got knocked on your ass."

He slowly turned his gaze up toward Antonia Black and felt his heart speed up in a way that had nothing to do with his fall.

It was getting worse. He could hardly look at her anymore

without being filled with an almost paralyzing ache of attraction.

She reached out her hand, her jet-black eyes twinkling with amusement, and after a beat of hesitation, he took it and let her help him to his feet.

For a moment after he stood, he let his hand linger in hers, allowing himself the luxury of feeling the tingling heat that seemed to generate from her skin into his. But then he dropped it, remembering the runaway horse.

"Did you see where Sunny went?" he asked.

She laughed. "She pranced right into the barn. I'm sure one of the grooms has her by now."

He nodded and winced, already sore from the fall. "She got stung," he said.

"Oh," said Noni, "I know. I saw the whole thing."

He smiled and rubbed his neck. "Hot horse," he said ruefully.

She smiled back. He felt his chest squeeze in response. "Hot horse," she agreed.

She looked him over. "You sure you're all right?"

He nodded. "I'll probably be sore, but nothing is broken."

"Good," she said.

They gazed at each other for a moment.

"Are you going to Hendy's party tonight?" he finally said, needing to break the tension.

Her mood suddenly changed. She frowned, and a red flush touched the creamy skin of her cheeks and chest. "Yeah, I guess," she said in an abrupt tone. "Anyway, if you're really okay, I'm going to head on home." She quickly turned to go. "I'll see you at the party."

He watched Antonia walk away, heading for her truck. He had the impulse to call out, stop her, ask her what was wrong. But before he could act, Noni swung up into her truck, her platinum blond hair streaming behind her, slammed the door with a bang, and was gone in a cloud of dust.

He clenched and unclenched his fist, reminding himself that every time she slipped away, it was better for both of them. Less complicated, safer.

Nothing good, he reminded himself sternly for the ten-millionth time as he started back toward the barn, *could come from anything happening between us.*

She is my boss's sister. She is a Del Campo. I would only end up hurting her.

The words were his litany, but lately they were starting to lose their power.

He shook his head. Being stern with himself wasn't working anymore. He could feel that he was starting to weaken. Being around her at work, being her friend and confidant, without ever hinting at his real feelings, had begun to exhaust him.

It was a part he knew he could not play much longer. All his good reasons for keeping his distance, all the rules of the barn and vows to himself that he had clung to over the years, had started to feel weightless compared to his growing feelings for this woman. The many times he had repeated to himself that it was unprofessional, that he wasn't fit to be in a relationship, that he didn't deserve her, that she was too fragile...it was all beginning to feel as insubstantial as a fairy story. A cautionary tale he'd heard as a child, meant to keep him away from gingerbread houses and wolves in the woods.

Because she was different these days. She was stronger and happier and more stable. And her happiness made her all the more irresistible.

And maybe, he thought, *I'm different, too...*

He turned back around at the barn door, watching the lingering trail of dust that her blue truck had left behind. He thought of a moment in the barn earlier that day, when he had held the head of a pony for her while she bent over its hind leg, hammering in a new shoe. For just the quickest second, she had looked up and met his eyes, and a devilish smile had danced over her mouth. It had been the kind of carefree grin he would never have imagined on her face when he had first come to know her. It seemed to prove that she was finally mended. Certainly, she was a changed woman from the one he'd met all those years ago.

* * *

Eight Years Earlier

The barn had been fizzing with gossip for days. Lorenzo's boss, Alejandro Del Campo, had flown to Berlin to find his newly discovered half-sister. She was a scandal no one in the Del Campo family had even known existed before reading Carlos Del Campo's posthumous will.

There were rumors circulating all over the farm about the mystery woman. The grooms were whispering that Alejandro had bailed her out of jail, a student rider swore she heard that the sister was an opium addict, the Argentine vet said she had been living on the streets, doing what she must to survive.

Of course, not one of those things had turned out to be true, but on the day that Alejandro had first brought Antonia to the barn, anything seemed possible and none of it was good.

Enzo had been leading out a little black mare named Hex for training—she'd recently started to get spooky on the field and he'd wanted to pinpoint, what, exactly, was setting her off—when Alejandro slid open the doors and entered with a small blond woman trailing behind him. The usual buzz and chatter of the barn suddenly stilled.

The woman immediately stopped to look at a pony, and turned away from Enzo, so that his first impression was just a swath of pale, creamy neck and long, silky white-blond hair, the kind of hair so fine and smooth that it looked like it couldn't be bound, as if it would just slide right out of a clip or hair band. At first glance she seemed a child, sylph-like and vulnerable, in an oversized black button-down flannel, baggy faded jeans, and worn work boots. But when she turned her head and glanced at Enzo, he'd felt himself go still.

This was no child.

She was stunning. With high Slavic cheekbones, a wide and generous mouth, a heart-shaped face tapering to a stubborn little chin, and most startling, Carlos's eyes. Large, slanted, and raven dark, hauntingly shadowed in her pale face, with long, sooty lashes and dramatic black slashes for brows. Except that, unlike her father, whose gaze had always looked a bit dulled by overindulgence and self-satisfaction, this woman had eyes that glowed like live coal—filled with raw intelligence, hurt, anger, and challenge. She looked like a desperate, wild thing who had just been trapped into captivity.

Her beauty was undeniable, but it wasn't just her physical presence that moved Enzo. He recognized something in her—a fierce and anguished aura—that made him want to reach out and touch this woman, to gentle her, to comfort her, to find out exactly what had happened to make her this feral, and to fix it in any way he could.

The pony beside him had nipped him then, impatient to get outside. Enzo swore in pain, and Antonia laughed—a silvery sound that sent electric chills down his spine. For a moment, her whole face lit up. She was transformed. She lost that hunted look, and she was, if it was at all possible, even more beautiful than she had been seconds before.

And then her smile had slipped away and her eyes had clouded back over, and Enzo realized that he would gladly spend the rest of his life doing just about anything to try to make her laugh again.

She walked over and scratched Hex's ears. "She wants out," she said. Her voice was soft and husky and thoroughly American—not a trace of the Argentine accent that the rest of her family, and Enzo himself, sported.

Hex closed her eyes and nibbled at Antonia's hair. Enzo smiled. "She likes you," he'd said.

Antonia arched a dubious brow. "She likes to be scratched."

The sleeve of her shirt fell back as she continued to rub Hex's neck, and Enzo had been shocked to see all the scars— some shiny white and healed, but others still pink and raw— that dotted her hand and wrist.

Without thinking, he reached out and touched her hand, tracing the marks under his fingertips, feeling the tight, raised flesh, and then, an incredible heat that seemed to emanate from her skin. She felt like she was burning with fever.

She went absolutely still, met his eyes defiantly, and then shook him off.

"Not that it's any of your business"—she flipped her hand over and showed him a small tattoo of an anvil on her inner arm—"but I'm a metal worker. Burns are just a hazard of the job."

He felt hugely relieved, and then annoyed with the force of emotions that were raging through him. What business was this of his? Why should he care how she got her burns?

"A farrier?" he asked, trying to hide behind polite conversation.

She shook her head. "No, mostly casting, lately." She looked around the barn, a hint of speculation in her wide, dark eyes.

Then Alejandro had joined them and Enzo had suddenly been shocked back to reality.

His boss's little sister. A member of the Del Campo family.

If ever a woman had been off-limits...

Alejandro led his sister away, eager to show her the rest of the farm, and Enzo had been left with Hex, who was starting to paw the ground in her eagerness to get out of the barn.

In the field, Enzo rode the pony, trying to figure out what she was shying away from, but his thoughts kept returning to Antonia. The silken curtain of her hair, her obsidian eyes, the way her skin seemed to burn from within, her scent— something sweet and hot like black pepper and cinnamon...

Under him, Hex suddenly tensed and Enzo broke from his reverie to take note of their surroundings. There it was—an old black garden hose on the field that someone had left out. It looked too much like a snake to the sensitive little mare. He'd tell a groom to take care of it right away.

He rode the pony back in, wondering whether he'd see Antonia again, wondering where she was staying...

He shook his head.

He had not felt this way in years. Perhaps he had not felt this way ever. And it shook him to the core.

* * *

The dust had cleared now, the truck was long gone, and Enzo finally went to find Sunny and make sure she'd been taken care of. He knew he would see Noni later that night, at Lord Henderson's end-of-the-season party, and thought that he might ask her, then, what had made her so angry.

Ducking back into the cool, fragrant barn, he flashed on her face again—that slightly wicked smile—and he felt his whole body tighten in response.

He closed his eyes for a moment, took a deep breath, and tried to banish her from his thoughts, push her away, in the same way he'd been doing for years.

But something stuck and held.

It was getting harder and harder to let her go.

Appendix

Each TEAM is made up of four PLAYERS. The players are designated positions from 1 to 4 and wear the corresponding number on their team shirts. Player 1 is primarily offensive, Player 4 primarily defensive. Normally, the most experienced and highest handicap players play positions 2 and 3, with position 3 being akin to the captain or quarterback of the team.

HANDICAPS: Each player is given a handicap from −2 (the worst) up to 10 goals (the best). Only a handful of the greatest professional players achieve the prestigious handicap of 10.

Polo is played on a large grass field—or PITCH—300 yards long and 160 yards wide. There are GOALPOSTS at either end, placed 8 yards apart.

The GAME begins with players lined up in the center of the field. One of the two UMPIRES bowls the ball between the teams. The players then use a combination of speed, skill, and teamwork to mark one another—and to score.

Players SCORE by hitting the ball between the goalposts. A pony can also score a goal for its team if it knocks the ball across the line between the posts. After each goal, and at the end of each chukka, the teams change playing directions. Play resumes with another throw-in.

CHUKKA: The number of periods into which a game of polo is divided. Players change out their ponies between chukkas. There are generally six chukkas in a game (in Argentina there are eight) and each chukka lasts approximately seven minutes.

HALFTIME: At halftime, which is typically five minutes, the custom is for spectators to walk onto the polo field to tread in the clumps of turf—or DIVOTS—kicked up by ponies.

The horses ridden in polo are known as POLO PONIES, whatever their height. Originally, no horse taller than 13 hands and 2 inches (54 inches) was allowed to play the game. Though the restriction was removed early in the twentieth century, the terminology has remained.

Polo ponies can be thoroughbred or mixed breed. What matters is that they are fit (they might run a couple miles during each chukka), strong, disciplined, intelligent, and love to play. Some of the finest ponies are bred in Argentina. Most ponies begin their training at the age of five, and this can last from six months to two years. As with their riders, it takes many years to master the game and most ponies reach their peak around age nine or ten. Barring accidents, a pony can continue to play until eighteen or twenty.

During a game, a player will use as many as eight ponies—known as a STRING OF PONIES. The higher the level of competition, the more ponies in a player's string.

ABOUT THE AUTHOR

Ignacio "Nacho" Figueras is one of the most recognized men in the world as the global face of Ralph Lauren's polo line. Hailed by CNN as the "David Beckham of Polo," Figueras is also captain and co-owner of Argentina's award-winning Black Watch team. He has been featured on *Oprah* and *60 Minutes,* and *Vanity Fair* readers voted him one of the most handsome men in the world.

Nacho currently splits his time between the United States and Argentina with his wife, Delfina, and their four children.

Jessica Whitman lives and writes in the Hudson Valley, New York.

You can learn more at:
NachoFiguerasPresents.com
Twitter @NachoFigueras
Facebook.com/NachoFigueras